GW00771233

Remember Tomorrow

Amanda Saint

Retreat West Books
https://retreatwestbooks.com

For Jemma

It is during our darkest moments that
we must focus to see the light.

~ Aristotle

CONTENTS

Part I

Now

2073

Zealot

Moon Phase: Waxing Crescent

MY GRANDSON MEANS to kill me. His name is Jonah and he has the glint of the zealot in his eyes. The people here follow him like sheep. Not that there are any sheep anymore, but they used to be known for following where anybody led. I should have known that the new way of life we'd created and the happy, peaceful times wouldn't last. All you need to do is look at the history books to know they never do. Even here in our tiny, isolated community hanging on a cliff side facing the sea, the evil that men do is coming back to haunt us again. We've ended up living in a future that's more like the past. A world filled with darkness, superstition and dread when I'd thought we were creating one filled with love and light.

He's just seventeen, Jonah, but he seems to have completely taken charge of things. All of the youngsters hang on his every word, carry out his every demand, and so does his mother, Dawn. She's my firstborn. I had her when I was seventeen, and she had Jonah when she was that age too. The witch hunts in England were in the seventeenth century. Is there some kind of sign in this, some connection? Whether there is or not, Dawn has hated me since long before Jonah was born. Maybe if I'd told her the truth from the start things could have been different between us. Maybe she's the one behind all this. She's always been angry, bitter, about things even before she found out we'd lied. But when Jonah first started preaching his sermons he was filled with love and peace, saying how thankful we should be that the old ways were wiped out and we had this chance to start again in a world that was fair for all. But, as times became harder and food more scarce, his preaching became judgmental, controlling, the old-style fire and brimstone, rules and sins, including pointed remarks about potions, spells and witchcraft being the Devil's work. I stopped going then but he was clever, is clever, and he did it so gradually that I don't think people noticed it was happening. But now they're all afraid that if they don't live how he tells them to they're all going to hell. At first even I believed that it was all harmless and that he'd get bored of it. Be my grandson again.

But I was wrong.

Even so, I have to carry on as normal. It's all I can do.

Which is why I'm here at the edge of the path leading from my cottage to the big house where he lives, loitering in the shadow of the woods and trying to pretend I'm not scared. The sun's high in the sky, so it's probably around eleven and I have to get some food. I've barely eaten for days. Instead I've been eking out a few bits of veg and hiding away in my cottage wondering how it's all come to this. Now there's no food left at all. The heavy humid air presses down on me as I watch the big, ivy-covered manor house that used to be filled with love when Rachael was alive. The blank, dark windows reflect the grey sky and the house looks as dead as Rachael is. Now that Jonah and Dawn have moved in.

I can't see anyone so I creep forward, heading around the side of the house that will take me on the quickest route to the food gardens and polytunnels. I quickly crouch down, tuck myself up against the corner of the house when I hear his voice ring out in the quiet morning. I peep around the corner to see where it's coming from. They're all in the clearing by the orchard. Jonah's standing on a small, wooden lectern they've made, his pale face shining out against the dense leaves behind him. His long blond hair flows around his shoulders and he's wearing a dark robe tied at the waist with a rope. Where has he got these things? Obviously cultivating the Jesus look crossed with a monk. Something about this makes me more scared than anything else that has happened so far. I stay hidden behind the corner of the house, listening. There's no way I can get any food without being seen. I'll have to go hungry. But I want to hear him, find out how he's keeping them all under this religious spell. I'd been imagining that he still just preached directly from the bible but he's telling it like a story.

'Greed is one of the worst sins against God and your fellow man. It is something that everyone has to fight against in their nature, for we are all created as sinners and must find the true path to goodness. Once, a wealthy farmer created a beautiful vineyard so that people could have grapes to eat and wine to drink. He left it in the care of his farmhands and at harvest time sent a man to collect his grapes. The farmhands had decided that as they were the ones who had tended and harvested the grapes they were the ones that should keep them and profit from their sale. Who in this story are the greedy ones?'

A long silence follows before Jonah speaks again. 'Come. You must have an opinion. Who should reap the benefits of the vineyard? The man who invested the money to create it, or the men who invested the time and effort to make it bring forth fruit?'

Can this even mean anything to the young people here? They've never been involved with money. They'll only know about it from the books they read. The ones I saved for them so we could learn from the mistakes of the past. That turned out well.

A young girl, a slight tremble in her voice, speaks. 'They should share it. They all had a part to play in the grapes being there, so they should all get a share. Just like we do here with our fruit and vegetables.'

'Yes, very good. That's right. Everyone who helps to create food should get a share in the food. What do we think of those who do not help in our garden but expect to take some of the food we grow? Of those that sneak around in the dark stealing food they haven't helped to nurture into life?'

The people murmur amongst themselves. This is about me. Does he know I'm here? Or does he always use a story to show how I'm the sinful one?

'Not only do they steal, they curse the plants they have taken from. Our lettuces will no longer grow where they have always flourished. Is this coincidence that a thief, a thief who is also practising witchcraft, the Devil's work, takes one of our precious lettuces and then the rest start to wither and die?'

What's he talking about? There were only a few lettuces left when I took one the other day. And if they aren't growing properly anymore it's because they aren't replenishing the soil. The youngsters are slapdash in their approach to the vegetable gardens. Pulling up food that's only just ready to eat and quickly sticking new seedlings in the same hole without adding compost and giving the soil some time to rest. Ignoring me when I try to explain to them how and why they should do it differently.

'No, it's not a coincidence. We know she doesn't believe in the ways of the Lord. We know she worships false idols and casts spells.' He rifles through the pages of the bible sitting on the lectern in front of him.

'Samuel says: "For rebellion is the sin of witchcraft, and stubbornness is an iniquity and idolatry."' He flicks more pages over, 'And Micah: "I will destroy your witchcraft and you will no longer cast spells."'

Another long silence, broken only by a robin chirruping and the swish of waves far below.

Then his voice rings out again, 'Revelation 21:8 says that the fate of all cowards, unbelievers, the corrupt, murderers, the immoral, those who practice witchcraft, idol worshipers, and all liars, is to burn in the fiery lake of sulfur. So I say to you, as Peter said so long ago, be alert and of sober mind. Your enemy the Devil prowls around like a roaring lion looking for someone to devour.'

'Hallelujah,' a lone male voice cries out.

'Hallelujah indeed!' Jonah shouts. 'And I say to you that you must keep your own souls safe from the Devil. He will tempt you through these unbelievers and immoral people. The Lord will know if you falter, if you lie and show us a false face, and he will tell me what your punishment shall be. Lying and denying the Lord will not be tolerated here any longer. Do you hear me? Now let us praise Him, praise Him.'

I press myself hard against the wall, as if it can make me invisible, make the situation less mad. The bricks digging in my back are the reality, not this. Not this. People are getting to their feet, murmuring at first then it gets louder and louder, all of the voices singing out together. 'We love you Lord, we obey you Lord, we follow your word. We love your son, Jesus, Lord. We love your son, Jonah, Lord. We love you all. We obey you all.' They chant those same lines over and over again.

What is he doing? Telling them he's the son of God? Placing himself in the Holy Trinity and booting out the lowly ghost? This is too much. He's worse than my Mum was. She was a religious maniac too, but she had nothing on Jonah. But could this be where it's all come from? Can it be passed down through the genes? I peep round the house again and they are all there, hands in the air, swaying and chanting. I swallow bile. What's happening to my egalitarian, forward-thinking community? Even Tess is there. Not that she's ever really with us anymore. Her mind has gone elsewhere. But there's no sign of Berry.

I can't listen anymore. I hurry towards the path back to my cottage. Will he call out after me that he knew I was there, knew what I was trying to do?

When I get home Berry is in my kitchen. 'I was just going to leave this here,' she says gesturing to a bowl on the table. 'I wasn't sure where you'd gone. Sorry, it's not much. Just what I saved from my dinner last night.'

I grab the bowl and start stuffing the cold stew into my mouth. Nodding a thanks at her. Not able to stop myself from devouring the food.

'Oh Evie. What are we going to do?' She sinks down into the chair next to me, rests her hand on my arm. She's always been one for touching once she trusts you. Ever since she was a toddler and first learned to speak, she'd just appear at your side, arms outstretched, saying, 'Hug.' Her sweet nature means that everyone here loves her back, even Jonah. But she's strong as well as sweet. Still here feeding me when everyone else has been quick to follow Jonah's orders.

'I don't know, Berry. I wish I did. I just don't understand why he's turned on me like this.'

She pulls me into a sideways hug and rests her head on my shoulder. 'He'll come round, surely he will. He's always loved you the best. I'll talk to him.'

AS DUSK STARTS to fall I creep up back through the woods again, determined to see Michael. There's no way my easy-going boy can believe all this about me. There must be another reason he hasn't been to see me. I keep to the edge of the woods as far as I can then scurry past the big house, not looking towards the kitchen window where light spills out, making everything around it seem much darker. If I don't look they can't see me. I rush across the driveway towards the row of cottages where Michael lives in the end one with his family. I need to get inside quickly in case Jonah or Dawn come outside. But when I knock on Michael's window it's Olivia who comes to the door, her pregnant stomach filling the gap. My fourth grandchild. How is it that I've got all this family here yet, apart from Berry, nobody to talk to, nobody to take my side, back me up?

She doesn't move to ask me in. 'What do you want?'

I blink back tears. I can't show anyone how much this is all getting to me. I have to make them believe I am stronger than I feel. 'Is Michael home?'

I hear a chair scrape on the floor then he appears behind her. 'Hello, Mum.'

Olivia tuts at him, mutters, 'We talked about this. Get rid of her.' Then she leaves him alone to face me. I thought he would take me inside, that we'd sit round his kitchen table drinking tea, chatting, laughing, like we'd done so many times before, but he steps outside, shutting the door behind him.

'C'mon I'll walk you home.' He gently pulls me away from his door by my elbow.

But I snatch my arm back, anger surging through me,

'No. I won't go home and be fobbed off. Why haven't you been to see me? Why aren't I allowed in your home anymore?'

He smiles sadly, pity in his eyes. But something else too. I can't name it, but it makes the hairs all over my body stand on end. If Michael casts me out too I really am in trouble.

'Olivia is scared. Jonah's threatening us. Saying we won't be fed if we have anything to do with you. That if we still see you then we'll be forced out. And then what would we do?'

'This is mad. He's just a child. Why has he taken against me like this? Why don't people tell him no? What's he done to everyone?'

Michael shakes his head. 'I don't know. But they all believe him. Do anything he says.' He pulls me into a hug and rests his chin on the top of my head. 'I'm so sorry, Mum, but I have to think of the twins, Olivia, the new baby. Why don't you try talking to him? Coming to his sermons? Pretend you believe it all.'

Just like his father. Willing to do anything for a quiet life. But I have always stood up for what I believe in and I'm not going to change that now. I push Michael away and walk away without saying another word.

But before I get too far, Michael calls out in a soft voice, 'Be careful, Mum. He said today he's giving you until the next full moon to prove you're not a witch.'

I turn to face him. 'Then what?'

'You know. You're the one that taught him what they do to witches.'

Then he goes inside and shuts the door and Olivia comes to the window and pulls the curtains closed.

Cross

Moon Phase: Waxing Crescent

THE SOUND OF footsteps on my front path wakes me from a restless sleep. The sun's barely risen. It can't be Berry as she's never up this early. I peek through the curtains. Jonah's standing in the garden, staring at the house. He doesn't say anything, doesn't move. He's holding the bible in one hand and something I can't make out in the other.

After a while, he opens his bible and starts to read. 'Submit yourselves therefore to God. Resist the Devil, and he will flee from you.' His voice is loud, clear, full of conviction. Does he really, truly believe all this stuff? I'm starting to think he might.

I can't bear to listen so I leave him to it and crawl

back into bed, burying my head under the pillows and pulling the duvet right over me too. His voice fades to a faint, distant murmur. The voice that used to tell me how much he loved me, that used to question all the things people had done in the past that he was now doing himself. After a while I can't hear him anymore, so I go back to the window. Wait for a few moments to see if he'll start again. When there's no more sound I pull the curtains open, suddenly brave and not caring if he's there, or at least that's what I tell myself. But the garden's empty. He's left something on the path though. I wait for a while longer to make sure he's really gone then go out to see what it is.

My hand trembles as I reach down to pick it up. A wooden cross. Carved into it another bible passage. 'The fear of the LORD tendeth to life: and he that hath it shall abide satisfied; he shall not be visited with evil.'

I stride to the end of the garden where it stops at the cliff edge and fling it over the wall into the sea, which is dark, oily, barely moving. I stare at it trying to take its stillness into my mind. Remember all that Connor taught me about thoughts and feelings and not letting them control me. Try to dismiss what's going on with Jonah and that I'm being ostracized, pretend that I'm not scared. This will pass. My old friends, my children, will see sense. But it doesn't work. My mind chases anxious thoughts in all directions, spinning round and round. Jonah's becoming obsessed and the witch trials of so long ago show that people's minds are easy to manipulate, especially when they're hungry. It didn't end well for many innocent women then and I'm getting the feeling it's not going to end well for me now. Is it my fault for teaching him about all this stuff? What's he going to do to me? What can I do to keep myself safe? Is there anyone at all that can, or will, help me?

I turn and walk back towards the herb garden. It covers almost the entire space behind the cottage, going up the hill in terraces. Connor built it for me when we first moved in. When Dawn was just a toddler and Michael yet to be born. I look over to the willow tree where Connor's buried, sending him my love wherever his energy is now, wishing it was still here with me. I kneel in front of the herbs, gather what I need for protection, thanking Rachael for teaching me so well and wishing she was still here too. Knowing that if she was then none of this would be happening. All the houses, the gardens, the stockpiles of food, clothes and everything we needed when the world as we knew it was wiped out, all of it was Rachael's. I knew from the very first moment I saw her on the day I arrived here, pregnant with Dawn, scared out of my wits at having run away from home and the only way of life I'd ever known, that there was something special about her. It shone from her face as she smiled with such love and acceptance at the grubby gang of strangers that had arrived to live with her, at me and Connor holding hands feeling so grown up, when really we were just kids. She'd wanted to teach me about the herbs and the spells straight away, but I resisted for a long time. Thought the spiritual side was all nonsense. If I'm honest, there's still a part of me, deep down inside that I try not to listen to, that isn't one hundred percent convinced that the spells work. I know the herbs work as I've seen the truth of it but I'm sure that the times when I've only used them to help people and not bothered with the incantations, they've still worked. Maybe not as well, nor as quickly. Or is that just my imagination? Rachael would tell me to believe though, that it's in believing that we make things true. So today I definitely *do* believe that they can help me.

In the kitchen I take a glass jar from the cupboard and fill it with a mixture of salt, garlic, bay leaves, dried basil, dill seeds, sage, anise, black peppercorns, fennel and cloves. Breathing in the tang and earthiness as I drop them in, counting to four as I breathe in and to four again as I breathe out. Calming myself and ridding my home of the negative energies and fear that Jonah left behind.

When the jar's full I place the lid on top and shake it nine times while softly chanting the spell that will help protect me. 'Salt and herbs, nine times nine. Guard well this home of mine.' Then I place it on the mantelpiece over the fire in the living room. Trying to cling on to the belief that it really can keep me safe from Jonah.

Then I head down to the beach to gather seaweed that has been left behind by the tide. If I'm not going to be getting vegetables from the gardens I need to make other plans. But the seaweed needs to be dried before I can eat it, so I still don't have anything other than herbs and water to keep me going. I'll have to wait until dark again and go and get some veg. No matter what Jonah might be preaching I did help grow it and I am entitled to my share. But I fall asleep on the sofa reading my book and I'm woken by voices singing. I blink, looking around the room, not sure if the singing was part of my dream. It's dark again but there's a glow coming from the garden. I can still hear singing, a low dirge-like sound with no clear words I can decipher. What now? But I can't bring myself to go and look.

It carries on for ages but then, finally, silence. The glow in the garden remains steady the whole time even when the singing stops and I hear people moving away to the path up through the woods. I finally find the courage to stand and go and have a look. I'm panting as if I've been running. In the garden is a burning cross. Like the Ku Klux Klan. Or a message that he's going to burn me at the stake?

I put the fire out with water from the rain butt. Once the flames have gone, I can see there's something tied to the cross. Charred and blackened, it's difficult at first to tell what it is. Oh my God. A kitten. I stifle a sob and squeeze my eyes shut as if that can make it not true. The barn cat recently had a litter, he must have stolen one from her. Why? Why would he do such a hideous thing?

There's no way I'm going up to the vegetable gardens now, so I make more herb broth. I'm eating it at the kitchen table when I hear someone outside again. A squealing sound, which is quickly cut off, followed by Jonah's voice ringing out.

'Witch, we will not make things easy for you. You cannot infect us with your evil ways. You must repent and come to the Lord. All of your familiars are deserting you.'

Familiars? What's he on about now? Something gives me the courage to go out there and just be his Nan again. I wrench the door open and he's there with a dead kitten in each hand, their heads limp and hanging at an odd angle.

'For God's sake, Jonah,' I shout. 'What are you doing? I'm your Nan, why are you doing this to me?'

He flings the dead kittens at me and I leap backwards.

'You dare to take the Lord's name in vain. Blasphemy. Another sin to darken your already blackened soul.' He moves away, walking backwards keeping his eyes pinned on mine. 'Your human relationship constructs mean nothing to me. I am divine. Your chances for redemption and saving yourself are running out now, Evie.'

Eggshells

Moon Phase: Waxing Crescent

IT'S BEEN QUIET for a few days now so maybe he's getting bored of it. Maybe he's realised how silly it all is. The sun is shining and I'm filled with hope as I head out to gather some fresh herbs to go in my seaweed soup. This hope dies instantly though when I open the front door. They've made a shrine of boiled eggshells on the doorstep. Six of them, in egg cups with the ends smashed in. They must have read about this in a book as well. There's surely nobody alive now that could have told them about this old custom, apart from me. Already then it was a part of history that had mainly been forgotten. I can see and hear my Nana now. I would've been about four or five and we were in the front room at her house. It was boiling hot as she always had a fire burning in the grate no matter what the temperature outside, the reflection of the flames flickering in the blank TV screen. No TV before 5pm was her rule. Apparently, only common people sat around watching TV from the moment they got up. Her favourite record, *I'm Only Sleeping*, was playing in the background. Nana was sat in her chair to the right of the fire and I sat on a little cushion next to her. The table was in between us and we had just finished our lunch of boiled eggs and toasted soldiers made from airy white bread.

Nana reached over and took my empty shell out of its cup and used the teaspoon to bash the bottom of it in. Then she placed it gently back in the cup. 'To stop the witches making a home in it,' she said.

I didn't question it. Just accepted that this was the truth and from then on I always smashed the bottom of my egg shells and I taught my brothers to do the same.

I smile at this memory. Nana and I were always great mates. She always took my side when Mum was trying to force her religion on me and I wasn't interested. What happened to them all? The family I left behind when I came here. What had I been thinking of? Why did I cut myself off like that? I should've been stronger and told Mum that it was my life, my choice, despite what she thought. Easy to say now. I'm sure they would all have died when the end times came. They had no food stores, nowhere to grow their own food, no idea how. I'll never know what happened to them.

I shake off these thoughts. I have enough to deal with in the now without dwelling on the past that can't be changed. I sweep everything up into the dustpan and take the shells to the little poly tunnel next to the herb garden, where I grow the more delicate herbs that aren't hardy enough to be outside. The ones that originally come from tropical places, cloves, cardamom and the such like. The egg shells are good for keeping the slugs away and now that everyone is shunning me I haven't had any eggs in ages. Berry brings me what she can but it's hard for her, she has to be careful or she'll end up in trouble like me.

I don't know what to do with myself. My days used to be filled with work of one kind or another – planting, harvesting and caring for the veg gardens, looking after the hives, making potions for the ailments people had, teaching the kids. Now it's just me here with my memories. I'll start to drive myself mad if I just hang around dwelling on how things used to be and imagining what madness might come next if Jonah doesn't see sense soon.

A biting pain in my hand brings me back to what I'm doing. A horsefly's sitting on my finger. I shake it off and see the red swelling coming up already. I've broken up the eggshells too much and they'll be useless now for keeping the slugs away. I must keep my mind more focused. I shake the soil and tiny fragments of shell from my hands and head indoors to clean up and treat the sting. My first thought is to put honey on it but I better be careful with it. The hives are cut off from me now, like the veg gardens. Even though it was me that managed to get them going again after they were all ruined. Instead I dab lavender tincture on it. I've got plenty of that.

A loud thud on the door startles me and I knock the bottle of tincture all over the kitchen table. The pungent smell of lavender surrounds me, catching in my throat and stinging my eyes. Another thud is followed by giggles and shouts. I yank open the door and a group of kids run away from me back towards the woods, squealing and laughing. One of them is brave enough to stop and turn to shout, 'Witch, witch, witch, we'll burn you at the stake.'

They are only kids but I let all the emotions I've been bottling up since this started come firing out. I pick up a rock they'd thrown at the door and throw it at their fleeing backs. 'Go on, get away from here. I'll put a curse on you, you'll see.' Then I'm panting, shaking, swallowing bile. My head spins and I grip the door frame to hold me up. What's the matter with me, saying stupid things like that? It'll only make things worse.

When I've calmed down I follow the kids up the path. It's time to sort this out. I can't just drift around any longer pretending that it isn't happening.

This time I don't loiter around at the edge of the woods trying not to be seen. Instead I march straight up to the house and let myself in through the kitchen door, like I've always done. My hands are shaking so I stuff them in the pockets of my jacket as I face Jonah across the kitchen table. Wearing the same robe I'd seen him in when he was preaching the sermon, he's sitting at the table by himself reading the bible. Does he never stop with all this?

He smiles at me but it doesn't reach his eyes. 'Evie. Welcome. I hope you are here as you have seen the light, are ready to repent.' He gestures towards the chair closest to me. 'Sit, let us talk.'

Why is he being like this now? What's going on? But surely this is a good thing – a rational conversation rather than throwing accusations at each other. So I sit down. 'I don't believe I have anything to repent for, Jonah. All I've ever done is help people.'

The fake smile drops from his face and he shakes his head. 'Such arrogance. We all have things to repent for, even me, and out of all the people here in our community you are the one with the most to atone for.'

'Like what? Using the plants the earth provides to help people when they're sick? Working to keep the community fed? Teaching the kids to read, and how to grow food? How are these things to atone for?'

'Magic is the Devil's work.' He stops and looks down

at his bible.

For a moment he looks like what he is, a young boy on the cusp of manhood with no clue about the world, and with that thought my courage returns. 'Don't be silly, Jonah, all this spouting of religious dogma. What are you hoping to achieve with it? There's no need for things to be like this.'

His head drops further.

Am I getting through to him?

He mutters something in a growly, guttural tone and then suddenly he's towering over me, banging his hands down on the table. I leap up, the chair clattering to the ground behind me and I trip on it as I stumble backwards, landing on the floor with a hard crack that sends fiery pain shooting up my back and down my legs. I scrabble back towards the door keeping my eyes fixed on him all the while. What's he going to do now?

'In the name of Jesus, I condemn thee,' he shouts, spittle flying across the room and landing on my cheek. 'You have forsaken his ways, his teachings, and are infecting the innocent with your evil. There can be no more of this.' He bangs his hands on the table again as I struggle to get to my feet.

I've just managed to stand up when the door on the other side of the kitchen opens and Dawn appears. Her dark hair's stringy and her face sallow; she looks uncared for, maybe a bit unhinged. Have they all gone mad? What is happening to them?

'Dawn.' I smile at her, hoping to appeal to some good feeling she may have buried deep inside for me. 'Please, what's this all about? You know I've never meant any harm to anyone.'

She shakes her head. 'You've always been a liar and willing to do anything to get your own way. Always.'

'That's not true—'

Jonah cuts me off. 'Yes, it is. She's told me all about how you were when she was a child. The things you let her believe that were your vicious lies. Get out. We won't have your evil here in our home any longer.'

'Dawn, I did lie but not to hurt you. Surely you must know that. And this, this was Rachael's home. It was Rachael that taught me about the healing, the herbs. I know you loved her, you know she wasn't evil, so how can I be?'

She walks towards me. Relief swells up in my throat, a smile hovers at the edges of my lips ready to stretch all across my face. She knows. I lift my arms to embrace her but she reaches behind me, pulls the door open and shoves me through it. I stumble but don't fall this time and the last thing I see is the two of them sinking to their knees, hands clasped and heads bowed. Then I run. My legs barely hold me up. There's nothing I can do. They really believe it. They think I'm evil, a witch, doing the Devil's work. I rush through the woods back to the safety of my home. Slamming the door shut behind me. If only we had locks. What will they do next?

Mistletoe

Moon Phase: First Quarter

WHEN I'M NOT thinking about how hungry I am, I'm worrying about when they're next going to appear. So as soon as it starts to get light I head up there. At the top of the path I wait in the shadows of the tree, watching to see who's about before I venture any further.

Nobody's around. It's very early and although the sky's lighting up, the sun hasn't yet risen above the hills. Soft mist hovers above the ground and there's a slight coolness in the air. A light shines out from Karin's window; her cottage is next door to Michael's, which is in darkness. I can see shadows inside as she moves around. I knock gently on the door, which has a bunch of mistletoe hanging above it. The other cottages in the row, all three of them, have it too.

When Karin opens her door and sees me she shakes her head. 'No, Evie. You can't be here.'

'Please Karin, let me in. Talk to me.'

I push against the door as she tries to close it, keeping my voice low so as not to draw attention to the fact that I have dared to venture up out of my witch's enclave. For a moment it seems like she's not going to relent but then she pulls the door wider and ushers me in.

Two candle lamps are burning—one on the table and the other on a shelf by the stove, where the kettle is just starting to boil. Karin is pale in the muted light, dark circles under her eyes. She's so thin and drawn. It's only been about six weeks since I last saw her but the difference in her is drastic.

'Are you OK? You don't look well.'

I touch her arm but she pulls away and goes to stand by the stove, opening the door to put another piece of wood on the fire that's already roaring, then keeping her eyes fixed on the kettle.

'What do you want, Evie? Why are you here?'

'I want to find a way to stop this witch madness. Why is everyone behaving like this and believing the crazy things he's saying? You know me. You know it's not true.'

She removes the whistling kettle from the stove and pours the hot water into a teapot. The smell of nettles fills the room as the water scalds the leaves. I sit down at the table when I see her take two mugs from the cupboard. I'm not being thrown out yet.

When she joins me and pours us both a cup, I try again. 'What's going on, Karin? Why is everyone turning against me?'

She shrugs. 'He's convincing, and people are scared.'

'Scared of what? What is there to be scared of? Definitely not me.'

'No. But you should be scared of him, Evie. He means all of this. He's going to do you harm.' Her voice breaks at the end.

'Why? How has this happened? Why has he turned against me like this? Has he said anything to you? Or has Dawn?'

She shakes her head. 'They're not going to say anything to me. I'm out of favour too. Old, useless, no good to them.' She starts to weep. 'We haven't got enough food anymore. The rains haven't been coming like they used to. They want something, someone, to believe in, and someone to blame. He's giving them that.' She croaks out, pressing her fingers to her eyes to stem the tears.

'But why me? When all I've done is help people. He used to love me.'

'I think he's scared of you. He sees you have power through your herbs, that he only has through his words, which he has stolen from people with bigger and better minds from the past.' Her tears have stopped, replaced by anger. 'He's stupid. And so are all the others. But stupid doesn't mean they aren't dangerous. You have to be careful, Evie.'

A lump burns in my throat and I blink back the tears that are so quick to appear nowadays. How had it got like this? 'Can't you talk to people for me, tell them that it's madness to think I'm trying to hurt anyone?' I gulp the tea. Can I can ask her for something to eat?

'It won't make any difference. Nobody will listen to me. It's the young people that are the ardent believers. They don't know what we do, have no memories of before. This is it for them and he's providing the guidance they think they need. Giving them something to believe in and something to judge. We both know that this is how humans are and what's happened hasn't changed that.'

I can't argue against this. After all, I've spent most of my life trying to fight against human nature. People used to believe in consumerism and corporations when I was young, but before any of that came along they believed in all this kind of nonsense that Jonah's spouting now.

'I'm sorry but you have to go, Evie, before you get me in trouble.'

'Can you give me any food, Karin? I have nothing to eat but seaweed and herbs.' I stretch my hand towards her and squeeze her hand. 'Please?'

She goes to the stove, puts a pan on it on to heat. 'You

31

can have this, it's leftover from my dinner last night. I don't have much appetite lately.'

A few minutes later she places a brimming bowl of stew in front of me and I devour it. It's so hot that I can barely taste it, but my eyes show me the beans, the potatoes, the carrots, the tomatoes. As I swallow the first mouthful goosebumps break out all over my body.

It's gone in seconds and as I push the bowl away from me, I say, 'Why has everyone got mistletoe on their doors?'

'Apparently it keeps witches out of your house.' She smiles and I see the friendship we've shared for many years is still there in that smile.

'But I'm in here, so either it doesn't work or I'm not a witch. Which do you believe is true?'

Karin comes around to where I'm sat, pulls me to my feet and into a tight hug. 'You know the answer to that, but I'm not strong enough to help you or stand up to them. I just want to live quietly until I die, which I've got a feeling won't be long now.'

'I knew there was something wrong. What is it? Come home with me and let me help.'

She shakes her head. 'There's no helping me now. I need a lot more than your herbs can give. Anyway, maybe there is something in all this heaven and hell stuff and I'll get to be with Al again.'

As she starts to push the door closed behind me, I

look back and somehow know that I'm never going to see her again. I turn back and hug her tightly, the tears falling down my face as I say goodbye to my friend.

As I walk away from her cottage, Jonah appears from around the corner of Rachael's house. He stops dead when he sees me then starts reciting more bible passages at me. Does he never just have a normal conversation with anyone anymore?

'He that believeth in him is not condemned: but he that believeth not is condemned already, because he hath not believed in the name of the only begotten Son of God. And this is the condemnation, that light is come into the world, and men loved darkness rather than light, because their deeds were evil. For everyone that doeth evil hateth the light, neither cometh to the light, lest his deeds should be reproved. But he that doeth truth cometh to the light, that his deeds may be made manifest, that they are wrought in God.'

By the end his voice has risen to a shout and I can hear doors opening in the cottages behind me. I stumble towards the back of the house then sprint as fast as my poorly-fed legs can take me down through the woods, but I can hear him still behind me. 'Heavenly Father, in the name of your sons Jesus, and my very own self, I bind and break all witchcraft, curses, spells, and all powers associated with it…'

The rest of it is drowned out by the sounds of my feet

hitting the path, my heart pounding in my head.

I go back to bed when I get home. Hide beneath the covers. I can't stay here. There's no pretending anymore – I'm not safe.

The sun has risen high by the time I hear footsteps coming to the front door. I sit up, clutching the covers. Have I got time to get downstairs and out the back door? Where will I go if I do?

I hear the front door creak open and know that I'm too late anyway.

Then a soft voice calls out. 'Evie? Where are you? It's me, Berry.'

A reprieve. I rush down the stairs to see her. I know that no matter what Jonah does and says that she's always going to love me. I squeeze her tight then hold her away to get a good look at her. She's so like Tess when we first met. But that's where the similarities end. Tess was always so fiery and fierce, quick to tell you what she thought about everything. The day I first met her she'd been protesting in the streets about a fast food place having stolen her Nan's cat and turned it into burgers. Even after we all came here to live a quiet life off the land, she started singing in a protest band. Berry, though, is quiet, measured. You can see that so much is going on behind those big brown eyes, that she thinks before she speaks. Whereas Tess rarely speaks anymore even though she seems happy enough, so I suppose that's all that matters.

But I miss her, and Berry does too.

Berry hands me a basket covered in a cloth. It's heavy so I put it down on the table.

'He's really frightening people now. He's told everyone that you put a curse on Karin earlier. They all saw you there when he started shouting and now she can't get out of bed.' She sinks into a chair, trying to reassure me with a smile but I can see the fear in her eyes.

'I knew she was sick and I asked her to let me help but she said I couldn't. That she needed more than herbs could give.' I rummage through the basket. Four eggs, a bunch of kale, six carrots, several runner beans and three large potatoes still covered in mud. A handful of strawberries, an apple and a plum. 'Thank you. I've been starving.' I pull her into a hug.

Berry nods and pulls back, 'I know. Karin's been sick for a while. She's got a lump in her stomach and feels sick all the time. Vomits whenever she eats.'

I sink into the armchair by the Aga. It sounds like cancer of the stomach, just like Rachael had. Is there something here, something we're doing that's causing it?

'You're in trouble, Evie. The next full moon is getting really close now. If you don't start coming to his sermons and believing in his God by then, he's saying he's going to prove to them all that you're a witch and put an end to it himself.'

'Prove it how?'

Berry shrugs. 'I don't know. But you have to do something. I tried to talk to him but he won't listen. Even though I always thought he would stop, come good, I think I was wrong.'

The next full moon is just days away now. I have to come up with a plan, to try and take back control of this situation or make my escape. I tell Berry to gather some gooseberries to make a juice for Karin by boiling them then straining the liquid. But I know it's probably too late to make a difference. 'Stay with her, feed her the juice as often as she can take it.' I wrap up some dried and powdered willow bark in a piece of paper. 'Add a teaspoon of this to it for pain relief. Send her my love.'

Now that they believe I've put a curse on Karin, they'll be back soon. What am I going to do?

Pisspot

Moon Phase: Waxing Gibbous

I'VE BEEN EKING out the bits that Berry brought me and venturing out into the woods to gather mushrooms. It's been two days since she dropped off the basket. As soon as it starts getting dark, I go to bed. Eager for another day to be over. Hopefully another day nearer to things getting back to normal. To this madness ending. But as I settle down with my book, I hear chanting from many voices drifting down through the woods and then I know. Karin is dead.

I cry for her, remembering when she'd first come here. Tess and I had gone looking for survivors and brought her and the others back with us. We were starting again then with hope, and love. How did we end up like this? I leave the tears to fall into the pillow as I drift into sleep, pretending I believe that Karin's death doesn't mean more trouble for me.

Next thing I know Dawn is wrenching me from my bed. She pulls me by the arm and I hit the floor. The sun is starting to rise so it's just light enough for us to see each other but Dawn can't meet my eyes, as she grips my wrist.

'Dawn, what are you doing? Please stop.' My voice is weak, all my strength drained by the searing pain in my shoulder as she drags me across the floor towards the door, the scrapes on my knees from the floorboards. I manage to tug my arm free and get to my feet, but she grabs me again, holding me tighter this time and pulls me roughly down the stairs behind her.

Downstairs in the kitchen, Jonah's lit candles all around the room. He's sitting at the table muttering incantations. He looks up as Dawn pushes me towards him. 'You cursed poor, wretched Karin, a defenceless old woman, and now she is dead.' He's gripping a wooden cross in both hands and he thrusts it forward so it's just inches from my face. 'Your ungodly powers are strong and I underestimated you but not anymore.'

I fold my arms under my breasts, trying to hold them up and cover myself at the same time. The vest top I wear for bed is tiny and I feel even more vulnerable without clothes to protect me.

'I told you your chances for repenting were running

out. They are gone. Now there is just the proof. The proof that I will show to everyone of your witchcraft, your evil intent, your curses and magic.' He bangs the cross down on the table then shouts, 'Your Devil's work.'

He waves his hands over a large glass jar sitting on the table in front of him, blessing it, 'We must try to contain the evil you are spreading. It cannot be allowed to go any further. You must urinate in the jug now.' He hands it to Dawn who presses it into my hands, still avoiding eye contact.

'What? I'm not doing that.' I try to push it back into Dawn's grasp but she turns away and I have to hold onto it, so it doesn't smash on the tiled floor.

'You will do it. This is how you can prove your innocence. You will pass your water into the jar and we will add a snip of your hair, your fingernail clippings and boil them all together and bury it in blessed ground. If you're not a witch then you will be fine, but if you are, as we believe, a Devil's handmaid, then you will no longer be able to pass water and you will die. As you will deserve to for the evil thoughts and intentions you harbour against us. The curses you have put on our food.'

'I will do no such thing. Where has all of this come from? I've never done anything bad to you.' I turn away from him to Dawn, who's staring at the floor, as if she can't meet anyone's eyes anymore not just mine. I have to try again though. 'Dawn, you have to stop this now. You must be able to see how mad this is. You know I'm not a witch, that I mean no harm, that I love you.'

Her head snaps up and her eyes slide briefly across mine, but she remains silent.

'Don't talk to her,' Jonah says and I don't know which of us he's directing this instruction to. 'We won't leave here until you've done it. We won't let you leave the room and sooner or later you will have to urinate.'

I don't want to admit that I already need to, quite badly. I always need to go as soon as I wake up. Especially now I'm older. So to get rid of them, knowing that they can do whatever they like with my piss as it won't do anything to me, I take the jug and walk towards the door into the living room.

'No, you will do it here where we can see you and make sure you don't apply any more sorcery to it.'

I shake my head. 'Leave me with some dignity in this madness.'

But he stares me down. I can't believe that this boy/man with his smooth hairless face and staring eyes had managed to completely take control of us all. That he's intimidating me into pissing in a jug in my kitchen in front of him.

'Look, Jonah. I don't know why you're doing this. I'm the one who taught you about all this. I'm not a witch. I'm a healer and your grandmother. I would never try to hurt you, or your mum, or anyone else.'

He shakes his head as if he can banish my words from his ears.

'I know who you are. That makes no difference whatsoever. I see you for what you are. That's what matters.' And with that he closes his eyes and a stream of incomprehensible words flows from his lips as he holds the cross, clenched tightly in both hands again, above his head and thrusts it towards me repeatedly. I have no idea what language it is, or if it's even real or just something he's made up.

'Jonah, please—'

Dawn pushes me from behind, a quick hard shove to the shoulder. 'Just get on with it.'

Jonah's eyes are wild, boring into me as he continues to chant and mutter his incantations. Maybe if I do it, they'll go. Leave me alone.

With shaking hands I put the jug down on the floor, pull my knickers down and crouch over it. Immediately the wee I've been desperately holding in comes gushing out. Splashing hot on my hands where I'm holding the jar. I bite my lip, keeping my eyes on the floor. I can't look at either of them anymore. What is wrong with them? Dawn comes up behind me and roughly cuts chunks of hair away. When the gush of wee has slowed, I clench my pelvic muscles to stop anymore coming out. Quickly stand and pull my knickers up, wiping my wet fingers on them as I do. I step away from the jug and back towards the door. I have to get away from them.

'Get her fingernails,' Jonah says.

Dawn steps towards me with the scissors she used to cut my hair but I hold my hand up to stop her. Quickly bite my thumbnail off and hand it to her. I don't want her to touch me again.

'More,' Jonah says.

I bite them all off, grimacing at the taste of wee coating my fingers, then pour them into Dawn's upturned hand.

She puts the hair and nails in the jug with the wee and then they leave without saying anything more. As Dawn follows Jonah down the garden path, I see some of my wee slosh out of the jar onto her hand. She raises it to her lips and licks it. I feel a visceral tug low down in my stomach and swallow back bile. Is she completely insane now, like her son obviously is?

I have no idea what they plan to do with the jar. Where they think they'll find blessed ground to carry out their mad plan. But I do know that whatever it is, it won't give the results they want so they'll be back for more. How long before they come back again with the next anti-witch remedy he's concocted from the books?

I run upstairs and dress in the clothes I'd had on the day before that are heaped on the chair next to my bed. I'll go to Heddon's Mouth. Surely they'll take me in there after the help I've given them before. I'll wait until dark then sneak off. They won't know I'm gone until it's too late. I have to see Berry before I go though, convince her to come too. She's been learning the herbs too since she was a young girl. How long before they turn on her too?

Sacrifice

Moon Phase: Waxing Gibbous

BERRY ARRIVES A couple of hours later. 'Evie, things are not looking good. You have to go,' she says as she comes through the kitchen door. 'I saw Jonah and Dawn coming back from here with the jug and I followed them. They poured it into a bottle then buried it while chanting their made-up prayers and rhymes.'

'I know. I'm going tonight. You should come with me.' I'm stirring a pot of herbal soup on the range. Rosemary, thyme and ransom so it will be delicious and health-giving but it won't keep me full for long or give me much energy for my journey.

'Jonah's really fired up now. He's been preaching all morning.' She holds out something wrapped in a cloth. 'I brought you this.'

When I pull it open, the smell brings saliva gushing into my mouth. A cooked chicken leg.

'I saved it for you from my dinner last night. Jonah sacrificed a chicken yesterday in a ceremony to help protect us from your evil. He's saved the blood and is keeping it in a bottle.' She shakes her head and pulls another cloth package from her pocket. 'He's confused. He's reading the bible, books about voodoo, all sorts. I've tried again to reason with him but it's as if he's possessed.' She lays down the cloth on the table and opens it up. Shiny blackberries.

'What are the others saying?' I shred all the meat from the chicken leg and drop it into my herb soup, popping a bit into my mouth.

'Nobody is saying anything. They're either too scared to stand up to him, or they really believe. I can't tell which is true and when I've tried to speak to people, they won't talk about it to me.'

I gesture for her to sit down and place a cup of water in front of her. Thankful that she's here, still on my side. Just a few months older than Jonah but so different. They were both brought up here in the same way. We taught them all from the same books that I saved from the library, but one had gone down the path of prejudice and vengefulness, the other compassion and love. My nana used to talk to me about nature versus nurture when I was young. She'd wanted to be a research psychologist but couldn't afford the fees so had just taught herself from books. She was interested in whether we are what we are because we would always have been that way, or because of the environment we grow up in. Well, looking at Berry and Jonah I would have to say that nature wins. Although Jonah had Dawn while Berry had Tess as a mother, so maybe there really is a bit of both sides influencing how we turn out.

Berry shares some soup with me, just a tiny amount as she insists I need it more. And she's right. I have no idea what the journey to the next bay will be like. It's many years since I left here. Afterwards, we wash up together both of us silent and staring out at the sea, which is flat and grey.

Then we sit side-by-side on the old sofa next to the range and I hold her smooth, strong hands in mine that are becoming gnarled and veiny, weakening slightly now with age. 'Berry, come with me. They're going to start on you next, I'm sure. Because I've been teaching you.'

She shakes her head. 'No, they won't. Not yet anyway. He loves me. Wants to marry me, he says.'

If only things had turned out differently, imagine how happy an occasion the marriage of my grandson and Tess's daughter would have made us all. Instead, it fills me with dread.

'But surely you don't want this?' I squeeze her hands

to show her how much I believe this would be wrong.

'No, of course not. He's not right in the head. There's something missing in him. But I can distract him for a few days, so he won't know that you're gone. It'll be too late when he realises and you'll be there. Then I'll come too.'

'Assuming they'll take me in.' I stand and put a kettle on for tea. 'They might turn me away. Then what do I do? And what about Tess, can you just leave her behind?'

'They will help and yes, I'll leave Mum. She doesn't even know who I am anymore, and Hazel and Stan will look after her. You're right. He will turn on me, especially when he feels spurned.' She pulls me to her and gives me a hard hug, a kiss on both cheeks. Wipes the tears from my face then her own with a gentle finger. 'Keep safe and I'll see you soon.'

'If I'm not there, at the hotel, it means they wouldn't take me in. So I'll wait at the beach, in the old kiln there. It will provide some shelter. Do you know how to find it?'

She nods and stands up to go. 'I will find you. Now I have to go. I don't want Jonah to find me here.' She kisses me again on the cheek. Then she's gone.

I spend the morning harvesting what herbs and plants I can to take with me. Pack them all away in a box inside my rucksack. I pull some up gently by the roots and wrap them in cloths so that they can be planted again. I can start a new garden if the people in the old hotel will let me make it my new home. When the sun gets too hot to work, I sit under the willow tree and chat to Connor.

'You wouldn't believe how things changed after you'd gone. All of those times we speculated on how the world was going to turn out. Never like this. Never did we think it would be like medieval times again. That religion and superstition would take over again. Are we just on a cycle? Will they use those books to start commerce and capitalism again next?'

I stroke the grass that covers where Connor lays then roll over onto my back, watch the clouds chase each other across the sky. Gulls screech far down below and a soft breeze swishes through the trees. My home. I can't even imagine not being here. Nearly forty years since I first arrived. And now I have to run away. How has it come to this? What will Michael think about me going? Will he at least wish I'd come to say goodbye? Or does he really not care now he's got Olivia and his own family?

I shake these thoughts off. No time to sit and think about all this now. I go inside and pack the few books I'll be able to carry. The encyclopaedia of herbs, my book of Chinese medicine, and *The Mayor of Casterbridge*. A novel of human nature from a past that came long before me but that has a message that resonates many hundreds of years later in an England that nobody could have envisaged would come around again. Then I sit at the kitchen table and write a letter to Michael, hoping that

Berry will see it before anyone else does and pass it on.

I don't tell him how hurt I am that he hasn't felt able to support me, instead I say how sorry I am for all the things I did wrong. The lies, the leaving, the lack of motherly love while I was off trying to save the world. If he does get to read it maybe he'll understand that in the end I really did realise that it was my family that was important. That I would have stayed anyway even if the world as we knew it hadn't ended. Know that I love them all.

Just as the sun is going down, I hear a noise from the front garden. I peep around the curtain in Michael's old bedroom. Jonah's lackeys are there, sticking branches into the ground. Another of their old witch protection charms, no doubt. They make a line of them across the grass in front of the kitchen window and then another on the other side of the front door in the grass in front of the sitting room. Then they chant over them and leave.

When I'm sure they aren't coming back I go outside to take a closer look. Hazel, holly, ash and rowan branches. I'm sure it means something to them but I have no idea what it's supposed to do. I go back in and sit at the kitchen table, staring through the window, watching the mist rise from the trees on the cliffs and the waves crashing onto the rocks below. Preparing myself to do it. To leave my home. What's going to happen to me?

Running

Moon Phase: Waxing Gibbous

SOMETIME AROUND MIDNIGHT, I set off. I stop just before the house half-way up the lane. Some of Jonah's gang live in this house and I don't want to get caught. The only sounds I can hear are the leaves rustling in the trees and water tumbling down the cliff behind the house. But there's light coming through the window, which looks directly out on to the road. I crawl on my hands and knees past the end of the path until I round the corner then leap to my feet. When I get to the bridle path I take the axe I've bought with me and chop my way through the brambles. It's hard going and by the time I get out the other side I'm scratched and dishevelled, exhausted and wondering if I should keep going or find somewhere to sleep. Then I hear shouting in the distance behind me. I don't know whether it's anything to do with me or not but can't take the chance, so I find some strength from somewhere and push on, stumbling on roots and brambles, pushing branches aside. Even though I've kept fit all these years I'm still getting on. Fifty-five is pretty old again now that we don't have all the artificial ways of keeping people alive.

The clouds clear and the almost full moon lights my way. I'm stopped by a wall of brambles covering the path completely. I hack my way through for what seems like hours then the path opens up beyond it. It's been tidied, the heather and gorse cut back from the well-trodden path. The people from Heddon must have done it. Why did they stop here and not carry on to see us? I sit and rest for a while, lie flat on my back with my head resting on the rucksack. Alert for sounds of people following me. But there's nothing. Nobody here but me and the moon and the stars. Even the gulls are silent, sleeping. An owl hoots somewhere far off. My eyes start to droop so I force myself to get back up and carry on.

The sun's just coming up when I reach the old hotel. I bang hard on the front door, thinking I might need to wake them, but someone appears straight away. An outline in the shadows but they don't come any closer to the door. Will they remember me and how I helped them?

'Who's that?' A woman's voice calls out.

'My name's Evie. I've come from Woody Bay. I need your help.'

The woman opens the door. It's Daisy, whose child I saved that night when I was here with Michael. I could sob with relief but I swallow it down. I don't want to scare her.

'Evie, it's been so long. Come in, come in.' She ushers me through the door. Her hair's greying now, her skin lined and ruddy from the sun, and I know I look the same.

I follow her through to the kitchen where there's a fire going in the grate and candles are burning. Do they have bees too for the wax? A book lies face down on the table next to a mug that has steam rising from it. It's all so normal and so welcoming. I can't believe that just a few miles away from our bay everything is still so sane.

'What's wrong?' Daisy says as she pours hot liquid from a pot into another mug and hands it to me. I sink into the nearest chair and cup it in my hands. Only now, as the adrenaline drains away, do I realise how utterly exhausted I am. While we sip our tea and the light outside grows steadily stronger, I tell her about what's been happening. It all seems even madder now that I've got away.

Daisy keeps shaking her head, her eyes widening further as I tell of the persecution and the things they'd been doing.

'Well you must stay here with us,' she says when I reach the end of the tale. 'My boy will be so pleased to meet you. He knows all about you and how you saved his life. Many times he spoke of coming to see you but something has always stopped him. It's as if we all know that our valley is a good place and we shouldn't leave it.'

'Really? I can stay?' My hands tremble so I put the mug down on the table. Slump back in the chair, a huge breath that I hadn't realised I was holding sighs out of me. 'I can stay? You're sure.'

'Of course, Evie.' She reaches across the table and squeezes my hand. 'Finish your tea and I'll get a room ready for you.'

IN THE ROOM that is now mine, I strip down to my vest and knickers and stretch out in the bed, falling into a heavy sleep immediately.

The sun is still shining when I wake but I feel like I've been sleeping for a long time. I pull on my clothes and head downstairs. The front bar area's empty but I can hear voices. I walk to the back where floor to ceiling windows used to make up a whole wall overlooking the garden. One of the panes has been filled in with inter-twined branches and mud. The other panes are cracked but still in place and I can see Daisy is in the garden along with several other people.

I head down to join them, my legs shaking as I walk down the stairs. I can barely lift my arms and every step burns through my thighs.

Everyone's sat around, either on the grass or at the old picnic tables left over from the days when people came here to socialise and holiday. Apart from the fact that everyone's dressed in clothes that have obviously been made from old bedding and curtains, it looks like it could have been those carefree olden times that none of us had known in real life, just from books and the screens.

A woman with long white hair sits on a bench facing away from the house but she turns when she hears me pull the door closed behind me. Amber.

Her face breaks into a smile. She has hardly any teeth left, but she's still beautiful to me, the light shining from her eyes, 'Evie. It's so lovely to have you here with us again.' She pats the seat beside her and when I sit down she grips my hands in hers. 'You are welcome here.'

After I've had some food, Amber and I go for a walk. She leads me down to the back of the garden, past a pond luminous with algae. A weeping willow's fronds stir it around as they sway in the breeze. We cross the pond on a crumbly wooden plank and join the path that slopes gently downhill alongside the river. She holds my hand as we walk and looks at me often, smiling, but neither of us speak. A blackbird's song filters softly down through the trees that line the hill. My shoulders are no longer up around my ears and in noticing that, I realise how tense I've been for a very long time.

When we reach the stony beach, we sit on a large flat rock close to the river's edge and watch it tumble into the sea. The heat shimmers over the water and the sea seems to bleach into the sky. It's one of those weird days that are bright but grey too. I keep glancing up at the path on the headland, expecting Jonah and the rest of them to appear at any moment, but nobody comes.

'Daisy told me what's been happening.' Amber shakes her head. 'It's hard to believe. What brought all that on?'

'I have no idea. Maybe we shouldn't have cut ourselves off, shouldn't have read all the books about the past. Perhaps it's my fault for teaching them all about our history.'

She shakes her head again. 'I don't see how it can be your fault. I was taught all sorts of things about history when I was young, and it didn't set me off wanting to kill people and thinking they were devils. It must be something that was there in him already.'

We both go quiet and watch the sea, see the clouds starting to lift on the horizon so you can see the hills in Wales. Was Jonah always going to turn out like that no matter what I did? Was what happened with Dawn when Connor died behind it all? Had she put him up to all this – still angry at me after all these years? I'll never know. I'll never get to ask them and get a rational answer. They've both gone mad.

As we approach the house again, an hour or so later, Amber says, 'We should have a celebration tonight. To welcome you to our family.'

I clasp both her hands in mine and squeeze them gently. Then pull her into a hug, the biggest smile I've felt in ages lighting up my face, tingles rushing all over me. I have a new home.

I GO AND lay down again, still exhausted from my flight but glad that we had walked to the beach otherwise my legs would have seized up completely. I sleep deeply again for a couple of hours and when I wake with a gasp, the sun is just going down. My face is wet.

In my dream, I was weeping. Lying under the willow where Connor is with a deep, wide trench surrounding me. So deep and wide I would never be able to cross it without a bridge. The tree had withered and died, its fronds blackened and charred as if it had been burned. The garden surrounding it was in tatters and the house, my home, which should have been right there in front of me, was a small speck far away. A siren, like the one we heard on the journey down here so long ago, wailed continuously and Berry was shouting something that I couldn't quite hear. Panic in her voice. I couldn't see her, but she felt close by.

I wipe the tears away. It's the first dream I've had in a long time. They've returned and left me with a message that I cannot go back. Not that I want to. But is it a sign that they've burned the house down, that Berry is in trouble now too? I shake my head. Maybe we can go back for her. Maybe with the support of everyone here, I can stand up to him.

AMOS, WHO WAS just a child last time I was here, helps me to fill a shallow bath with water carried up from the big pot that simmers constantly on the kitchen range. I sink into it gratefully, really feeling my age for the first time.

I dress in the only other clothes I brought with me – faded jeans and a black t-shirt – and head down to the bar where I can hear lots of voices. I can't believe my eyes when I get there and everyone's drinking beer, which they're pulling from the pumps.

'What...how?' I say.

Amos laughs and hands me a glass. 'They had it all here. There's a little brewery down in the basement. We haven't got any wheat, or hops, but we've been making it with corn, which we grow up in the fields beyond the woods.'

I sip at it, amazed again at how different things are

here compared to my Woody Bay. Why had it all gone so wrong there? Was it my fault? Would the same happen here now that I'd come to stay? I shake the despair away. No, it wasn't my fault and there was no reason it should happen again.

The beer has an unusual taste but not unpleasant. After the first glass my head is already a bit light, so I decline to have any more until after food. Plates of baked potatoes, salads and omelettes cover the table. It's all delicious and the room is filled with laughter. It doesn't feel real after everything I've been through, especially after I've had another glass of beer.

We light candles in holders on the walls, on the shelves, bar and table, and then Amos pulls out a guitar, and Willow some small bongo drums, and the singing and dancing begins. I'm safe. All I had to do was come to the next bay along. Everything that's been happening is starting to seem like a bad dream. They haven't come after me. The people here are happy, joyful and obviously have plenty of food and love to go round. We just need to get Berry here and everything can be good again. But maybe Jonah will chase her. After all, he wants her, he doesn't care about me. Is probably glad I've gone.

I push all these thoughts aside and focus on staying in the moment. As Connor taught me – that's all there is. The singing, the dancing, the love I can feel all around me is my reality right now.

After another glass of beer, Amber and I both say goodnight and leave them all to it.

THE NEXT MORNING I wake just as it's getting light. I listen to the birds stirring in the trees, the cheep and chirrups of the chaffinches and tits. So many of them now. Then I hear footsteps on the gravelly path coming down from the cliffs. Oh God, is it them? I listen harder. It doesn't sound like a big group. Just a couple of people and I don't think Jonah would come without all his lackeys to back him up. I creep to the window and peek out of the curtains.

I rush downstairs and meet them just as they come through the door into the bar.

'Berry!'

She drops her big, heavy rucksack to the floor and rushes into my outstretched arms. 'I was in bed last night and I couldn't sleep and I knew I couldn't stay there. So I got up and left.'

'I was on lookout duty and saw her appearing through the mist this morning. I wasn't sure if she was real at first,' Amos says.

I can tell by his tone he's entranced by her. And why wouldn't he be? She's beautiful inside and out and it shines from her like it did from Rachael. 'Lookout duty?' I say.

He nods. 'We thought it would be a good idea for now.'

So much trouble because of me. I squeeze his arm, grateful that these people seem to think I'm worth it.

He smiles and takes my hand. 'You'll be okay. I'll go make us all some tea.'

I lead Berry out to the garden and we sit in silence, holding hands, watching the sun rise over the hills, shining on a new day, a new start.

Free

Moon Phase: Full

BERRY IS GIVEN a room next door to mine. I sit on her bed and watch as she pulls things from her rucksack. She's brought lots more of my clothes as well as her own. And more herbs, although from what I've seen so far it seems likely that there'll already be a good herb garden here. But more is always good.

After breakfast, Daisy takes us on a tour. They've got two fields of corn, two orchards filled with apple, pear, plum and cherry trees. One field is filled with root vegetables – potatoes, carrots, turnips, swedes, beets. Another with squashes and pumpkins, courgettes, cucumbers, and more too far away for me to see what they are. It's all flourishing. Three more fields are lying fallow.

In the gardens behind the house are raised beds with salads and herbs, spinach and chard. Runner bean canes where peas grow too. Hoverflies buzz around going from plant to plant doing their pollinating job. Even a bumble bee tumbles from a foxglove, drunk on pollen. You can feel the life energy from all of the insects and the plants filling the air. It's been so long since it felt like this at Woody Bay. After the bee hives were destroyed, it took me so long to get a new one established and it never flourished in the same way as before. Insect life on the whole had been scarce. I'd thought it was the climate, and I realise now it was, but the human one that had been created. The one filled with fear and hatred had infected everything. You just had to look at this place filled with love and joy to see what a difference it made – insects and healthy crops galore.

'We lose some to the rabbits and deer,' Daisy says with a smile. 'But that's okay, there's plenty for us all.' She points to a space at the end of the raised beds. 'You can plant your herbs there.'

She leaves me and Berry there and heads back indoors.

Berry smiles at me. 'I've got a good feeling. How about you?'

I nod but there's a knot of apprehension in my stomach still. I can't believe it's that easy.

By the time Berry and I head back indoors at the end of the day, there's a new raised bed in place filled with the herb plants we'd brought with us. It's been a long time since I did any planting and it feels so good to have spent time with the soil and the plants again. There's a good ache in my back and dirt crusted under every fingernail. I relax into it. Letting myself believe that we're free. That we got away and all of that is over now.

WHEN DAISY COMES to wake me, I'm still in the same position I'd been in when I first lay down. It feels like I've hardly slept at all but it's dark, just the candle Daisy's holding providing a faint flickering light around us.

'Evie, come on, get up. They're coming. Amos was out on the path and he saw their torches. They'll be here in about forty minutes.'

I push myself out of bed, every muscle in my body complaining, and start dressing. 'I'll go now. Tell them I was here and left. Get Berry up.'

She grabs my shoulders, 'No. Stay. We won't let them hurt you. We'll tell them we're happy for you to be here with us. I've spoken to everyone and we all agree. We're not scared of them.'

I shrug her hands off and carry on dressing. 'No. I won't put you in danger too. You don't know what he's like. What his band of followers are like.'

She tries to persuade me but I have to go. I can't be here when they arrive. I know they'll get me.

I rush into Berry's room, shake her awake. I don't even have to tell her. She nods and gets up, dresses quickly and takes my hand as we run down the stairs.

Daisy walks with us to the path Amber and I took the day I'd arrived, out through the back of the hotel gardens.

'We'll hide on the beach. Tell them I was here, that I rested for just a night then set off up through the woods towards Heale. Say I told you I was heading for Barnstaple eventually, and you haven't seen Berry at all.'

She hugs us both tight. 'I'll come get you when they've gone.'

I turn to leave but she grabs my arm. 'Wait. I remembered that I have a letter for you from Tom.' She pushes it into my hand. 'He left it here years ago, the last time we saw him.'

I glance at it. His handwriting in black on a tatty blue envelope. 'For Evie. Only open this when the lights come on.'

Tom. I haven't thought of him in ages and now here he is again. Always turns up when there's trouble. What on earth is this about? I haven't got time to think about it. I stuff the letter into my jeans pocket then run off into the night, stumbling on rocks that I can't see in the dark, pulling Berry behind me. The full moon is hidden behind clouds; branches whip my face as panic propels me forward. When I fall and twist my ankle I get a hold of myself. They'll hear us even if they can't see us if we carry on like this. Berry pulls me up and I lean against her, wincing at the pain in my ankle.

'Are you alright?' she whispers.

I nod but I'm limping as we start again more slowly, more quietly. The pain in my ankle wears off as we creep along. We cross the river at the first bridge so that we're further away from where Jonah and his gang will come down into the valley. The path from the bridge climbs steeply away from the river. Something rustles in the bushes and there's a splash. Maybe the otters have come back now that we're not polluting everything anymore.

We stop at the top of the slope so I can catch my breath then we head out towards the sea. The path is rocky and gravelly and the crunch of our feet seems so loud to me.

As we reach the top of the next slope the trees fall away, and the moonlight is glinting on the sea in the distance. Huge cliffs rear up either side of us, black and jagged against the paler grey of the night sky. I stop to take it in, in awe of the world's beauty that seems capable of surviving anything we do to it.

A couple of minutes later I see the flaming torches coming around the corner of the path near to the top of the cliffs, on the other side of the river. I pull Berry to a stop, pointing up there and then press myself back against the cliff side, gesturing for her to do the same. Hoping the moonlight won't reveal us to them. As the torches start to descend the path towards the hotel, we hurry towards the beach. The sound of the waves and the river tumbling down the rocky beach to join them drives everything else from my mind as we huddle up in the corner of the old lime kiln, cold, hungry and tired but too scared to light a fire. I hug Berry to my side for comfort and warmth. We've got a long night ahead. Please let them believe Daisy.

I pull Tom's letter from my pocket. I can't read it in the dark. What did he mean if the lights come on? What lights?

'Why has Tom left you a letter?' Berry whispers.

She was young when he left and barely knew him. Tess had always wanted to keep Berry away from him. Even after I'd decided to make the best of him being there, Tess couldn't forget what she knew. Never trusted him. Berry has no idea about all that came before me and Tess went to Woody Bay, nor what happened when Tom arrived there years later. Tess was pregnant with her then.

'We have history,' I say. 'We've known each other a very long time.'

Tom. Every single time things in my life have gone really wrong, it's been Tom's fault. If it hadn't been for him I wouldn't have come to Woody Bay. Jonah wouldn't even exist. Tom was my lover. He's Dawn's father. He vanished a long time ago. And now, when the grandson he left behind is going to kill me, here he is again.

Part II

Then
2035

Starting

WHEN I FIRST met Tom, I was seventeen. I was working in Coffair, the only coffee shop brand left in the world and a massive polluter, killer of rainforests, and abuser of workers' rights. My idea of hell but I needed money and it was either that or work in one of the clothes or gadgets shops. Equally bad. It was a Thursday. The book group, several silver-haired women who came in at the same time every week, had just left when one of the girls I worked with screamed. I looked up from wiping a table to see a crowd of protesters streaming through the door throwing balloon bombs – some filled with muddy water others with flour. The stench of rotting plants filled the room. River water. Toxic.

'Slave owners. Tax avoiders. Planet killers. Scum!' The crowd chanted as they rampaged through the shop turning over tables and chairs, throwing food from the fridges onto the floor and stamping on it. I bit my bottom lip to keep from smiling but I couldn't help myself and the laughter burst out of me. Tom was the protester closest to me and he looked at me in my slave uniform and grinned. Then, as quickly as they were there, they were gone.

When I finished my shift, Tom was waiting for me outside.

'Hello, laughing girl,' he said, pushing away from the wall where he'd been leaning, scrolling on his phone.

'Hello, protest boy,' I replied. Although he definitely wasn't a boy. A man. At least six or seven years older than me.

We went to a pub, the Ale House, another relic from the past, just like the book group. We sat in a little wooden booth covered in graffiti with beer mats all over the walls. My eyes stung and I recoiled from the stench of piss wafting through the back door from the toilets. Everything was covered in a layer of grime. Even so, I was impressed by Tom.

Here he was, with his grey eyes and golden hair, voicing all the things I said to myself in my head all the time. The things I tried to make my mum and dad see so that they'd stop with the breeding. It seemed as if they were on a mission to single-handedly keep the human race going, in the face of all the evidence that said we were on our way out.

'You should join us. You don't belong in that shop, but for now it would be good if you stayed. See if you can find out anything from the Coffair corp office that might help us.' Tom brushed his hair back from his eyes repeatedly as he spoke.

I shook my head before sipping the warmish brown beer he'd bought me. Vile. 'I really don't think I can help you there, unless you want to know about the number of alarming ingredients that go into the "egg" sandwiches.' I cringed. 'All I do is wipe tables, mop floors, fill up dishwashers and fridges.'

'You've not been there long though. You wait, you'll get sent on a staff day where they talk about goals, mission statements, and give you all sorts of info about their plans.'

'How do you know how long I've been there?' Was he some sort of nutter?

'We know lots. We have people who watch and take note of who's left, who's started, who looks like they might be up for helping.'

'Helping with what? Tipping up tables?'

He tapped the side of his nose, 'Well, it's a secret for now. But we like to make life difficult for Coffair and today's protest is a minor one.'

I stared across the scarred, sticky table at him. Not sure what to make of it all. Was he a deluded boy playing at protest or was he really doing something worthwhile? Whatever he was doing I knew already that I was going to help him do it.

But after a few weeks of seeing him it seemed like Tom was the real deal. His activist group, Countervaillence, was organised, determined to bring the government to account, to bring back control to the people and stop the corporations and rich elite from using us and the planet as their playthings. I really thought they could do it as well. Make a proper difference. They were making their plans from their dingy, damp office, one dark and mouldy room in the old converted car park by the canal. He had people researching new technologies, making constant Freedom of Information requests to government departments, all of which were ignored, organising petitions, protests, rallying people to the cause. He had lawyers working with him who sent official complaints to every corporation department they could. But nobody ever responded. He kept hinting that there was a lot more going on behind the scenes and that one day, he'd let me in on all of it. So I kept my ears open when I was at work but I never heard anything worth telling them about. I wanted to help though. I wanted to make a difference.

My first corporate away-day was coming up and Tom said once I'd been to that then he'd look at getting me out of there and working for Countervaillence properly. As well as all the volunteers who did it because they believed, he had paid staff working for him too. I had no idea where he got the money to pay them but that wasn't my problem. As long as he was going to pay me too, I wasn't too worried about how he organised it. I did wonder though. Who would fund a left-wing activist group? What were they hoping to get out of it?

The afternoon before the Coffair staff briefing, Tom took me to his office to tell me what he wanted me to do.

'You'll be taking notes like the good little employee you are but I want you to wear this too.' He pinned a badge onto my Coffair polo shirt.

'Why?'

'It's a microphone. It'll transmit everything they say back here so we can record it. Before you go into the first session in the morning just press it like this.' He stood me up and showed me in the mirror behind the reception desk. 'And keep it switched on until you leave.'

I nodded but wasn't convinced that the kind of information we'd be given at a staff day for table wipers and coffee heaters was going to be of any help in Countervaillance's fight.

Nevertheless, I wore the badge and it made me feel a part of something bigger, more important. Like I was more than just a wage slave. I took a few notes but barely listened to the tales of Coffair's new shops opening, new coffee farms they'd planted in Asia, how excited they were that climate change meant the bean belt was still expanding, profits and losses, goals and objectives. Did they really think that any of us minimum wage slaves cared? My granddad would have been mortified. Coffair was one of the corporations he used to get really riled up about when I was little. Him and Dad ranting away about them stealing land and keeping people in poverty, ripping out ancient forests. I wasn't proud that I worked for them but what was I supposed to do? When I told Dad, another light had gone out in his already fast-dimming eyes. But he patted my arm and smiled, said, 'Well done.' But now I'd be able to tell him I was doing something good. And maybe Granddad could still see me from wherever you go when you die and know that I was following in his footsteps after all.

The day went on for ever and all the food was coffee-flavoured, the only drink was coffee, so by the end of the lunch break everyone was edgy and wired. The din of everyone talking at once hurt my ears and I wanted to leave. But I stuck it out until the end then headed over to Tom's place as instructed, excited that I was going to be able to hand my notice in and start doing something more interesting.

When he opened the door he was naked apart from a towel hanging low on his hips, his hair dripping and water pooling around his feet. I could hear the shower still running somewhere behind him and a musky yet fresh smell wafted into the hall.

'Oh.' I stared past him hoping the heat I could feel in my cheeks didn't show in the shadowy hallway. 'I'm sorry. I'll come back later, shall I?'

But he smiled, took my hand and pulled me through

the door. 'No, no it's fine. Just give me five minutes. Make yourself comfy.'

Something about the way he was looking at me made my insides burn like my cheeks. When he came back, dressed in jeans and a long-sleeved black T-shirt, he leaned in so close to me that I could feel his heartbeat on my arm as he took the microphone off my collar. I held my breath. Hoping I didn't stink of coffee too badly. Wanting him to want me but not knowing what I would do if he did. He put the microphone in a plastic box on a desk in the corner then gave me a glass of red wine and took me out onto the balcony. We sat watching the swans and geese glide along the river, the sun glinting on the tiny waves created by the soft, warm breeze.

'You did really well today, Evie. Thank you for everything you've done for us so far. Have dinner with me. As a thank you and so I can get to get to know you better.'

I bit my bottom lip. I liked him a lot but I had no experience with men, flirting, sex. I giggled. 'OK, great.' My eyes watered as I'd knocked back the whole glass of wine. 'I'll need to go and get changed though.'

He stood and pulled me to my feet. 'No need. We can eat here. Just shower and you can wear one of my t-shirts. It'll be like a dress on you.'

He led me through the bedroom to his en-suite shower room. I was sure he'd be able to hear my heart pounding.

He was very tall, and I was very small, but even so the t-shirt he gave me, black with frayed cuffs that hung down over my hands and a hole in one elbow, ended in the middle of my thighs. I tugged it down as I walked back to the living room. I never wore skirts and dresses. Every time I moved I got a waft of his scent as I'd used the same shower gel. My stomach was all tied up in knots and, at the same time as I wanted to get as close to him as I could, I wanted to run out the door and go home to my attic bedroom, where I didn't have to deal with all these confusing feelings.

Tom was in the open-plan kitchen area, stirring a pot on the hob, and the smell made my mouth water. Earthy and sweet, I didn't know what it was but it wasn't anything like the stodgy stench that came from the tinned and frozen food we always ate at home. I smiled as he looked round at me. He turned the cooker off, put a lid on the pot then came and took both of my hands in his. Then he leaned forward and I took a deep breath in, glad I'd used some of the mouthwash I'd found in the bathroom.

'I really like you, Evie,' he said, right up close to my face.

I swallowed, the sound loud in the silent flat. 'I like you too.'

He came closer and I closed my eyes, waited for the feel of his lips on mine but it didn't come. Instead, he kissed my neck. Soft feathery kisses, and tiny little licks. Oh God. I couldn't breathe. My legs threatened to buckle so I clasped my arms behind his neck. The smell of the musky minty shower gel surrounded us as our skin heated up. He moved his mouth onto mine at the same time as he manoeuvred me onto the sofa. I wanted him to stop but I never wanted it to stop.

I WOKE IN his bed. Thrilled about what was happening but scared of what my mum and dad would say about me staying out all night. Tom was still sleeping so I crept out of the room, rescued the T-shirt from where it had been thrown on the living room floor, then rummaged in my bag to find my phone. Seven missed calls from Dad, twelve from Mum. Nine new voicemails and five texts. One of them from Leah who they'd also been calling to find out where I was.

I sent a quick text to Dad knowing he would be so much easier to deal with. He replied straight away. GLAD YOU'RE SAFE. YOU SHOULD HAVE LET US KNOW LAST NIGHT.

I knew I should have but it all happened so fast and I didn't have time to stop and say, like a little girl, oh I just have to ring my mum and tell her I'm staying out. What would she have said anyway if I had called her? She'd have told me to come home straight away.

I went into the bathroom and dressed in my Coffair

uniform, rubbed toothpaste on my teeth with my finger, and splashed my face with cold water. I had to be at work in twenty minutes and I wanted to make sure before I went in that Tom definitely had a job for me at Counter-vaillence.

His face was buried in the pillow, his wavy hair poking out the top of the quilt. I sat down next to him and gently pushed his shoulder.

'Tom…Tom?'

He didn't move.

I pushed his shoulder a bit harder. 'Tom!'

His eyes flickered but still he didn't wake up. I lost my bottle and left him there to sleep. I wrote on a notepad I found on the desk: *Had to go to work. Text me when you wake up. E x*

All the way to work I agonised over that kiss at the end of the note. Should I have put it? Would he freak out and think I loved him and was going to be a mad stalker type? But everyone put kisses on everything. It would be fine.

All morning I kept checking my phone, which stayed stubbornly silent after I received one hysterical text from my mum. By the time my lunch break came around I was convinced he hated me and now that he'd got what he wanted from the Coffair corporate day, I'd not be hearing from him again. But when I went outside he was there, leaning on the wall again, just like the first time I'd met him.

He smiled and took my hand, pulled me back into the shop and up to the counter where my boss was serving a customer.

'Evie is no longer working here,' Tom shouted. 'She's not being your slave any longer!' Then he turned and ran out the door pulling me with him. Both of us laughing our heads off at the look on everyone's faces as we left them all behind. We went straight to a clothes shop and he bought me a new outfit – black jeans, black and white T-shirt, and black pumps. I stuffed the Coffair uniform in a bin in the toilets inside the mall.

'Right, let's get you to work,' Tom said as I approached the bench on the bridge where he sat waiting for me.

'I've been working all morning and I need some lunch and a break first!'

We had a picnic on the bench but the sun got too hot after a while so we wandered over the bridge and down onto the towpath that led to his office. There was only one other person there when we arrived, a girl a couple of years older than me who looked as if she'd been crying. When she looked up and saw us coming through the door, she grabbed her bag and rushed out without saying anything but she gave Tom a filthy look. I never saw her in the offices again after that.

Tom shoved the papers the girl'd left on the desk she

was using into a drawer. 'You can sit here,' he said, 'and you'll start on a salary the same as you were on at Coffair plus ten per cent.'

I started off working on the online content – writing blogs and emailers, running the social media accounts. For the first time I started to feel like I might have a chance of a life of my own. I stopped handing over all my money to my mum and started keeping some back for me to go out to bars and restaurants with Tom, although he was very generous and often paid. It was as if he'd been sent to change my world, so that together we could change the whole world.

Beliefs

SEVERAL WEEKS AFTER I'd started working at Counter-vaillence, I came downstairs for work in a new outfit. The first brand new clothes that I'd ever brought with my own money. Usually I wore tatty old charity shop stuff. Mum was sat at the table, her swollen belly looking like it might contain more than just one baby again.

'New stuff. How can you do this to us? How can you spend your money on clothes you don't need when we're all going hungry?'

'Hardly. I still give you most of my wages. How is it alright for you to take nearly everything I earn and there be nothing left for me to have a life of my own? Maybe if you stopped having loads of babies—'

She started crying. Like always. Sat among the dirty dishes and piles of laundry, with the last set of twins, Aaron and Isaac, who had just turned one, sitting at her feet staring up at her. When they heard her hiccupy little sobs, they started wailing too.

'May God forgive you,' she croaked out, but I left before I heard anymore. Stomped off down the road, cursing her under my breath, and when I looked up Dad was walking towards me on his way home from a night shift driving the buses. He didn't see me as he was shuffling along staring at the ground. He looked so defeated.

'Alright, Dad?' I said as I got closer.

'Evie, love, hello.' He smiled. 'Off to work?'

I nodded and he shuffled on. I stared after his retreating back. When had he got like this? He'd been a big, boisterous man when I was little. Filled with booming laughs and always debating things with Granddad. It was Mum and her religious bloody mania. She'd done this to him. To all of us. I knew Dad didn't really believe in it all. He'd roll his eyes at me in church when she made us go. I stopped all that church nonsense as soon as I could. Told her I wouldn't go anymore. There were tears and threats, but I stood up to her. I wished Dad would more often.

I watched him turn into our path then hurried on, keen to get to work. I loved my new job. As well as writing things to recruit more people into the cause, I'd started to do more interesting stuff. Researching the latest reports and developments coming out of the universities. Not that many of them were doing proper work now as they were just another tool for big business. And who knows if what they put up on their websites was even true? There was no way we could check as we weren't allowed anywhere near them; as the only universities still going were in London. But I'd done some digging around for the names from research papers and journal articles way back in the past before they segregated us and some of the authors were doing their own thing now. They were all really old and tucked away in their sheds and garages still plugging away trying to make a difference. But they were pretty hard to find and you had to know where to look. None of the science journals published these kinds of things anymore – thoughts about the interconnectedness of everything, philosophy and science merging together to try and find the truth about the world, the universe, consciousness. Nowadays, the screens only churned out propaganda, the news reporters were no longer journalists and just said what they were told to, and the vast majority of people took it all as gospel. Never stopped to wonder whether what we were told was the truth or ask the bigger questions about what we were all doing here. We weren't taught to think for ourselves at school, to question, we were just taught to memorise things, pass tests, for what? I certainly hadn't needed any critical analysis skills working in Coffair and it was only because of Tom I'd got out, started to find out about all these amazing inventions, and that there were so many people trying to change things. I was so grateful to him. And I loved him. I couldn't believe that he loved me too.

As I reached the burger bar by the old train station,

there were lots of old people there with placards saying, "Meat is Murder" and "Animals are our friends not our dinner" – slogans from around the time I was born when there was a huge global trend for veganism. My granddad always used to wear T-shirts with these kinds of things on.

I stopped and watched as one of the old women launched a stone at the window. It didn't even make a scratch.

'Murderers, murderers, murderers!' she screamed.

A girl about my age came and stood next to me, her bleached blond hair glowing in the sunlight as if she was wearing a halo. 'That's my nan. She reckons they've been stealing cats and dogs and cooking them up for the burgers.' She handed me a leaflet.

'And have they?' I said.

She shrugged. 'Put it this way, Nan's cats have all disappeared, and lots of her friends have lost their dogs when they've been out walking them in the river park down by Portman Road. And where else are they going to be getting meat from? It's not like it's easy to come by nowadays, or cheap, but they sell their burgers for hardly anything.'

'I'm Evie.' I stuck my hand out to shake hers.

She gripped my hand hard and pumped it up and down vigorously. 'Tess.'

I stood and watched as Tess's nan and her friends were shoved away from the doors by the burger bar security guards. They only pushed them as far as the pavement, then went back and stood by the doors and watched as they took up their chants again, shoving leaflets at everyone walking by.

'Nice to meet you, Tess. I hope your nan finds her cats.' I waved at the old people and stuck my fist in the air to show solidarity with their cause. 'But I've got to be off to work.'

'Wait up and I'll walk into town with you.' She gave her leaflets to her Nan, hugged her, then we set off.

'So where do you work then?' Tess said.

I explained about Countervaillence and she got out her phone and showed me a website called Nature First.

'This is mine.' She grinned at me. 'Looks like we're all about the same things.'

'So where do you work then?' I asked.

'Nowhere. Help my nan out in her garden and we grow fruit and veg there.'

We chatted as we walked about all the things wrong with the world and how it had to be changed. As we reached the bridge on Duke Street, I knew I wanted to be friends with Tess so we arranged to meet again in my lunch break.

There was nobody in the office, so I made the most of the quiet to work on a plan for a series of blogs and videos I was putting together. Looking at how life for us in the feeder towns had stalled when they'd taken over the cities and shut us out, closed down the transport systems.

My dad told me that around the time I was born everything was changing really fast and new technologies were coming out all the time. But since they closed the borders and herded all the lowly workers out of London, the gadgets we used had mainly stayed the same. They just gave them a different name and made them look slightly different, so people would buy new ones.

I was going to find the scientists and technologists who'd been left behind when London was shut off and interview them. Surely they'd know about the advances still being made, and what it was like in London, as they must still be in touch with old friends and colleagues that lived there, even though officially we weren't allowed any contact with the city people. There was always ways to get round things. Dad had told me loads of stories from when he was young about how you could go to the city whenever you liked. He used to go there and see bands, go to exhibitions and museums. He even lived and worked there for a while when he was young. When he was my age, he'd been in a band and they played gigs all over London in the pubs. Then he got Mum pregnant with me and he had to come back to Reading and look after us. He always said he wouldn't have wanted it any different but when I was little, he used to talk all the time about how his life had been then. London had taken on a mythical status in my head, and in most people's my age.

What was it like there? Who were the people living there? What did they do? And why weren't we allowed in?

Tom hadn't turned up by the time I got hungry, so I texted him to say I'd gone for lunch and would be over by the Abbey ruins if he wanted to join me. Tess was waiting on the bridge where I'd left her a few hours earlier. I bought us some veggie wraps from the hawker stalls in Market Place when she said she had no money to get her own, then wandered over to sit under the trees lining the canal over by the Abbey. Even though we were well into Autumn it was still way too hot to sit in the sun for long.

'How do you live then without having a job?' I said.

'My dad works so we have a bit of money coming in. We get the government food package once a month, which has a tin of something, veggie stew, curry, stuff like that, for each of us per day. And with the food me and my nan grow, we manage. Just. Trade a few bits we've got extra to some of the local shops.'

She was ever so skinny. Her clothes were even tattier than my usual charity shop attire but she didn't look beaten down by any of it.

'It's not right, is it? The way things are. We have to find a way to change it,' I said.

I saw Tom walking towards us, coming from the direction of the river and the shanty towns. Where had he been all morning?

He leaned over and kissed me before sitting down,

pinching the last bit of my wrap out of my hands and taking a big bite.

'Oi, cheeky,' I said as I grabbed the final morsel back. 'Say hello to Tess.'

Tom leaned forward so he could see her. 'Hello to Tess.'

She smiled at him but something about her changed as soon as he arrived, became more guarded.

I told Tom about her blog and the things she'd been writing about, but was shocked when he offered her a job on the spot.

'Really? Doing what?' she asked warily.

'Working with Evie on the communications. We need people like you to help tell the stories.'

'What, and you'll pay me and everything?'

Tom laughed. 'And everything. Come back with us after lunch and we can chat about it.'

By the end of the day when we left the office, Tess had her job all sorted and was starting officially the next day. I'd spent the afternoon showing her the projects I'd been working on for the past couple of months. The three of us wandered up Duke Street, chatting, relaxed together now. When we got to Broad Street, Tess left us to meet a friend and Tom and I went for drinks. We sat in the pub garden in the final bit of sun in the corner, a bottle of white wine in an ice bucket on the table in front of us.

'Cheers.' Tom clinked his glass against mine.

As I swallowed the icy cold wine I could feel him watching me.

'Move in with me, Evie.' He took the glass from me and put it down, then took both my hands in his. 'I'm not going to lie. There have been a lot of girls before you but never anyone like you, and no-one that I've asked to live with me.'

I couldn't believe he wanted me to but I was nodding before I even thought about it properly.

When I got home, Dad had already left for work and Mum was in her usual spot at the table, surrounded by debris. Did she never stop to think that there could be more to life than sitting there surrounded by crap and continually popping out babies?

'I'm moving out.' There was a smug tone in my voice. She might not be able to have a life but I was going to.

'What do you mean? Where are you going?'

'I'm moving in with Tom.'

They'd never even met him. Mum shook her head violently. 'No, you are not. Don't be stupid you're still a child.'

'I'm seventeen, not much younger than you were when you had me and married Dad. And if I'm just a child how come I'm the one that pays the rent, buys the food?'

She stood up, her white-knuckled hands wringing a tea towel in front of her. 'That's what being a family is about.'

'Oh yeah? How come you don't do anything then? You just sit there. You take my money, treat me like a skivvy and do nothing but try and make me feel bad about myself with all the crap you talk about sins and hell. You're off your head!'

The twins started crying and she spun away from me to pick one up in each arm, resting them on either side of her enormous belly. Sam, born just eleven months after me, sat drooling in the corner as always, his mind somewhere far away. But he banged his hand down on the chair at the shouting.

I was in my stride now though and wouldn't be stopped. 'I'm sick of it. Let Luke get a job and pay for everything. I'm not doing it anymore.'

'He's still at school for another year. How can he?' She jiggled the twins to try and stop them crying.

'Not my problem. I'm going and you can't stop me.'

'If you do this then you are dead to me. You can never come here again.' Her eyes gleamed with triumph. She thought I'd back down. She was wrong.

'Fine.' I turned and left, slamming the door behind me.

I left the house ten minutes later with all of my clothes stuffed into cloth bags. I didn't care if I never saw her again. I had a new life with Tom and I was going to do important things that would change the world.

Queasy

FOR THE FIRST few weeks of living with Tom, I was the happiest I'd ever been. We had lazy days in bed at the weekend, walked along the river paths in the late afternoon sun, ate in restaurants, danced in clubs, worked hard at Countervaillence, and it seemed like my life was going to be that wonderful forever. But then I started to feel tired all the time, queasy, and the first time I puked in the morning as soon as I woke up, I realised I hadn't had a period in a while. But there was no way I could be pregnant. I'd gone on the pill a couple of weeks after we'd got together. I wouldn't let myself think about the weeks before that when we'd been having loads of sex and not using anything.

Tom had gone out early to visit his parents. They lived out in the east of Reading on the way to the old motorway junction, in a housing estate that had been built at the start of the millennium on the old bog ground. I'd asked if I could go too but he said not yet. They were difficult, sick, and it was hard enough for him to deal with without having to worry about what I was feeling too. So I walked into town and bought a pregnancy test in the supermarket, using the self-serve machine so I wouldn't have to face a check-out operator.

Back at the flat I sat on the toilet and peed on the stick, getting it all over my fingers. I washed my hands and watched for the second blue line to appear, praying to a God I didn't believe in that it wouldn't. But of course it did. Shit. What was I going to do? I didn't want a baby but there was no way I could get rid of it. I might have stopped going to church as soon as I could, but the early years of Catholic indoctrination meant that guilt and fear were still in there somewhere. And I was only seventeen. You can't be rational and wise and make good decisions at that age. Well, I couldn't anyway.

I lay on the sofa for hours, staring out the window at the sky and trying to imagine what it would be like to have a baby, be a mother. I couldn't. All I could see was my mum in that poky, dark house, crying all the time and the smell of puke and shit that was always around her. But whether I could imagine myself being a mother or not, I was going to be one. And I wouldn't be like her. I wouldn't have loads of babies, just one, and I had Tom and a nice place to live. It would be great.

I decided to keep it to myself for a while though. Luckily, Tom called and said he had to stay with his parents for a couple of days to sort some things out, so at least I wouldn't have to make excuses to not go out drinking and dancing. I had the whole weekend to myself to get my head around it and by the time he came home on Sunday night, I'd convinced myself that everything was going to be absolutely fine. Unexpected, yes, and not ideal, but we could work it out. Even so, I didn't want to blurt the news out as soon as he got home. One more day wouldn't hurt.

We spent the next day at the office and there were lots of volunteers around, planning their next raid on a Coffair shop, so we didn't spend much time together. Tess and I were working on a communications strategy – a mix of video, blogs and social media campaigns to try and get people thinking more and wanting to take back control of their lives, to be free again. It was a long day and I hoped that Tom wouldn't want to go out in town at the end of it. I didn't have to worry. When the door closed behind Tess, and we were alone, he looked shattered.

'Come on. Let's go home,' he said taking my hand.

WHEN I CAME out of the shower, towelling my hair dry and wearing my pyjamas, Tom was in the kitchen preparing dinner.

'Tom, I've got something to tell you,' I sat down on the stool at the breakfast bar, gripping the towel on my lap. Swallowing the nerves bubbling up inside me.

Tom turned to face me, the knife in his hand. 'What's that then?'

I needed to be close to him so I went and stood in front of him, rested my hands on his hips. God, what was he going to say? Even though I'd convinced myself that it was all going to be alright, I kind of knew I was lying to myself. Every time my mind had tried to create this scene it had skittered quickly away.

'I'm pregnant. I'm sorry. I did a test. I'm sorry.' I hadn't planned on apologising. Surely it was his responsibility too?

I stared intently at his face. Wasn't he going to say anything?

His jaw clenched and he turned away. 'You'll have to get rid of it,' he said and just carried on chopping the onions.

'Of course I won't get rid of it,' I said to his back. 'I couldn't do that.'

'But you know the statistics, Evie. The truth about the food, the future, what it's going to be like. You can't bring a baby into the world. I won't be a part of it.'

I gulped back a sob. I did know all of this but there was still a part of me that hoped things could be different. That there would be a way for us to sort it out, make it okay again.

'But—'

'No, don't say but. There is no but. If you're doing

this then you're on your own. I'm not having you here.' He still hadn't turned to look at me. How could he be so cold?

I reached out and stroked his back but his shoulders tensed and he shifted away from me. How had our normal evening at home turned into something so different, so horrible, so quickly?

'I know it's a shock but let's just take some time to think about it. We don't have to decide anything today.' I still hoped that we could sort it out.

'You don't get it, do you?' He turned, waving the knife at me to emphasise his words. 'The decision is already made. I don't want your baby and if you choose to have it then I don't want you either.'

'It's not just my baby, it's yours too.'

'How do I know that? I don't know what you get up to. You're not the only girl I have sex with so how do I know what you get up to when I'm not here?'

His unexpected viciousness stole my breath and I had to grip the table and bend over to try to get it back. I thought he loved me. I was such a stupid, idealistic, foolish girl. And despite everything I'd thought and said about my mum, I'd ended up pregnant by accident, just like her.

I turned and ran to the bedroom, pulling my pyjamas off as I went. I dressed in jeans and a sweater then grabbed a holdall that wasn't mine from under the bed and stuffed all my clothes inside. I kept expecting him to come after me, to say sorry, to stop me. But I could hear him chopping away in the kitchen and he didn't stop even as I slammed the door behind me.

Where was I going to go? I couldn't go back home. Dad would have welcomed me back but Mum meant it when she said I was dead to her. I walked along the river path towards Caversham Bridge. I'd never felt so alone before, or scared. Not only did I not have a home, I no longer had a job. Tom wouldn't keep me around at Countervaillance any longer either. I headed to the office. There was no way that I was going to leave behind all the stuff I'd been working on.

In the office, I created a new email address and cloud account and backed up everything from my laptop into there, and onto a hard drive which I stuffed in my bag, then deleted it all from the Countervaillence cloud. If he didn't want me and our baby then he couldn't have my ideas, my work, either. Wherever I was going to go, I could still think, still write and try and get the word out. I didn't need Tom. I stuffed my laptop into my holdall and walked out of the Countervaillance offices for the last time. I swiped at the tears running down my face. Even though I'd only worked there for a short while, it was where I'd become more conscious, where I'd been able to take the feelings and ideas I'd always had and turn them into something coherent. It had meant so much to me to be working alongside everyone there, realising that the world was a very different place to the one the screens would have you believe, thinking of ways to make a difference. It had taught me so much about myself too. I was not the same person Tom had found in the coffee shop. I could do whatever I needed to keep me and my baby safe and carry on spreading the truth. I just had to find somewhere to go.

To start with, I headed to Leah's house. I couldn't leave without seeing her and maybe she'd have some ideas. She wasn't in when I arrived, so I sat on the wall and waited for her. Only one street behind my old house but I felt a very long way from it and knew I wouldn't ever be returning to Belmont Road, no matter what happened. Leah didn't come home for hours and when she arrived, I had fallen asleep on the doorstep with my head on the holdall.

'Evie! What are you doing?' She stumbled towards me, her breath stinking of the cheap vodka she always drank.

It made my stomach turn. Her twin brother, Lloyd, was behind her looking just as drunk, along with another man, boy, I'd never met before. I tried to speak but it turned into a great, gulping sob and Leah crouched down, pulling me into her arms. 'What's wrong?'

I couldn't speak for crying so she pulled me to my feet and led me into the house. Sat me down on the sofa and hugged me until I'd cried myself out. Lloyd and his friend went into the kitchen and left us alone.

When I told her, she shook her head. 'I knew he was a wrong 'un. There's something about his eyes.' She squeezed my arm. 'Everything'll be alright. Let's go to bed and we'll sort it out in the morning.'

We went upstairs, changed into our pyjamas and climbed into her double bed, where we'd slept together so many times before. She'd lived in this house her whole life and her parents had left her and Lloyd behind in it when they moved to Jamaica last year. They'd wanted Leah and Lloyd to go with them but they chose to stay – didn't feel Jamaican as they'd been born in England. Leah couldn't figure out why they wanted to go either as her mum had been brought to England when she was a baby and her dad was born in England too. They said it was going to be a better place to be with the way things were. They'd left in the middle of the night and somehow got to Wales, got an illegal boat out to Ireland then another boat from there. They were the only people I knew that had left and gone to another country. If they could do it, could I? But the screens showed so many horrific stories about what it was like in the rest of the world. Including Jamaica. Huge hurricanes and so hot. Maybe it would be better to stay here. But was any of what they showed us even true? Leah fell straight into a drunken sleep but I was wide awake for hours, wondering what was going to become of me and my baby.

Leaving

WHEN I WOKE the next morning, Leah was up already and I could hear voices downstairs. After my morning puke, I found her, Lloyd and their friend sitting in the front room drinking tea and eating toast.

'Hey, sleepy,' she said and patted the sofa next to her. 'This is Connor.'

Connor looked up and smiled. I nodded at him.

'So, little Evie, you've gone and got yourself up the duff then,' Lloyd said, shaking his head at me.

Despite everything, I laughed. Lloyd always had a way of making everything seem okay. 'Yep. Pregnant, homeless and jobless, that's me.'

'Course you're not homeless. You can stay here,' Leah said.

'I know I can, thank you, but I want to get away. I don't want to be here where I might see Tom or my mum. And I stole all the info from Countervaillance—the stuff I've been working on. He won't like that.'

'Oh, it's too early to think about all this. Go and get a cuppa and relax for a bit. We'll sort it out.'

She was right. Tom had no idea where Leah and Lloyd lived, even though he'd met them several times on nights out, so he wouldn't be able to find me. If he was even looking. In the kitchen, I made tea and a slice of dry toast. I took my cup and plate back into the front room and sat down next to Leah with my legs tucked up under me. The TV was on, some old nature programme showing whales jumping up out of the sea.

We watched in silence for a while then Lloyd did a big loud yawn and stretched. 'Right, I'm going in the shower.'

Leah went off to make more tea and I was left with Connor, who smiled shyly at me but didn't say anything. I carried on staring at the TV, although I wasn't taking in anything.

Leah came back and handed me another mug of tea, 'Here you go. So, what are we going to do then? I think you just stay here. Fuck Tom and fuck your mum. Don't worry about what they say or think. Me and Lloyd will help you look after the baby.'

I shook my head. 'I just want to go somewhere else. I've never been anywhere. I was thinking about your mum and dad last night. They're the only people I know who ever went anywhere else.'

'No, they're not. Remember my Auntie Shona? She left as well when we were little. Went off to that hippy place by the sea. She's still there. Grows vegetables and all sorts!' Leah shook her head in wonder. She barely even ate vegetables, let alone grew them.

'See, it can be done then. Don't you ever wonder what else is out there?'

Leah laughed. 'Not really. But then I'm always either sleeping or getting off my head and dancing away.'

THE THREE OF them went out, leaving me by myself. All day they were gone and I lay on the sofa staring at the TV but thinking about leaving, and the more I thought about it the more convinced I was that I had to go. I'd already discovered that loads of what the screens told us was lies so maybe there was a place, like Shona's hippy commune, where I could go with my baby and have a completely different life to here.

When they came back, Lloyd was carrying a bag of takeaway and we sat round the TV spooning dahl and turnip curry onto our plates and scooping it up with chapatis.

'I want to go where Shona is.' I said after we'd finished eating and cleared away the containers.

'What? How? We don't even know where she is,' Leah said.

'You're still in contact with her though, aren't you? Email her, ask if I can go.'

I was scared but determined.

'But how will you get there? And why do you want to go? Just stay here.'

Connor butted in. 'I can help. I've got a friend with a boat. He takes people places, going by the old canals and that.'

'C'mon, Leah. I'm done with it here. I want to find out what it's like out there. See somewhere else.'

'Well, I'm not letting you go on your own,' Leah said. 'If you even go. I'll mail Shona and see what she says.'

IT WAS A week before we heard back from Shona and by that time I'd convinced Leah and Lloyd that it was a good idea. Would be an adventure. Shona said, yes, of course, all are welcome at any time. She was in a place called Woody Bay and we needed to get ourselves to a beach just outside Bristol, in a place called Portishead, and she'd come pick us up from there. On a boat. It was the only way we could get to her other than walking, she said. She sent links to a map of the beach and said if we looked for Lynton on the map further west, that she was near there. It looked so far away and I couldn't imagine what it would be like to see the sea, to go on it in a boat.

The next day we went to see Connor's friend, Bhav, who was one of the boat people that I'd sat and watched from the balcony in Tom's flat. He had one of those old narrowboats and he would take us to Bath on the canal, which was as far as his boat could go. We'd have to sort something else out from there.

'We can leave in a week's time,' Bhav said. 'You need five hundred pounds cash, food and drink for the journey, and enough fuel to get there and get me back. If all goes well it should take about six or seven weeks to get to Bath.'

As we were walking back to town I was convinced that escaping was a dream that wouldn't come true. 'So that's that then,' I said.

'What do you mean?' Lloyd came and put his arm around me and pulled me into him.

'I haven't got that much cash, and I have no idea where we could get fuel from.'

Lloyd stopped and turned me to face him. 'Evie, don't you worry about that. If this is really what you want to do, then I can sort it all. I know people that can get anything. Leave it to me and Connor.'

Connor nodded and pulled a big wad of notes from his pocket. 'I've got nearly £300 just here. More at home.'

'But you don't even know me. Why would you pay for this?'

He smiled. 'Because I want to. You need help, I can give it. You want to leave and I'm up for that too.'

I swallowed the burning lump in my throat. Stepping forward, I leaned in and kissed him on the cheek. 'Thank you. So much.'

Our eyes met and something in the air between us changed, became charged. I felt a warm tug of lust throb between my legs. His smile spread further across his face as he felt it too, but I stepped back, turned away and carried on walking. Not now. The last thing I needed was to get involved with someone else. Besides, it was probably just my crazy pregnant body. Not me. I still loved Tom, didn't I? I shook my head to clear it of thoughts of him. He obviously didn't love me and never had done. I had to forget him. But that didn't mean I should rush into anything else.

The next day Leah and me were heading home after a trip to the tinned food shops. You could only buy a few at once so we'd been around town to different shops to get enough for the journey. We were tired, hot and sticky. My phone rang.

'Where are you? How come you've not been in work?' Tess said.

'I've left. I won't be back.'

'I thought something was up. Tom's not been in either until yesterday and he's barely said a word when he has been here. What's going on?'

When I told her, she said she wanted to come with us. But I couldn't say yes without talking to the others first.

Leah agreed straight away and said Lloyd would be fine with it too, but it was Bhav that we had to get the okay from. I told Tess to come round to Leah's later and that we'd go speak to Bhav. We dropped our bags of tins off and headed back down to the river.

Bhav was working on his engine when we arrived and had to put the floor back in place before we could climb on. I was curious to see inside as we hadn't come on board yesterday, just stood on the towpath and made the arrangements. Half of his roof was covered in solar panels and the other half with wooden planters filled with herbs and salads, which he said we could also use on our journey. There were two small wind turbines on each end as well. Gutters around the edge of the roof funnelled the rain down into the bottom of the boat somewhere.

It was bigger inside than I'd imagined and kitted out like a proper home. There was a bathroom and two double bedrooms, as well as a galley kitchen with dining table and an area with a sofa and a wood burner. I was getting excited about setting off on this adventure.

'Your friend can come, no problem, as long as you don't mind sharing the bed space with her,' Bhav said as he sat down opposite us at the table. 'You girls can have one of the bedrooms, I have the other, and Connor and Lloyd can sleep here.' He patted the seat. 'This folds down into a double bed too.'

TESS JOINED US over the next few days on our food gathering sessions and we started taking it straight down to the boat. There was an area at the front, which Bhav told us was called a cratch, that he had built storage space in and we filled his cupboards with our tins of soup, vegetables, lentils and beans. Bags of rice, pasta and potatoes.

Lloyd and Connor were doing the same with fuel and there was a space under the dining table where the fuel cans were being stored. Everything was coming together. We were going to get away and I wouldn't have to deal with Tom ever again. But a couple of days before we set off, Tess and I were approaching the boat when my phone rang.

I nearly didn't answer it when I saw it was Tom.

'I can see you.' He said as soon as I answered.

I looked over towards his flat and he was standing on the balcony staring at us.

'I can see you too.' What was that tone in his voice? How was this call going to go?

'What are you doing, Evie?'

'What do you mean?'

'What's with hanging out on the boat opposite where I live?'

'It just happens to be by where you live and what I'm doing on the boat is none of your business. You made it very clear you don't want anything to do with me.'

'It makes no difference to anything that you stole that info. We can just get it again. And what are you going to do with it anyway? Who's going to take any notice of you if you're not with us?'

'Is that all you want to say? You're not interested in talking to me about our baby?' I glared at him even though I was too far away for him to be able to see it.

'Don't do this. Whatever it is you're doing with the boat people. Get rid of the baby and come home. We can start again, pretend this never happened.'

'But it did. I wouldn't be able to pretend. I don't want to do that.' I hung up. There was no point. How could he be so heartless? How could he not have any feelings at all for the baby that was part of him? As he watched me, I threw the phone into the river and turned away. I could feel him still staring at me though as we climbed on board Bhav's boat. Well, let him stare. I was done with him now. He wasn't the person I'd thought he was, he'd just proved that once and for all.

We spent the afternoon checking things and making sure we were ready. At four o'clock I said I had to go and do something by myself.

I hurried off over the bridge and back towards town. He'd be arriving to start his shift at about half four and I wanted to be there before then. I got there in time and even had ten minutes to wait. When I saw him walking down the road towards the depot I stood up from the wall I'd been sitting on and ran towards him.

'Dad!' I flung myself at him, hugging him tight.

He dropped his bag on the floor and hugged me back. 'Evie, love. It's so good to see you.' He held me away from him, his eyes searching my face, then pulled me back in for another hug.

I hugged him back hard. If only I could take him with me.

We went and sat down on the wall together, held hands as I leaned against him and told him everything that had been going on.

'Oh, Evie. You should have come home, we'd have sorted it out.'

'No, we wouldn't. It would have been awful. She would've made sure.'

He smiled sadly and didn't deny it. 'Will you be OK?'

'Of course I will. Say goodbye to the twins for me.' They were the only siblings I liked. Luke was a pain, always thought he knew best about everything, and Samuel – there was no way to bond with him, you couldn't have a conversation of any kind. I felt bad though for thinking that. 'And to the others too,' I added.

I got him to write his mobile number on my hand then walked into town and bought myself a new phone. One that Tom didn't know the number of.

That night, Leah, Lloyd and Connor went out. A last chance to see their friends, get wasted with them and dance in the clubs. Tess and I stayed home and watched a film in our PJs, eating Chinese food from the takeaway at the end of the road.

'There's something not right about Tom,' she said.

I looked at her and nodded, thinking she meant how he had behaved towards me.

'He's up to something there that I can't quite put my finger on. But he isn't all that he seems.' She licked curry sauce from the corner of her lip, 'I've seen him coming out of the train station a couple of times, the security guards know him. He's been going up to London.'

'But how can he? We're not allowed. What would he be doing there? You can only go in if you've got a service job there.'

'I don't know. But he has and there's something not right.'

I thought about all those times he'd disappeared for hours on end, sometimes staying away for days. Maybe she was right. But what did it matter now? We'd be gone in a couple of days and we'd never see him again.

The next day we packed up everything we were taking with us from Leah and Lloyd's house, mainly clothes, some bedding and a few old photos in frames. They were quiet as they looked around at all the things they had to leave behind. All the memories of their mum and dad, their grandparents.

'You don't have to do this,' I said. 'I can go by myself, with Tess. You can stay here.'

Lloyd shook his head. 'No, it's time for an adventure.

I think Woody Bay is going to be a good place.'

That night we all moved on to the boat. It was a bit claustrophobic with all of us crammed in together but we'd get used to it. And it wouldn't be forever.

We sat around the woodburner even though it wasn't lit and Bhav showed us the route on his paper maps. We'd head down the Thames a bit towards London then turn off onto the Kennett & Avon canal and cut back up through town, which would lead us all the way to Bath eventually. How we would do the next part of the journey we hadn't yet worked out. Shona said when we were near Bath we should get in touch again and let her know when we would get to the beach. Bath was one of the rich folk cities that people like us weren't allowed in anymore. So we didn't know how far we'd get or whether the canal would have been blocked off. Even if it hadn't there was no way we could go right into the city – they'd arrest us straight away.

The next morning we set off at sunrise. I stood next to Bhav, who was barely moving the wheel that steered the boat, and watched Tom's flat as we floated by. It was in darkness. Nobody was up apart from us and the birds. The only sounds were the chugger, chugger, chugger of the boat's engine and the cheeps and whirrs of the morning bird song. It was the start of Winter now and there was a bit of a nip in the air. I hugged myself and slid my hands up inside my sleeves. We passed King's

Meadow shanty town where a few kids were at the water's edge. They shouted when they saw us and started running alongside the boat. When we got to the locks and Bhav pulled the boat up next to the towpath they tried to get on board but he chased them off, waving a metal bar he grabbed from the boat.

Tess came out and joined us, yawning and barely awake. 'Adios Reading,' she said and waved.

We grinned at each other. What was it going to be like out there?

Bhav came back from chasing the boys away, beckoned to us to join him on the towpath and showed us the metal bar, which bent in the middle at a forty-five degree angle and had two different-sized holes in the top. 'This is a windlass. You use it at the locks to wind the paddles and let water in and out.'

He showed us then gestured for me to take over. I wound it until it wouldn't go any further and water was gushing into the lock.

'Now the other side,' Bhav pointed.

I walked across the narrow wooden beams that lined the lock gates and opened the paddle on the other side too, then went back over and stood with Tess and Bhav watching the water fill the lock. As it rose, I felt like I was filling up too. With new life as my baby grew inside me and with new experiences that would make me a different person.

Once the water reached the top of the lock we had to open the gates to let the boat through. It was hard work as the sludge had built up at the bottom of the gates. We had to get Leah, Lloyd and Connor out as well to help us push them open.

We turned right onto the canal just before the old business park where all the tech companies used to be. The old office buildings were now filled with the poor people who had been turfed out of London. It was a place where you could get whatever you needed but you had to be known. You couldn't just go there, or you'd be unlikely to get out again. Lloyd knew people there. It was where he'd been sorting the fuel. It was hard to believe that the cheeky, funny boy I'd known my whole life had turned into this savvy man. Who could sort things. It made me feel safe that he was with us. But then he'd always been super smart. When we turned thirteen the teachers had started saying he could be one of the lucky ones that got taken into university then a job in the city in one of the corporations. So he'd stopped working so hard at school and deliberately started doing things wrong, told us to do the same.

'Fuck that. I don't want no job in the city where they watch you all the time, control you. Do you?'

I didn't know. I idolised both Leah and Lloyd though, so always did what they did back then. But we didn't know what went on in London. It might be amazing for all we knew. We might have missed the chance to do something brilliant there.

We passed through the Oracle shopping mall just as it was getting properly light. A gang of crows was pecking through the litter on the riverside café floors, left there from the night before. I remembered Dad when I was little telling me all the names for groups of animals. A murder of crows. Was seeing them at the start of our journey a bad sign? There was a light on in the Coffair branch where I used to work and where I'd first met Tom. I looked back as we turned the corner that would lead us out of town. I couldn't believe that I was leaving and I would never see any of it again. Seventeen years old and I had never left the town before. I had no idea what it was going to be like anywhere else. Was I doing the right thing?

Sirens

BHAV'S BOAT WAS slow. We had to keep stopping and he'd open a box in the floor to pull out weeds that had got wrapped around the metal propeller. Sometimes there were big bits of plastic too. The water stank and he wore big, heavy duty rubber gloves that went right up to his elbows. I'd have to go away, wait inside until he'd put the lid back on, as the smell made me gag. The canal was filled with rubbish and clogged up in places too, so we'd have to fish things out with a long pole with a hook on the end that Bhav kept tied to the roof.

'A long time ago there used to be dredging boats that would come along and clear it but it's just up to us boat people now so it's going to be hard going a lot of the time,' he said.

By lunchtime on that first day we'd only got as far as Burghfield, about six miles from where we'd set off. It would have been as quick to walk. We stopped before the lock and tied the boat to pins that Bhav hammered into the ground. There was nobody around. The sun glinted on the water, the trees and bushes were still wearing their

Autumn reds and golds, and it felt like a different world already. Everyone was in high spirits.

Bhav went off to collect firewood for later while Connor and I prepared lunch, a salad made with leaves from the planter boxes with tinned beans and bread. I was grating carrots to go with it when Connor touched my arm. He was holding out his hand towards me and when I looked down it was one of the carrot ends that he'd carved into a rose.

'Wow. That's beautiful. How come you can do that?' I realised I knew hardly anything about him. I'd been so consumed with myself, what I wanted, how to get away and find a new life for me and the baby.

'My dad taught me. He used to work in a restaurant and started off as the veg carver while he learnt to cook. You know the Thai place down by the Abbey? He worked there – was head chef in the end. He was taught to cook by my grandma. She was from Thailand originally.'

I looked more carefully at his features and could see now that he was part Thai.

'Don't your parents mind that you're leaving?'

'My dad's dead. He died when I was twelve. My mum got married again, she had a baby last year. She's busy with her new life. Don't think she really wants me around to remind of the past.'

He looked sad briefly but then he grinned. 'If you ask me nicely, I'll teach you to carve vegetables too.'

I laughed. 'I'm not sure I need to know but thanks.'

He nudged me gently in the side and went back to putting food out on the plates. When he touched me, I felt that surge of lust again. I pushed it away. It would complicate things and the last thing I needed was more complications.

After lunch, Leah and Lloyd went off to see if they could find any other boats further up the canal who could tell us what it was like. Bhav had heard that some parts were difficult to get through as they were either too silted up or the water was too low. It had been a long hot Summer and Autumn with hardly any rain. Stuff that I'd read from the end of the last millennium had predicted more rain because of climate change but for the past few years it had been really dry. It did rain, obviously, but the floods that had been so common at the start of the new millennium had stopped and Reading was never overrun with water anymore the way it used to be. I'd seen old pictures of the Thames and the Kennet bursting their banks and water spreading for miles, into people's homes and washing away roads.

Leah and Lloyd came back, saying they'd found an old abandoned pub.

'It's been ransacked,' Leah said, 'but there are a few useful things we could stop and get. Some pillows, plates, glasses and some stools and tables that could be chopped up for firewood.'

Bhav arrived, his arms filled with old branches. 'There's not enough room to load up with firewood. We'll have to gather it as we go along.'

'But there's an old wooden rowboat there too. We could tie it to the back and tow it filled with enough wood to last us for weeks,' Leah said.

Bhav shook his head. 'No, let's keep it simple. Towing all that will mean we use more fuel. It'll be hard at the locks. There'll be plenty of wood lying around.'

Leah looked like she was going to argue but she thought better of it. Once we got through the lock we stopped again at the pub and got some of the bedding. It smelt a bit musty but it was clean enough. We stocked up with more plates and cutlery, glasses and mugs too.

We chugged slowly along for a few more hours then Bhav said it was time to stop for the night. The boat could only go so long in one day. It was old, needed its rest just like he did. I wondered how old he was. He had grey hair at his temples but the rest of it was dark still, hanging down his back in fat, felty dreads. He had baggy eyes, the circles underneath them almost black. There was a framed picture on the bookcase inside of a young man in a turban and I couldn't decide if it was Bhav, or maybe his dad. For some reason, I felt nervous of asking him questions about his life. As if I would be prying. He seemed very private. That evening I watched him as he made dinner with Leah and he seemed more relaxed around her than with the rest of us.

The journey to Bath carried on pretty much the same for about ten days. We were all getting to know each other more and feeling more comfortable. I'd caught Connor looking at me several times and noticed that he always tried to be near me as much as he could. He was funny and made me laugh a lot. Had this real feeling of peace around him. I could tell he was a good person. If only I'd met him first rather than Tom. But there was no way I was going to get involved with anyone else. I was going to look out for me and my baby and that was it. Friends only.

We passed lots of places that I'd heard about from my dad, or read about in my research. When we came to Aldermaston a flash of memory came to me of being on Dad's shoulders in an angry crowd. Of people shouting and waving placards. The nuclear weapon protests. I could only have been about two or three. Dad told me about it later, how the government was spending money on weapons while making it harder and harder for people to get welfare, education and healthcare, saying they couldn't afford it. But the protests made no difference anymore. The police surrounded the protesters and started hitting them with batons, firing water cannons at them. Dad managed to get us away unhurt, but he'd never taken me to another march again and he stopped going soon after that himself. I couldn't remember anything else apart from that brief moment on his shoulders, my hands gripping his hair and seeing the tops of other heads all around me. The noise of the shouts. I couldn't believe that I'd probably never see him ever again.

We passed through a town called Newbury with no problems. It was pretty deserted and the few people we did see just nodded and carried on. Then we got to Hungerford and that's when it all went wrong.

We'd just come out the other side of the town, which was empty and derelict, then passed under a bridge when a siren started to wail. Bhav slowed the boat to a stop, staying out in the middle of the canal, and we all looked around but couldn't see anyone. Bushes and trees lined either side of the canal and the towpath was overgrown, covered in old litter. Lloyd ran inside and came back out with a shotgun, which I had no idea we had, and Bhav pulled a smaller gun from the inside of his jacket. It was as if I was watching a movie. Where had all these guns come from?

There was a lock up ahead in the distance but there didn't seem to be anybody around. The siren wailed on. It was like the ones you heard on old films set in World War Two that they'd shown us at school.

'You should go inside, Evie.' Connor shouted to be heard over the siren, pushing me towards the door. 'You need to keep the baby safe.'

I headed for the door, my heart hammering so hard in my chest I could hardly think, my hands instinctively going to my belly. Leah pushed past me and went first. I thought she was scared too but she came straight back out with a gun of her own. I couldn't believe we had so many guns. Again, I was struck by my naivete. I'd obviously been living in a very different reality to everyone else. Tess took my hand, pulled me down the stairs and into the cabin. Before she shut the door behind us, I saw Connor pulling a knife out of his backpack.

Tess and I huddled together on our bed as Bhav steered the boat over to the towpath and killed the engine. We couldn't speak because the siren was so loud. She hugged me to her side while I cradled the tiny swell of my baby, and I knew I looked as scared as she did. We watched the towpath through the window but nobody appeared. Then the siren stopped. The sudden silence hurt my ears almost as much.

There was no sound from outside so Tess crept out and opened the door. I followed close behind. Leah and Lloyd were on the towpath watching in opposite directions. Bhav was still standing on the boat, his gun pointed up towards the bridge in case anyone appeared there.

Connor was crouched on the roof by the planters peering through binoculars to the lock. 'There's a house there, next to the lock. I think there might be people in it.

But I can't really see,' he said.

'What should we do?' I said.

'Wait here with the boat. We'll go down there, see what's going on,' Lloyd said, gesturing at Connor to join him on the towpath. 'Leah, get back on the boat.'

'I'm coming with you,' she said.

My heart was hammering. What would they find? Why had these people set up a siren? Was it to protect them from others or so they could be ready to attack as people approached? I wanted to turn around, go back to Reading. I'd deal with Tom and my mum, if I ever bumped into them, but I couldn't deal with this. For the first time I realised why my mum found comfort in prayer; if ever there was a time to call on God for protection this was it. But I couldn't make myself. I didn't believe in her Catholic God, never had and never would.

We could hear Bhav moving around outside but nothing else for ages. Then there was a shout from down by the lock. Leah.

'Oh God, Tess, what's going on?' I ran to the front of the boat and looked out of the window but I couldn't see anything.

The door at the other end opened and Bhav stuck his head in. 'I'm going down there to see what's happening. Lock this door, shut the curtains and look in the storage box under the seat. There's an axe in there that I use for wood chopping. Keep it close.'

Tess went for the axe while I ran to the door and locked it then pulled all the curtains on the towpath side shut. We sat together on the sofa, the axe resting on Tess's lap. I was about to speak when we heard a single gunshot and a scream. Then silence again. I gripped Tess's arm and she looked at me in shock.

We both screamed as someone banged on the window nearest to the front of the boat then on the roof. Then we could hear steps above us and someone was shaking the door trying to get in.

'Oh God, Tess. They're going to get in. They'll smash the windows.' My hands went instinctively to my stomach again. Was my baby even going to make it into the world?

We ran into the bathroom and locked the door. It was so tiny in there that I had to stand in the shower cubicle, which we'd never been allowed to use as there wasn't enough water. Feet pounded up and down on the roof then three more shots rang out and the footsteps stopped. A loud thud was followed by a splash. Whoever had been shaking the door jumped from the boat onto the towpath and it rocked from side to side. We heard feet running away.

Tess was shaking and dropped the axe onto the floor and sank down on the toilet.

'Wait here,' I said. 'I'm going to have a look.'

I picked up the axe and opened the bathroom door. It

was completely silent. I looked to the left and could see a body floating face down in the canal. A man. Not one of us.

I gasped as I realised I'd been holding my breath. More footsteps approaching, quite a few of them. This was too much. Please let it be Lloyd and Leah. The boat rocked as someone stepped aboard. Then a light knock on the door.

'Evie, open up. It's okay,' Bhav said.

I ran and opened the door and Bhav pushed past me then Lloyd and Leah were there holding Connor up between them. He was covered in blood but I couldn't see where it was coming from. I gasped.

'Connor. Oh God.' I reached out towards him. Dread heavy in my stomach. What if he died?

'Quick, Evie. Put some water on to boil.' Bhav rushed back out with some towels and a big first aid box.

Connor was lying on his back on the deck. His face white and clammy.

'What happened?' I said.

'They stabbed him. Nutters. There was only two of them but it was like they were everywhere all at once,' Lloyd said.

'Evie, water!' Bhav knelt down by Connor. 'Press this against you to stop the bleeding. I'm going to wash my hands.'

Tess was already sorting the hot water when I got

inside. She was pale too but less shaky than she'd been when we were hiding in the bathroom. We took the kettle out and a bowl. Bhav was back by Connor pressing the towels up against his side. Leah and Lloyd were still watching out for the other man who had run off.

Connor had two stab wounds in his side. Bhav stuck a big needle from the first aid box into the hot water, held it there for a minute or so, then threaded it with surgical thread and dropped the whole lot into the hot water, keeping hold of the very end of the thread. He held it there for a while.

'Connor, this is really going to kill, man, but stay strong. Have a swig of this when it gets really bad and hold Evie's hand.' He passed Connor a little bottle of vodka and Connor knocked back half of it straight away. I gently pushed his sweaty hair back from his eyes and gripped his hand, steeling myself. But I needn't have worried as he passed out at the first pass of the needle through his skin. Bhav worked cleanly and quickly, like a professional. He must have been trained to do it. When both wounds were sewn up he got antiseptic gel from the kit and smeared that over the stitches, then placed a large dressing pad over them.

'Here, hold this in place.' He stuck my hand where he wanted it then taped around the pad to keep it in place. 'There. I think he'll be alright. Let's get him inside and on my bed.'

Connor grumbled and moaned as we moved him but didn't come round. Bhav laid him down on the bed and I took his trainers off then swung his legs up and onto the bed. Bhav stuck another cushion under his head. We both eased his jeans off and pulled a blanket over him.

'Are you a doctor, Bhav?' I touched his arm. What we'd just done together had removed all the wariness I'd had about him.

He shook his head. 'No. I was in the army briefly in another lifetime. They teach you basic stuff like that so you can keep yourself alive if you need to.'

We joined the others who were all standing up on the deck now.

'We should go,' Lloyd said.

We all nodded.

'Yep, let's get as far away as we can before it gets dark.' Bhav started the engine. 'Leah, get the ropes. Lloyd, keep guard. Evie, keep an eye on Connor. Tess, make us all a cup of tea.'

Despite everything we all grinned and got on with it. I went and sat on the bed by Connor, willing him to be okay.

We travelled slowly for two hours, most of that time taken up with the six locks we had to get through. We all felt uneasy that we hadn't gone far enough. But we didn't see anyone else. Connor didn't wake up and we ate a bowl of soup each, pretty much in silence, and then went to bed. Bhav stayed in the table bed and Lloyd went in with Connor. I lay awake sandwiched between Tess and Leah. Were we even going to make it to Bristol to meet Shona? Life outside Reading was a lot more dangerous than I'd thought it would be. Were the screens right to keep everyone afraid to leave the towns? Maybe they were just trying to keep us all safe.

CONNOR REMAINED SEMI-CONSCIOUS for several days. We took it in turns to lift his head and feed him water and soup. Change his dressings. He was sweaty and clammy and deathly white but the wounds weren't infected nor deep.

We plodded along, making very slow progress. There were so many locks after we left Hungerford and many of them were in a really bad state and we had to scrape the bottom of the canal with Bhav's long sticks for hours to be able to move the gates. Other times, we got stuck in the middle of the canal when the bottom of the boat got caught in silt or rubbish. Sometimes the water was so clogged up that, as well as the engine power, we had to walk on the towpath and pull it with ropes too.

On the day that Connor finally woke up properly, we were all knackered. We'd spent the night before just outside a place called Great Bedwyn where we'd seen a couple of people out walking along the canal path, who'd just scurried away when they saw us. We were all nervous, wondering if people were going to attack us. Nobody was sleeping well so we were all up and ready to move on as soon as the sun rose. We spent the whole day getting through a series of nine locks that were really close together and we moored up for the night after the final lock, just as it was turning from twilight to proper dark. I slumped down on the sofa, my arms, shoulders and back on fire and my legs shaky. I'd barely eaten all day as we'd been so determined to get through all the locks and as far away as we could from the last village. When we'd first set off from Reading, I'd wanted to meet other people and find out what their lives were like but after what happened in Hungerford I was scared of everyone that wasn't part of my gang.

Leah, Lloyd and Bhav were outside, gathering firewood and securing everything on the boat for the night. Tess brought me a cup of tea and a bowl of leftover stew and I was just tucking into it when I heard Connor calling out.

'Hello?' His voice was weak, scratchy.

I put my bowl down on the table, smiling at Tess who was stirring the pot of stew on the stove, keeping it warm for the others.

Connor's face was still pale and clammy but he was back with us.

I sat down next to him on the bed. 'Hello. Nice to see

you again.' I smiled and tears prickled my eyes. That's when I knew. I'd been trying not to think about it as I was terrified he might die, but those feelings of lust were more than that. Connor was a good guy. He had a good heart. I picked up his hand and squeezed it.

He gave a wan little smile but squeezed it back. 'Nice to see you too, Evie. Is there something to eat?'

THE NEXT DAY Connor got up and managed to walk about a bit. We waited where we were for several days to give him time to get some strength back, and for us all to have a rest. It had been a stressful and tense few weeks. I spent as much time as I could with Connor, giving him extra food from my bowl, helping him dress and keep his stitches clean. But mainly chatting, and laughing, getting to know each other. He told me he was a Buddhist, that's where the calm came from. His grandmother had brought him up in the old ways from her country and he accepted whatever happened in life. Nothing is forever, nothing stays the same except the you that experiences it all.

'But if that's true, that would mean you never change and grow as a person,' I said.

'No. That's your personality, your external you. That can change. The eternal you, the consciousness, that's always there at the core. That never changes and it goes on after you die.' He laughed. 'You'll have to read about it, I'm no teacher of the Buddhist ways.'

I laughed as well. It kind of made sense but it went against all the scientific ideas I'd ever read about. And the eternal you going on after death sounded too much like the Catholic idea of heaven and hell to me. Whatever, if this was part of Connor it was alright by me even if I didn't really believe any of it.

The night before we were due to set off again, Connor and I were sitting on the bed together. Connor lay back against the pillows, and patted the bed next to me.

'Lie down, make the most of the last day of not having to open locks and pull on ropes.'

I relaxed into the pillows next to him. My belly had started to look much more pregnant now and I could feel his eyes on it as my T-shirt rode up. I pulled it down, ashamed that it was me and my baby that had caused all this trouble for everyone. But he pulled it back up again and placed his hand on my little bump, caressed it. My breath caught in my throat and he looked up at me. I leaned towards him then we were kissing each other, hard. His hands moved up onto my back and he pulled me towards him.

'Oh, sorry.' Tess was standing in the doorway, red-faced.

Connor and I pulled away from each other and we all started laughing.

'Don't be sorry, Tess. We're not are we, Evie?' Connor said.

I shook my head, kissed him lightly on the lips, but stood up and left the room. It wasn't the right time or place for me and Connor to start this. It would be weird for the others. And we'd have plenty of time to be together when we got to Woody Bay.

We had a good run over the next few weeks as there were no locks for ages, just silt and rubbish to deal with, which was a lot easier than getting the locks open and shut. But then we hit a place called Devizes and as we rounded a bend my heart sank. I was up steering the boat and the others were inside. There were locks ahead of us as far as the eye could see. I started steering the boat towards the towpath.

'I need some help to moor up,' I called.

Connor appeared and we grinned stupidly at each other, which we did all the time since we'd kissed. He'd understood when I said we should wait, but it was known that we were together even though we weren't quite yet.

'What's up?' he said.

I nodded towards the locks and he groaned. Tess stuck her head out the door. 'What we stopping for?'

'Locks. Millions of them.'

It felt like we never going to get to the beach to meet Shona. It would take ages to get through here and what if more nutters turned up? There was no way we could get away from them stuck between locks. I pushed these worries away though. We'd had no more trouble. Seen hardly any people. We were going to be fine, of course we were.

Waiting

WHEN WE FINALLY got near to Bath it was almost three months since we'd set off. It had taken so much longer than we'd expected. We ran out of fuel and the final two weeks of the journey we'd been using the long poles to push the boat along and the ropes to pull it. The food had started to run low and we'd had to ration it so everyone was hungry all the time. My belly was getting big and I tired really quickly.

We stopped and moored up in front of a barrier that had been built across the canal so that we couldn't get into the city where the rich folk were pampering themselves in the ancient Roman baths. We were opposite a turning on the left that went off into another canal. A faded sign half hanging off an old lamppost told us it was the Somerset Coal Canal.

'Do you think we can carry on and get a bit further on the boat if we go down there, Bhav?' Lloyd asked.

'Nah, probably not. I think it'll go the wrong way.'

Lloyd went to check the maps and Leah emailed Shona to find out if she'd sorted something for the next part of our journey. There were no phones at the commune so we had to wait until she went and checked her emails in the library, which she did once a week apparently. I couldn't imagine living like that and hoped they weren't going to take our phones and screens off us when we got there. Maybe they couldn't even get a signal?

Lloyd came back with the map and showed us the route. 'I reckon we could get a bit further before we have to leave the boat if we go down there,' he ran his finger along the blue line, 'to about here. We're gonna have to walk round the bottom of Bath anyway.'

'We'll walk over there tomorrow, check it out,' Bhav said.

THE NEXT MORNING Bhav and Lloyd set off early to have a look. Connor stayed with us. He still got tired pretty quickly so it would be good if we could stay on the boat to get a bit further. But when they came back they said it was impassable.

'Just round the first bend from the entrance a huge beech tree's fallen and it's completely blocked. We'll have to walk from here when we've heard from Shona,' Lloyd said.

Bhav was going to return to Reading but he couldn't do it by himself with no fuel. None of us could think of a way to get him some.

'You'll have to come with us, Bhav,' Leah said. I had a feeling she liked him, despite the massive age gap, he must be at least thirty, and that she was secretly pleased.

'What just abandon my boat, my home?' Bhav shook his head. 'I can't do that.'

'Why not? You wouldn't need it. Shona said there's room for everyone, food for everyone. What have you got in Reading to go back for?'

Bhav just shook his head again and wandered off to get some wood. It was Winter proper now and the days were shorter and a bit colder, but not that much. But it did get quite chilly in the evening and we'd been getting the woodburner going earlier and earlier each day. My dad had told me about Winters when he was young. Waking in the morning to deep frosts that pinched the end of your nose and fingers, covered everything in a layer of white icing. I'd never seen it apart from on the TV.

We waited for five days to hear from Shona who told us to cut across country to find the River Avon and follow its path to the sea. She'd collect us there and take us to Woody Bay. But as we didn't know how long it was going to take us to get there we'd have to let her know when we arrived and then wait until she could come for us.

It was a long distance to walk. We had no idea what we'd find on the way. On the map it looked like it would probably take us two or three days to get to the outskirts of Bristol, but then look how much longer it had taken to get to Bath than we'd expected. What would we do about food? Where would we sleep?

While we were discussing plans, another narrowboat arrived. We could hear it coming long before it rounded the corner and when it did, Bhav and Lloyd were waiting with their guns hidden but handy. If the past few months had taught us anything it was that you couldn't assume people were going to be friendly. There were two women stood at the tiller, with a scruffy dog sitting on the roof. When they saw us they slowed down and the one with the long blonde hair lifted her arm in a semi salute.

They started moving towards us again more quickly, until they pulled up and moored on the towpath just behind us.

'Hi,' the blonde called out as she stepped off the boat and tied it to the post. The other woman had short dark hair and she seemed much more wary.

'Alright,' Lloyd said and walked towards her. The rest of us watched. 'Where are you heading?'

'Here. How about you?'

'Bristol.' Lloyd took his hands out of his pockets so he was obviously thinking they were okay.

'We're meeting friends that are coming up from Bristol. Have you seen anyone?' She looked around as if they might be hiding somewhere. I had a funny feeling about her but I felt like that about everyone since Connor got stabbed.

'Nope, we've been here for a few days now and haven't seen anyone. Is it just you two?'

'Yes, just us. And Buster, of course.' She fondled the dog's ears. 'We're a couple of days early, I think. How are you going to get to Bristol from here? There's no way through on the canals now.'

As if we hadn't noticed the huge barrier that we'd stopped in front of.

'We'll walk from here.'

'What, and leave your boat?'

Bhav stepped down onto the towpath then and joined them. 'No, the boat's mine. I need fuel to get back to Reading but I've no idea where to get any.' He stuck his hand towards her, 'I'm Bhav. Don't suppose you've got any going spare, have you?'

She gripped his hand and pumped it up and down. 'Mia.' She gestured towards her friend, 'Erin. And no, I'm afraid we don't. We need all we've got.'

About half an hour later, three blokes and a woman, all of them dirty and hard-looking, arrived and went on Mia's boat. We were packing essentials in to the backpacks to leave the next morning when Mia shouted over, 'These guys have got some camping gear they'll trade with you.'

They tried to make Bhav give them his boat in exchange for a few tents, sleeping bags, and some cooking equipment.

'It's my home,' he said, 'and I'm not even going with them to Bristol so why would I give you my boat?'

Leah's head snapped up when he said that and she gave him a filthy look. I was unnerved that Bhav really meant it when he said he wouldn't be coming with us. He was so calm and capable and it made me feel a lot safer having him around. It was going to be scary enough being in tents instead of locked away in the boat. But I didn't feel like I could ask him to come. Why would he? He'd only ever agreed to give us a lift on his boat.

In the end, Lloyd struck a deal to give them some cash, a gun and a small box of bullets. The six of them set off back up the canal on Mia and Erin's boat, waving to us until they rounded the corner. I felt better that they'd gone.

We spent the day sorting out food and provisions for the walk. Figuring out what we could fit in the backpacks and what we really needed. Bhav was tinkering with the engine as if he was already removing himself from our gang. I took him a cup of tea. 'Please come with us, Bhav. Leah's right – you haven't got anything to go back to Reading for, have you? I lived over the water from your boat for a while and I saw you lots of times and you were always alone.'

He glared at me. 'What, you were there watching me all the time, were you?'

'No, of course not.' I reached out and touched his

137

hand. 'I just saw you now and then. But we've all become friends, haven't we? I've come to care about you. I'd like you to stay with us.'

He shrugged and bent back down to stare at the engine. It was clear he wanted me to go so I left him to it.

Leah smiled as I re-joined her in the food store. 'Leave it to me.' She winked at me, stuck a tin of soup in my hand and went to join Bhav outside. She whispered something in his ear, took him by the hand and pulled him out of the engine pit and they set off down the towpath together. I watched until they disappeared round the corner, hoping she could convince him. If any of us could, Leah could.

They were gone for a couple of hours and when they came back they were both flushed and glowing. Leah winked at me again as she went into the bathroom. I didn't say anything to Bhav as he got the axe from under the seat and went back out again. I watched through the window as he started chopping big branches from the trees in the field. What was going on now?

Leah came out of the bathroom, saw him and gave a smug grin. 'He's coming,' she said. Then went off and started dragging the branches he was chopping over to the boat.

I made everyone a lunch of baked beans and rice and we all sat out on the towpath in the sun.

'So, Bhav has decided he will come with us. We're

going to put the boat down there,' Leah pointed to the old coal canal, 'and block the entrance with branches so people won't know it's there.'

At first light the next morning we manoeuvred the boat over to the other canal using the poles, the branches that Bhav had cut sitting on the top. When the boat was just inside the entrance, Lloyd and Bhav went up on the roof and started pulling the branches down onto the deck at the back then dropping them into the canal. The first few sunk straight to the bottom but the next ones sat on top of them and a few leaves started to poke out. It was obvious we were going to need a lot more trees though. So we moored up on the towpath and spent the rest of the morning cutting and dragging more branches. By lunch time the side of the canal we were on had a pile of branches sticking out of the water for about three feet. It was going to be a long job.

Camping

WHEN WE SET off on foot at sunrise the next day, Bhav was quiet and withdrawn. The way he stroked and patted the boat as we left suggested he thought he'd never see it again. Even if he decided to come back once we'd got to Shona's safely, was it likely that the boat would still be there? Would our camouflage be enough?

I was going to go and comfort him but Leah got there before me. She grabbed his hand and kissed it. 'It'll be alright, Bhav.'

He smiled and they walked on holding hands.

Mia's friends had told us the quickest way to get round Bath and join the River Avon was to cut through the bottom of the Mitford Valley and go out past the old university campus. They'd just come up that way and not seen anybody. Leah was in charge of the crude map they drew for us. That first day we walked for as long as the light lasted. It was muggy and grey and everyone was quiet. We camped outside a deserted village. The old stone houses were crumbling and trees and bushes sprouted up from inside them. It was eerie that night inside the tents, which we pitched in a field at the edge of the village, next to a falling apart house that had a faded Bed & Breakfast sign still standing in the garden. The wind rustled the trees continuously and there was the haunting hoot of an owl all night long. I snuggled close to Connor, wishing we could just magic ourselves at Shona's without having to go through all of this.

The next morning though, as we sat around drinking hot tea and the sun was rising over the hills, muted by the mist, it was peaceful and beautiful, and I could imagine how it used to be in the times my dad had told me about. When people from the cities came to places like this for holidays and camped for fun. He said lots of people stayed in B&Bs where everyone sat around in the same room in the morning, eating their breakfast without really looking at each other or speaking beyond saying, 'Good morning.' Sounded really weird to me but I could see the attraction of camping and being out in nature.

Even Bhav seemed more cheerful. 'Right, we need to think about where we're going to get to each day so we can let Shona know when to send the boat.' He took the map from Leah and marked places to aim for each day, which would mean we'd need to walk for around four to five hours a day and camp out two more nights. We were meeting Shona at a beach just outside Portishead, called Kilkenny Bay. In just a few days we would see the sea for the first time in our lives. The sea. Almost as mythical as

London in my head.

It rained that day and as we trudged across hilly fields to our next destination, another deserted village called Queen Charlton, close to where we could pick up the Avon path that would lead us to Portishead, everybody was pretty miserable.

I'd worried that there would be trouble on this part of the journey but like Mia's friends had said, we didn't see a soul. The next day it was still raining and when we joined the Avon path we saw people for the first time since Mia and Erin had left us. Boaters living there.

We stopped to talk to a man who was sitting reading on a camp chair on the towpath, his feet resting on his boat. A big tarpaulin was tied to his boat on one side and a couple of trees on the other, sheltering him from the rain. When we told him what we were doing he offered to help. 'Camp close by for the night, and tomorrow I'll give you a lift right along the river to the mouth and then it'd be just a short walk for you. I'm Jack.' He stuck his hand out and we each shook it in turn, introducing ourselves.

I peered closely at his face when he got to me. Why would he offer to help us? What was in it for him?

'You don't need to do that,' Lloyd said. 'You'll be using fuel you don't need to for people you don't know. Cheers though.'

'It's no problem. My boat doesn't run on fuel. I in-stalled an electric engine I took out of a car and the solar panels charge it. I can get a spare one while I'm down there. There's thousands of them just sitting there in the cars that never got sold and never will.'

I wasn't sure what he meant but I wanted to take him up on his offer. I was tired of walking and even if he did try anything funny there was a lot more of us than him. 'Thanks, Jack, that'd be really great,' I said.

He smiled at me, 'You all look pretty tired and be-draggled. Come sit by the fire.'

We all climbed aboard and went inside and huddled round his wood burner to try and dry out. It was very like Bhav's boat inside except smaller. No bedrooms just a bed against the wall as you came in then a bathroom before you went into the kitchen and living area. That night we shared our fresh food with him that we had left from Bhav's planters and he shared his that was growing in the garden he'd planted in the field behind the towpath. He told us about the changes he'd seen in Bristol since he was a young man there. He was sixty-five years old.

'I've seen England go from being an affluent, forward-thinking country where all were welcome, to an insular, scared hell-hole where only those with economic power are wanted. It all started with that Brexit nonsense, when it was decided to go it alone and not be a part of Europe anymore. That's when the smart people got out. The rest of us just kept thinking that things would get better again, but they didn't, and they won't ever now, if you ask me.'

He scared me and made me depressed for the future of my baby. I wanted to say, we're not asking you, so shut up with your doomsday talk. But I bit my lip and held Connor's hand. Surely things were going to be all right once we got to Woody Bay. I was silent the next day as we set off to the beach where Shona would come and collect us, wondering if Tom had been right all along, and I should have just got rid of the baby. But I had to believe good times were still possible, had to be positive. I rubbed my hands over my bump telling it I would make sure things would be okay for us.

JACK STOPPED BY a tall stone wall that had steps leading up to the road above and tied his boat up. We all climbed up and came out by a row of houses, some terraces, some bungalows. There were no people around but dub was blasting out of a house somewhere behind the ones we could see. In the distance, the old motorway bridge and electricity pylons towered over the river.

Jack pointed towards them, 'C'mon. That's where we're heading next.'

My T-shirt was sticking to me under the backpack, which was thumping against me with each step, and I hoped we didn't have far to go. We followed the road alongside the river for about ten minutes, then cut up through a housing estate.

At the end of the houses a metal bar gate led to a dirt track that went off into a woodland and Jack led us through there. We passed under the motorway. The huge concrete pillars holding it up had deep cracks in them and looked like they would crumble completely pretty soon, ivy wounds its way up them and onto the road above. We came out on a lane by some big red, metal gates, which were open.

'Right, I'm going in here to get a new engine,' Jack said. He'd carried a little trolley with him from the boat.

'How much further have we got to go?' I said. I was intrigued by what he was doing and what he meant about the thousands of car engines that wouldn't get used. If it wasn't too much further, I wanted to go and have a look.

'Just over an hour, I reckon. A bit more probably as you're carrying loads of stuff.'

'I want to see where Jack's getting his engine from.' I turned to face the others. 'Don't you?'

Lloyd shrugged. 'Not really bothered to be honest, Evie.'

Leah and Bhav dropped their bags. 'You go, we'll wait here,' Leah said.

'Actually, I do want to see,' Bhav said. 'If he can run a boat engine on solar then I could too.'

'Yeah, but you're going to Woody Bay now,' Leah said.

'I am now, yeah, but that doesn't mean I'm going to

145

stay there forever, does it?'

Tess and Connor came as well. We followed Jack over to the red gates and through them, then we rounded a corner and in front of us were hundreds and hundreds of cars all sat in rows, the sun glinting off the rusted chrome and cracked windscreens. It was surreal to see so many of them just sitting there.

'What are they doing here?' I looked around the one closest to me. Small and red with headlights sticking up from the bonnet, which made me think of frog's eyes. Inside it the seats were black and white checks and covered in mould.

'They've always been here as long as I can remember. Well, not always these ones but they used to get shipped in all the time and sit here until someone bought them, or they'd get shipped out again when they didn't sell, then a different lot would arrive.'

I shook my head, it seemed completely mad to me. Had the government actually done the right thing in taking them away, stopping all that waste? I was very confused about what I felt about the government. On the one hand, they seemed to be doing everything they could to oppress us, control us and use the planet for their own ends. But then some of the things they'd done ultimately seemed to be good and would slow down climate change. It made my head hurt thinking about it all and trying to figure it out. Maybe I should stop worrying about it and just focus on me, my baby, and Connor. Worry about making the world a better place for us. But that was a selfish view. What about all the other people that needed the world to be a fairer place? Like the ones in the shanty town, even the ones who'd attacked us. If the world wasn't so out of kilter then they wouldn't need to live like that, behave like that.

Connor came and put his arm around my waist. 'We better get a move on.'

We walked back to Jack, who had a car bonnet open and was telling Bhav how he'd changed his boat over.

'Thanks for everything, Jack. Take care of yourself,' I said.

Connor shook his hand. 'Cheers Jack.'

'Come back and see me anytime. Bhav, if you want help with your boat just let me know.' He waved then walked off deeper into the sea of cars.

We turned and walked away to who knew what might come next.

Chickens

WE FOLLOWED THE route Jack had drawn for us on the map and passed deserted business parks and warehouses. Then we came to Portishead, which would have been a pretty place once. Old stone buildings lined the wide streets and the shops were still busy, people everywhere going about their business. But the grass verges were wild and overgrown, the roads potholed and cracked, the old petrol station was derelict. Nobody took any notice of us as we trudged through laden, down with backpacks and tents. As we headed out of the town towards the beach the houses got bigger and further apart, many of them looking empty and unloved. After about ten minutes we came to a huge allotment, filled with vegetable plots, sheds, poly tunnels and people working away, planting and pruning, harvesting and digging. We cut across a big green after that and through gaps in the bushes I could see glimpses of the sea ahead of us, but it was a dirty sludgy colour. Brown? I had been expecting a deep, soothing blue. Even so my stomach somersaulted, and I wasn't sure if it was fear or excitement. Probably both.

There were more houses around than I'd been expecting and I hoped people were going to be okay with us camping out while we waited for Shona. But all thoughts were pushed from my mind when we reached the beach. The sand was a grimy beigy-grey, and the waves that were rolling onto it had an oily, scummy sheen to them but that couldn't take away the awe I felt at finally seeing it. Even though Jack had said it wasn't even the sea proper here, still technically the river mouth and estuary. It looked like the sea to me. I sank down onto the sand and watched the waves. I was going to see this every day from now on. My baby would grow up never not having seen the sea.

We made camp and stayed for two nights. On the third day, one where the sun hadn't appeared from behind the dense blanket of grey cloud, a boat appeared on the horizon. We'd seen a few but they'd all stayed far out from the shore but this one got steadily bigger as it headed towards us. A woman dressed in wet weather gear appeared on the deck and waved as she dropped the anchor. I couldn't see her face as it was hidden by her hood.

'You'll have to wade out to us. We can't come in any further,' she shouted.

Connor took my hand and hefted my bag and his on to each shoulder and we went first. The water was freezing and when it reached my belly, I swear I felt the baby shrinking away from it. By the time we reached the boat, the water was up to my armpits and the woman reached down and hauled me up onto the little ladder then pulled me onto the deck. She pushed her hood back and I saw it was Shona.

She hugged me. 'Little Evie. You were just a kid and now look, having one of your own.'

I stood to the side while she took the bags from Connor then pulled him up too. 'Go down into the cabin.'

As soon as the others were aboard, Shona pulled the anchor up and went up to the man at the wheel of the boat who'd waved at us as we'd climbed up. He switched the engine on and we slowly turned around and headed back towards the horizon. There were hazy hills in the distance but we seemed to be going straight out to sea.

Shona came back and joined us, sitting down next to Leah and pulling her to her side. Kept her arm around her the whole way. I shivered in my soaking clothes, snuggled up to Connor, hoping he could warm me up but he was cold and wet too.

'We have to go out into the middle of the channel as there's sandbanks. When we get to Woody Bay, we might have to wait for a bit for the tide to turn before we can head in.'

Woody Bay. The name sounded so inviting, so safe. As if nothing bad could ever happen there.

The up and down of the boat on the waves made me

feel sick so I went up to the deck. Connor joined me up there. 'What's it going to be like in Woody Bay, do you think?' he said.

I rested my head on his shoulder. 'It sounds like it's going to be really lovely.'

He put his arm around me and squeezed. 'It does. A good place for us to be a family.'

My stomach lurched at the thought of it. Of giving birth without doctors or a hospital, of having to look after a baby, of being in the middle of nowhere forever.

WHEN WE GOT to Woody Bay the boat pulled up against a crumbly old concrete jetty. A stone wall towered above us. There were shallow steps carved into the side. I looked around trying to take it all in. I'd never imagined that places like this existed in England. The beach was rocky and the waves crashed up against huge boulders, grey, brown, others with a pinky-purple tinge. A waterfall tumbled down from the tree-covered cliff and crashed onto the beach just short of where the waves rolled in. It looked like there was a little house or something at the edge of the beach, with two arches leading inside it.

Shona came up next to me. 'They're old lime kilns. There's books where you can find out all about them. Come, follow me.'

We climbed up the stone steps in the wall and they

led up to a flat grassy area where we waited for the others.

'Everyone, this is Marcus. Marcus, this is everyone,' Shona said as the boat driver finally climbed over the wall and joined us.

Marcus's short afro hair was greying at the sides and he had deep grooves running from his nose down each side of his mouth, as if he smiled and laughed a lot. He smiled around at us all now. 'Welcome to Woody Bay, everyone,' he said and beckoned for us to follow him up a steep path. 'Come, let's get you indoors so you can have a bath and a rest.'

We traipsed behind him up the path. On one side, there was a wall with a steep drop to the sea below, where it crashed against huge jagged rocks. The path split into two and we went right. It was even steeper and my heart hammered. It was hard work carrying a baby around as well as me. We rounded a corner and the path levelled out in front of an old cottage that looked out over the bay below. In the distance on the other side of the bay, I could see a big house that looked like it might fall off the cliffside at any moment, as if it was suspended in the trees that surrounded it on all sides.

We carried on past the cottage then turned off the path and walked up through some woodlands. We emerged to see a huge house in front of us, surrounded by acres of gardens. Poly tunnels and greenhouses were covering much of the land and behind them it looked like there was an orchard. We walked round to the right of the house and there were several smaller houses too. It started to rain as Marcus held open a door into the big house and ushered us all in.

We came into a big kitchen where a woman was sat in a chair to the side of a huge old fireplace, knitting. She looked up and smiled. 'You're here safe. Welcome. I'm Rachael.' Her face beamed love and gentleness out towards us. Her brown eyes sparkled and it was impossible to tell how old she was.

It was as if the journey finally being over had made us all mute. We smiled but nobody said anything. Rachael laughed. 'You look dead on your feet. Shona, take them upstairs and let them get settled.'

Shona led us out through a small door and up the stairs. We came out on a landing where a big bay window overlooked the sea. There were several doors going off either side of the corridor. 'All of these rooms on the left are empty,' Shona said. 'The one at the end is a bathroom, but take your pick from the rest. Come back down to the kitchen whenever you want to.'

We all stood there for a moment after she'd gone then Leah stepped forward and opened the first door she came to. 'I'll take this one then,' she looked back at Bhav and gave a lewd wink. 'Want to join me, Bhav?'

He blushed and glanced over at Lloyd as if to check whether it was okay then followed her in and pulled the door shut behind them.

Connor and I went in the room next to them and we heard two more doors shut as Tess and Lloyd went into their new rooms. The room was a good size with a huge fireplace and floor to ceiling windows overlooking the gardens. A big old cast iron bed took up a lot of room and I dropped down onto it straight away, swung my legs up and lay back. It was blissful after sleeping on the floor of the tent and cramped up in the boat for so long before that.

I patted the bed and Connor came and lay beside me. We held hands and stared at the ceiling, neither of us saying anything. I fell into a deep sleep immediately.

When I woke it was almost dark and Connor wasn't in the room. I rolled off the bed and looked down into the garden. It was raining hard and there was nobody around. The rain bounced on the roofs of the tunnels and greenhouses then rolled down into guttering that fed into water butts. I could hear faint voices coming from the kitchen but I headed off for a bath before joining them.

I pulled on my leggings and a long jumper I found in the chest of drawers in our room. Most of the clothes I'd packed when we left were too tight now, and not warm enough. It felt damp and chilly in Woody Bay, as if Winter might still mean that.

Downstairs, Leah, Tess and Shona were sat at the kitchen table peeling a huge pile of potatoes and Bhav was standing at the cooker stirring something in a big pot. It was warm and cosy. I felt tears coming and tried to swallow them down, but I couldn't stop a small sob escaping. Leah patted the chair next to her and when I sat down she hugged me to her side with one arm. 'It's okay. We're safe now.'

I nodded. 'I know. Sorry, I don't know why I'm crying.'

Shona laughed. 'Because you're pregnant!'

'Where's Lloyd and Connor?'

'Outside somewhere with Marcus, he's showing them round the place.'

The door opened then and they all came bustling in. Lloyd had a basket filled with carrots and Connor was holding eggs.

'Chickens, Evie. Loads of them,' he said holding them out towards me.

It was a completely different world to the one we'd left behind.

The next morning I realised how different. Rachael showed me around. The fifteen large poly tunnels were filled with fruit and vegetables, two greenhouses with herbs, spices, things I thought only grew in tropical places. Trees had been cleared on the hills behind the gardens so that they got the sun for the maximum amount of time every day. Irrigation systems kept everything watered. Bee hives buzzed in the corner. The orchard had apples, pears, plums, cherries. Everything was so lush, and there was so much food.

'What do you do with it? There's way too much for just you, Shona and Marcus.'

Rachael nodded. 'We sell it to shops in Lynton. We've got a horse and cart and we go once a week to Combe Martin and Ilfracombe to the markets there. We trade. We store. We make sure we've got enough to survive whatever might happen.'

She took me into a large shed. It was lined with tables, one of which was covered in trays containing herbs and leaves, flower petals. Bunches of leaves and flowers were hanging on the walls too.

Another table had pestle and mortars, jars filled with powders and pastes, all labelled.

'This is my pharmacy,' Rachael said. Turning to face me she put her hand on my arm. 'There's something you need to know about me. I'm a witch.'

I laughed, thinking of the Halloween witches dressed in black with warts and flying broomsticks. 'Yeah, right,' I said.

'Yes, I am. It's not what you think. I'm a green witch.' She smiled as she said it, told me about the reverence for nature and the energies present in everything.

'I inherited everything from my aunt. She married a rich man and spent his money travelling the world to collect seeds and plants. She brought me up here after my parents died when I was ten, taught me all I know, and I want to teach it to you, Evie. I could tell as soon as I saw you that you're the one to pass it all on to.'

I smiled but didn't commit to anything. What did I know about nature? I'd grown up in a concrete city where the only green was littered parks that nobody looked after and peeling trees with black spotted leaves. And what did she know about me? She'd only just met me.

Next we went to the basement under the big house. She'd filled it with supplies that she said would last fifty years when we finally couldn't get anything from the shops anymore. Candles, solar torches, cans of food, clothes, bedding, poly tunnel sheets, blankets, rucksacks, bottles of wine, oil lanterns and bottles of citronella oil, panes of glass for the greenhouses and house windows, brooms, and a whole lot more. A long tunnel had been dug out leading deep into an underground cavern. I shivered when we arrived, goosebumps breaking out all over me. It was filled with vacuum-packed bags of rice, oats, different types of flour, beans, pasta, pulses stacked high going on for rows and rows. It was overwhelming.

'Won't it all go off?' My breath showed white. I hugged my arms around me and rubbed the tops to try and keep warm.

'No, the sealed containers and the temperature down here mean it will all last for a lot longer than they tell us food will. The rice and pulses will be good for around twenty years, the pasta and flour for a decade or so. But we can rotate it for as long as we can still get it. Eat the older stuff and add new to replace it.'

I shook my head, not sure if it was in wonderment or at the potential madness of it all.

Rachael turned to walk away. 'But this is not to be the first place to turn. It's more important to know how to be self-sufficient than to rely on this. You have to learn.'

She seemed so sure that we would need it all. That the shops would be gone, that there would be a time when only the self-sufficient could survive. Then she started talking of fairies and fey folk, spells and magic. Was she completely nuts or completely sane? I couldn't decide but something was telling me that I'd made the right decision in coming here. Me and my baby and Connor could have a good, safe life here. Like Rachael said, where we'd be okay whatever might happen. Wouldn't we?

Part III

Later
2050

Reawakening

FIFTEEN YEARS SEEMED to fly by. Dawn was born a few months after we arrived. We chose her name to signify our new life, a new beginning in a world that seemed to be ending. Being away from Reading, and living like we did in nature, put everything in perspective. You couldn't see clearly when you were living it but, from here, it was easy to recognise how mad and unsustainable it all was.

Our son was born almost three years later. We'd said no more kids but he came along anyway, even though we'd tried to be careful. We named him Michael Boon-Mee, after our dads. Connor said that Boon-Me also means lucky boy in Thai so it seemed fitting, right.

Rachael had taught me about the herbs and I'd been glad to learn but I wasn't so sure about the magical side of things, the spiritual elements. I always felt a bit stupid, fake, when I did it. She was always patient with me though. I settled into our new life with joy and ease, like I'd been made to live this way and been born in the city by accident. But then I started to get restless. To feel like I needed to do more. Whenever I went into Lynton and chatted with Nathan, the librarian who had become my dear friend, he was always telling me about how bad things were getting in the cities. The old feelings I'd had when I first started working at Countervaillence started to re-emerge. Our life in Woody Bay, making sure we were safe and prepared, was no longer enough. I wanted to help others too.

I dug out the old laptop and hard drive that I'd stolen from Countervaillance all those years ago. Obviously, things were going to have moved on a lot since then but I thought it'd be a good place to start to get my mind working in that way again. The research papers I'd been reading back then were about food security, energy, population growth, clean tech developments, all of the things that needed to be better managed for the benefit of people rather than profits. I couldn't believe all this time had passed and things were still getting worse rather than better. That those in charge couldn't, or wouldn't, see the irreversible consequences of this endless pursuit of money and power while they polluted the planet and made it virtually uninhabitable for the rest of us. Why were people putting up with it?

I knew Connor wouldn't want me to get involved in anything again. Ever since we arrived here he'd said how that was it, we should never leave. He reckoned we were lucky to have ended up here and had to do everything to keep our family and little community safe, the love we all had was enough to sustain us. So I was secretive about it and only tried to find the old websites when he wasn't around. I searched for the alternative news sites I remembered, the ones that told how things really were. But I couldn't find them. I hadn't been online much, only to email Leah, who, as predicted, hadn't been able to handle the quiet life here and had gone back to Reading with Bhav after just a few months. Marcus had dropped them back at the beach where we'd been picked up and they'd walked back to the boat, which was exactly as we'd left it. Jack had helped them get some fuel. They couldn't get one of the electric car engines up there as it was too heavy to carry all that way. When I asked Leah about how things were in Reading, she was always so blasé. Few shops were open in town anymore, there were more restrictions on the food you could buy for eating and cooking at home, but she said people were just carrying on as normal. The clothes and homeware shops that were open were still filled with people buying stuff they didn't need. The fast food restaurants were packed out all day long as the food in them was cheaper than the supermarkets, and they could get more of it. What was wrong with people? Couldn't they see?

I knew Nathan would have some idea of what was happening with the kind of stuff I was interested in. I'd have to ask him as I didn't have a clue where to start catching up on everything I'd missed while I'd focused on growing food, learning about healing herbs and having babies. If anything, the info and the people that I wanted to connect with would likely be even more hidden than when I'd had to search hard to find them before. The corporations would definitely be controlling search engine results even more tightly by now. There were probably loads of new websites that I'd not even heard of.

So, the next day, I set off on the long walk into Lynton. The path ran along the edge of the cliffs, the sea hundreds of feet below, cut up past the Valley of the Rocks and the old monastery, which was long abandoned, and came down through the north of the town. It took a good two hours at a steady pace. Lynton was a pretty town but a bit down at heel now that the tourist trade was a thing of the past. The rich city folk were the only people that took holidays and they didn't want to hang about in damp and rainy Devon, even though there was nowhere near as much rain as there used to be, when they could get super-fast jet planes and be on Caribbean island resorts in a couple of hours. Apparently, they'd herded all the people that lived in the islands on to just one, apart from those needed to cook and clean for them, and taken over the rest and turned them into one big five star resort. Or so the story went. Who knew what you could believe about anything?

Most of Lynton's young people had left and gone to the satellite towns like Reading and Bristol, where the recruiters found the workers they needed to keep the cities running. And where there were still shops, bars, cinemas and restaurants for them to then spend the money they earned in. All of this meant that Lynton had a bit of an old and dusty feel to it. Whenever I went into town I was one of the youngest people around.

When I got to the library, the doors were locked but the lights were on inside. I banged on the door and after about five minutes, it opened a crack and Nathan appeared. His wiry grey hair sprouting out wildly in all directions always made me think of the old Tom and Jerry cartoons I used to watch with my nana when Tom used to get electric shocks.

'Sorry, we're not opening until later today, Evie,' he said. 'Can you come back in a couple of hours when you've done whatever else you came in town for?'

'I only came in to come here.'

'Oh, okay then. Seeing as it's you. In you come.'

I squeezed through the little gap and then he shut the door and locked it behind me.

'What are you doing?' I asked.

'Sorting new stuff out. Had a big delivery yesterday – another donation from a rich dead man I've been pestering for years.' He laughed. 'I've got a big list of them and send regular begging emails. Some of them have still got hearts despite being wealthy.'

'How do you know about them? Aren't they all in

London? How can you contact people inside the city?'

Nathan gave me a searching look. 'They were too old and too arty to be deemed of any use, so they got left outside with the rest of us,' Nathan said.

We turned the corner into the reception area and there were boxes everywhere.

'Some lovely stuff in there so far.' Nathan stopped by the box he'd been emptying. 'You go off and get whatever you want while I get on with this.'

I lifted the bag of books I'd brought back. 'I'll leave these on the desk.'

Upstairs on the third floor, I headed for the engineering section. Connor wanted a book about hydropower. The solar panels we had at home were going to start wearing out, he said, and it would be too hard to get the parts we needed. He was going to try to build something simple that would let us generate power from the rivers, waterfalls and sea that surrounded us. He remembered seeing something about water wheels, so I searched for that.

I found a book in the history section in the end about the Pelton Wheel, which had been invented way back in the 19th century. I found another about generating electricity at home through renewable energy. Flicking through it I saw instructions on how to build hydroelectric generators to place in rivers, and also a whole section on building biomass boilers that could provide hot water and electricity. I put them both in my bag for him. Then I searched for books about activism from the early part of our century. I knew that there had been big global organisations lobbying for change, with members from all around the world getting involved in petitions and protests. From what I'd been reading online, these kinds of things didn't seem to work anymore though. Governments all around the world were puppets on the strings of the corporations. They were the ones that had control of the food, water, energy and clothing supplies, and they blatantly ignored all protests knowing that whatever happened we had no other choice than to keep on buying what they sold. But maybe looking back at the things activists used to do, and what they had achieved by it, could provide some inspiration for me.

An hour or so later I had almost filled my bag and headed back down to pick a couple of novels to take home too. Nathan was still busy emptying boxes and cataloguing their contents. He stood up when I approached and moved towards the desk to check the books out for me. He made me laugh with his insistence on these old-fashioned processes when he knew every single person that came in and borrowed books and where they lived. He'd been born in the last century, the previous millennium. His heavily wrinkled face and gnarly hands had so many stories ingrained in them and I loved the rare occasions that I got to spend time with him just chatting.

He'd told me once that he could remember a time before everything was online, before online even existed. That once the internet came along he'd known that we were in trouble. Guessed that little by little our freedom would be taken from us but that it'd happen so gradually nobody would notice and when they did it'd be too late. Consumerism and fear would have become so firmly entrenched in people's minds that they wouldn't want to go back. They'd think it was worth it to have security from the terrorists and as long as they had their nice comfy homes and money to spend, it didn't really matter.

At the time we'd had this conversation, I'd thought about all those people in the shanty towns around Reading. They didn't have nice comfy homes, so why weren't they rebelling? But then I went back to my safe haven in Woody Bay and didn't think about it again. Until now.

As he picked up the book about the Pelton Wheel and scanned it into his system, I said, 'Nathan, what's the best search engine to use if I want to find real information?'

He squinted at me over the top of the computer screen. 'Real information?'

'Yeah, you know, not the stuff the corporations want us to know but real news. I used to use a website called Planet Awake but that was so long ago and I don't know where to look now.'

'What sort of thing is it that you want to find out

about?' He picked up the next book on my pile. Called *Social Disorder and Creative Protests in the 21st Century*, it'd been published a couple of years before I was born and was based on an academic's PhD research. He rifled through the rest of the pile, which were all on a similar theme. 'Ah, I see.'

I smiled. His tone let me know he approved.

'Come, let's make a cuppa and have a chat.'

We took our tea out to the little back garden that went up the cliffside in terraces. Nathan led me up to the top one and we sat on the bench looking out over Lynmouth Bay. The sea glinted in the sunshine and the cliffs glowed orange.

'What's brought all this on then?' Nathan asked, blowing on his tea and staring straight ahead at the view.

I shrugged. 'It's always been there, I've just not taken much notice of anything else since I got here. Too wrapped up in bringing up the kids, learning from Rachael, you know.'

He nodded. 'Maybe you should just carry on focusing on that. You've got a nice life there, Evie.'

'But what about the people that haven't? And how long can it stay nice, even here, if everyone else just carries on the way they do?'

He smiled sadly at me. 'What makes you think you can change people? There have been protesters and activists trying for years to change things and look where we are now.'

'I have to believe. I do believe. I remember what it was like in Reading where as long as people had money to buy things, to party, they didn't care about what else was going on. I had kind of been like that too. Even though I was working at Countervaillence, I'd been buying clothes and eating out all the time. Consuming all the things that I knew were making it all worse. But somehow I managed to live with those two sides of myself. Believe that because of my job I was doing something to help the millions of people that were being made homeless every year because of climate change, while I was buying the products that were at the heart of it all. I think that's just the way humans are. We all do that to a certain degree. There were shanty towns filled with people that didn't have nice homes and things, but they weren't doing much to change things either.'

'Countervaillence?' He spun round to face me. 'You worked there?'

I nodded. 'You've heard of it?' I was surprised. It hadn't seemed like our reach was that big. But then again, a long time had passed and loads would have changed by now.

Nathan frowned. 'Have you been keeping in touch with people from there?'

'No. It's a very long story but things didn't end well when I left. It's part of the reason why I came here.'

He shook his head. 'I can imagine with what I've heard about them.' He stood and held his hand out for my empty mug. 'I have to get on. I need to have a think about how I can help you.'

It was weird. I felt like I was being dismissed. I followed him back to the counter to collect my books. Nathan was silent the whole time. I wondered if our conversation and my mention of Countervaillence had offended him in some way but as he handed me the last book and I turned to leave he added, 'Come and see me again next week, Evie, and in the meantime maybe you should have a word with your friend, Tess, about all this too.'

'Tess? What's she got to do with it? She worked at Countervaillence for a little while too. Did you know that?'

'I didn't. But I do know that she's involved with things that mean she might well be able to help you.'

I stopped and looked back at him. What did he mean when he said he'd heard things about Countervaillence? But he was walking back to his boxes. I headed for the door but then turned back. Nathan was at the desk typing urgently on his laptop, a look on his face that I found hard to interpret. A strange mix of unease and what could have been pride. The boxes forgotten behind him. So I left him to it. I'd ask him when I came back next week.

As I trudged back home, laden down with my books,

I thought about what he said. Tess. She'd moved down into the next valley along by the Heddon river, opposite the old hotel, and we didn't see her that much anymore. She was living with Matt, a local bloke who grew weed and played in a band, had moved in with him around the time Michael was born. What was she up to?

Cleansing

IT WAS MID-MORNING, hot and sunny, and I was in my herb poly tunnel planting some new Echinachea. I'd just harvested a load to dry out for tea.

'Hello, Evie.' As if my thoughts of her and conversation with Nathan had summoned her, I turned and saw Tess's smiling face peering through the half door at the other end of the tunnel. She'd let her hair grow into dreads and taken to wearing tie dye clothes made from old white sheets. She was very different to the clean-cut young girl I'd first met when she was handing out flyers about her nan's cats being turned into burgers.

'Hey, hello yourself.' I dropped the plants I had in my hand back in their box, hugged her tight and took her into the kitchen for tea.

We chatted for a while about what she and Matty had been up to, Connor's and my latest ideas to keep us powered and fed. Then I told her what Nathan had said.

'So what are you up to?' I asked as I pushed a plate of my homemade ginger biscuits towards her. She looked like she could do with some food. It had probably been four months since I'd seen her and she'd lost a lot of weight.

'Not much, I just like to keep informed. Always have done ever since we came down here. Go on a few protest marches in Bristol, sing a few songs.'

I remembered when we were on Bhav's boat on the way here she'd always been on her laptop. When we first got here, she'd been keen to keep me involved in the work we'd been doing at Countervaillance but I'd been too caught up in Connor and having a baby, then after that having another one. Learning from Rachael.

'How are you getting to Bristol? Have you got a boat?'

'No, a car. We got Jack to sort us out so that it runs on solar panels. We park it up where all the others are and walk into the city from there.'

I nodded. 'Nathan knew about Countervaillence. After I mentioned it he virtually rushed me out the door. But he told me to come back again this week. I don't think I'll get there though for a couple of weeks as there's too much to do here. Harvest time.'

'How come you're so fired up all of a sudden? And our life in Reading was so long ago now, what does it matter?'

'I feel like I'm coming out of a trance. One I've been in since Dawn was born. I want to get back to work, to try and make a difference, so that things will be alright for her and Michael in the future.'

She smiled but didn't say anything.

'So I thought I could start by writing things again. Sharing information and making it available to everyone in ways they can understand.' That had always been what I was good at.

'People don't want to know, Evie.'

'That's a shitty attitude, Tess. And not like you. Why are you going on marches and singing protest songs then?'

She shrugged. 'It's good to feel a part of something. I suppose some part of me feels like we can make a difference but most of the time, it's just a party scene. Sometimes I feel I'm too old for it all. Should just settle back down here with you, grow food and potter about.'

'Oh shut up, Tess. We're only thirty-two. And you'd go mad pottering around here. Believe me I know.'

We laughed and she stood up and came round and hugged me.

'You're right,' she said. 'I'll come back soon with my laptop and show you some sites. Show you some of the things Matty and I have been involved in when we travel around for gigs. There's this protest group in Bristol as well that we go on the marches with.'

'Can't you show me anything now? On my laptop?'

'No. It's not safe. I'll have to install an app we've designed so that you can get online without them tracing it back to you. Don't go searching for anything about this in the meantime.'

I looked down at my hands. 'I already have.'

'Well don't do it anymore. It should be okay if you've only done it a little bit then stop.'

She left, promising to come back in a few weeks and help me. I didn't know how I was going to wait a few weeks to get started and find out the answers to all the questions that were racing around in my mind. Now that I'd started thinking about all of this again I felt consumed by it. How dare they think that we'd all sit by and be their slaves while they trashed us and our planet. When I thought about the supposed health shops, with their rows and rows of herbal supplements made in factories by big corporations and sold in polluting plastic bottles, I seethed. Just another moneymaking ploy. They didn't care about keeping people healthy. There was too much money to be made from pharmaceuticals, and hospital treatments. My dad had told me that when he was young healthcare was free for everyone and then the same year they closed the borders they started charging everyone extortionate amounts of money to see a doctor, or have an operation. So only the rich could be healthy.

I tried talking to Connor about it all that night when the kids were in bed but he wasn't interested.

'It doesn't matter to us, does it? We've got our lives here and we'll be okay,' he said.

'That's a very selfish view. It should matter to us. It does matter to me.'

But he just shook his head at me and headed back out into his workshop, where I heard him hammering away.

I didn't believe that we would be okay in the long-term and I definitely didn't think things were going to be okay for Dawn and Michael unless changes happened soon. I'd brought them into the world, I had to try and change it for them. Make it better, safer, fairer. I could run a blog that people could access through the secret networks Tess had set up. I'd talk about all the things that people should be worrying about rather than blindly carrying on as if everything was going to be the same forever. As if it wasn't all going to come crashing down around us soon. The food, water, fracking, the social cleansing. Why couldn't they all see what was happening? Or maybe they could and really didn't care. I'd read a book from the library called *Selfie*, about how we all became so self-absorbed and the age of individualism. When community died and all anybody cared about was themselves. But I couldn't believe that everyone was like that. If we could fight back before it was too late, get some momentum going, we could get enough people to stand up to them. But the people I'd reach through a blog like that were not really the ones I needed to convert. I had to find a way to reach the people who didn't already think about these things, or if they did just pushed those thoughts away, believing that they couldn't really make a difference. But I also wanted to get out there and start instigating some positive changes.

I started by writing a blog about social cleansing. Surely that was more obvious to people than the environmental issues, the controls. I remembered from my childhood those TV programmes about clean houses where people who were not great housekeepers were paraded for all to mock. Their dirty hovels prodded and poked by clean freaks with their noses turned up and a bottle of bleach spray in hand. Viewers saw it as a way of feeling superior to others, so I thought I should play on this to try and get people reading. And keep it succinct. Attention spans were short, and getting shorter.

Are You Clean Enough?

Back in the days when religion guided the people it was said that cleanliness is next to Godliness. Although the vast majority of people now worship at the altar of a capitalist rather than a religious shrine, being seen to be clean is as important as ever. Perhaps even more so. What will people think if you don't have a spotless house? Washed, ironed and up-to-date clothes replaced regularly? How can you face your friends if you haven't got all of this?

Well, ask yourself this: are your friends clean enough? Are any of us? Surely, if we were considered clean we'd be allowed to live in London and the other big cities, wouldn't we? Or at least to visit them. But we can't – we can only go to serve. We have no freedom of movement, no chance to make things better, or just different, for ourselves. No further education, no proper healthcare, no voice. It's been decided that we're not clean enough, and never will be.

We are the dirty worker bees in this crumbling, rotten hive.

The rich elite that we have to serve in order to get by have been pushing us out for years. Removing us from their sight. Banning us from their cities. They started the process gently, calling it gentrification, but it's social cleansing. Face it.

Why are we putting up with this? It's time to take our rights, and our land, back.

I say we ARE clean enough.

I was pretty pleased with my first effort and made a note to find a video to insert at the end of Jenny Cargin, an activist and politician who had tried to change things and started to come close. My dad had spoken of her endlessly when I was growing up. In the few years before I was born she'd been the leader of the other party that used to exist, the one opposing the ones in power, back when we got to vote for who was in charge. Jenny Cargin had big ideals and ideas about a better, more equal, world for all. She'd started to gain real momentum and it looked like she was going to win the election. But then, the press had started to vilify her before, conveniently, she'd been killed in a car accident.

The following year, they'd started the social cleansing programme in earnest and within a couple of months everything had changed. The cities were no longer accessible, cars and travel were banned. Unless you'd been taken inside the enclave when it happened then the only future for you now was one of working in the service industries until you died. Or not having any work at all and having to find some way to scrape by. There was no retirement anymore. You had to carry on working to pay the rent or you'd be homeless. There was no more welfare, no more pensions.

What was going on in the rest of the world that it didn't matter that they were doing this to us? Why did nobody step in on our behalf?

Driving

BY THE TIME Tess returned, I'd been busy writing and had a dozen blogs ready to go. I'd been looking into how online had changed since I'd last been involved. Although people did still read blogs, they preferred videos and pictures. So I'd been keeping the words to a bare minimum and just writing notes of the videos and pictures I wanted to find to go with them until she got me set up on the untraceable web.

She brought me a new tablet that was set and ready to go. 'Completely safe. You can search for anything on there and they won't find you. Make sure you post your blogs from here too so that they can't trace that back either. Here use this programme to run it.'

She showed me the software that had been designed by the drummer in Matty's band for the activists to use. Apparently, you could write and publish untraceable content on the main web. That's what I really wanted to do, get it out there in the mainstream. I went straight to Planet Awake to see what sort of things they were publishing now. Back when I'd first discovered the site, when I was working at Countervaillence, it had loads of info and was a great resource. But it was no longer there. The homepage had a message saying: 'This website has been removed for non-compliance with Regulation 101 which states that all website owners must register their personal details.'

As far as I could remember it had had millions of social media followers. Where had it gone? How could a site like that, with so many people following it, just disappear with nobody protesting? Or maybe they did. What would I know? I'd been tucked away in my Woody Bay for years not bothering about anything outside of it.

Tess was doing something to my laptop to make it untraceable too, when Dawn came running in.

'Mum, look. Hazel gave me a chick to look after.' Her face was all shiny with excitement, as if she hadn't been looking after chicks all her life. For a moment I saw the little girl that she'd been until recently, before she turned into a surly teenager. It was hard to believe that she was fifteen already.

'Can you help me in the garden and make it a little home?'

'I'm busy at the moment, Dawn. Just go and put it in with the others up at Rachael's and then we'll do it later.'

'But then it won't be mine. It'll just get mixed in and I won't know which one is which.'

'Does it really matter?' I muttered, turning back to

Tess.

She stomped off and later, when Tess had gone and I'd had time to feel bad about it, I went outside and saw that Connor had built a little house for it down by the wall at the end of the garden. They were sat on the ground outside it together, watching the chick peck around in her new home.

'Sorry, Dawn, I should have helped,' I said as I sank down next to her.

She shuffled away from me, so she was pressed right up against Connor. 'Dad did it anyway. Much better than you could have.'

Connor smiled and rolled his eyes at me over her head. But they were always doing this lately, ganging up together against me it felt like. Just like I'd done with my dad. But my mum had been a nightmare with her religious mania. I wasn't like that.

Before I could think of how I could make it up to her she got up and walked off, saying pointedly, 'See ya later, Dad. I'm going up to Rachael's.'

'Be back for dinner,' I said and she huffed but didn't look back.

Connor scooted over to sit next to me, put his arm round my shoulders and squeezed. 'She'll be okay when she comes back. Remember what it's like being that age. A little kid one minute, convinced you're a grownup and know everything the next. She's all over the show.'

I smiled and dropped my head onto his shoulder. 'Oh, wise one.'

'Yep, Aristotle, Confucius, Camus, none of that lot come close to the depths of my insights into the human condition.'

I poked him in the ribs. 'And oh so modest with it.'

He pushed me back on the grass and started kissing my neck. 'My vast knowledge tells me we should make the most of having the place all to ourselves and get naked in the garden in front of the new chicken shed. It will do much to realign the planets and fix all that is wrong with the world.'

Part of me was annoyed that he was having a little dig even then, but I soon forgot about it as he carried on kissing me and sliding his hands up under my top.

'What about Michael?' I gasped.

'Gone into town with Shona and Marcus. Won't be back for hours.'

So I stayed where I was and let him pull down my jeans. I could get on with saving the world tomorrow.

Shaking

THE EARTH MOVED. I'd never felt it do that before. It was just a slight roll and at first I thought I'd imagined it. I was digging in the potato patch and I stood up and looked around.

Connor was chopping wood in front of the store and he looked up at the same time. 'What was that?' he said.

We'd seen on the screens that the earthquakes in the north had been getting worse as the energy companies spread their fracking further and further. There had been pictures of old villages where houses had fallen into huge cracks that appeared in the earth. There had been video footage of people walking away with a few bags of clothes. I'd seen an interview with a man with his family. 'We have nowhere to go. Nothing left and nobody is going to help us. The government don't care, they've sent no help and they never will,' he said.

Others said that even if their homes hadn't collapsed, they would have had to leave soon anyway as the water was contaminated so they couldn't grow food in their gardens and allotments anymore. Everyone outside the cities and the satellite towns that served them had to rely on their own food supplies. There were hardly any shops open anymore and those that were had hardly anything in them. I wasn't sure whether I believed it all though. Were they just showing things like this to scare us all into moving into the towns where it was easier to keep an eye on everyone?

'I don't know.' I put the spade down and walked towards him. As I did it happened again. A bigger roll this time and there was a sound like a thunder clap way off in the distance. I stumbled and Connor stepped forward and caught me. 'What should we do?' he said.

I shrugged. What could we do? Surely we couldn't be feeling earthquakes here that were happening in the north? There were no more movements after that so we just carried on with our work but there was a strange feeling in the air.

Dawn and Michael arrived home from school, which was not a proper school just the local kids being taught by Hazel, who lived up the lane from us with her family. She had kids around Dawn and Michael's age, and some younger, and she taught them and a few others from the houses down in the Heddon valley, in a classroom she'd set up in her house. We all sat round the kitchen table sorting the potatoes into piles for eating now, storing, and making into vodka. Connor had convinced Rachael to let him have some of the yeast and barley she had in the stash to make our own.

'That was an earthquake today,' Dawn said.

'Well, it felt like it but we don't know for definite.' Connor was always slow to believe the worst.

'It was. Hazel said that the energy companies have set up a new fracking site over Minehead way. They switched it all on today and that was what we felt,' Michael said.

'She said they were building another one too and that would be switched on soon,' Dawn added.

'Did she say where it would be?' I asked. I felt like saying I told you so to Connor, he who had kept insisting that we'd always be okay down here.

But they'd lost interest now. 'No. Don't think so,' Michael said. 'Can I go now? I said I'd meet Joe.'

'Off you go,' Connor said.

As the door shut behind him, I couldn't help myself. 'Looks like the real world is reaching us even down here then,' I said.

Connor just shook his head and refused to be baited.

'Doesn't look like all your little activism blogs have made much difference does it, Mum?' Dawn sneered at me in that way she'd developed recently. She'd always been a daddy's girl. When I was being particularly selfish and immature, I wished we'd told her the truth so that she'd know Connor wasn't her real dad and love me best. Stupid, I know. But sometimes I found myself acting like the teenager she was.

'To be fair, Dawn, I haven't even published them yet,' I said, knowing that I should let it go but not able to.

'Too little, too late. As always,' was her parting shot as she ran off upstairs to her room.

I blinked back tears. She didn't really hate me. It just seemed like that now. We'd get past this bit and be close again.

Later that night there were a couple of small rumbles and ground rolls and I snuggled up against Connor in bed, hoping he could melt the cold, hard lump of fear that was growing inside me.

'What if it's too late and there's nothing we can do now that will make a difference?' My voice cracked.

He kissed the top of my head and squeezed me tight but didn't answer. Which was, I suppose, an answer in itself.

But the next morning he brightened right up again. 'I don't think it'll get any worse,' he said. The kids had left for school and I was going into Lynton to see Nathan.

'What makes you so sure?' I said, moving the plate I was scrubbing to the side so he could put his mug in the washing up water.

'Just got a feeling, a good one.' He grinned, kissed me on the cheek. 'See ya later.'

As I tidied the kitchen I wondered if he just couldn't admit he was scared. I knew it would get worse. You only had to look at what had been happening everywhere else to know that we would be in for bigger quakes. They didn't behave like normal quakes either, apparently. Because they weren't natural they were bigger, longer, more dangerous. It couldn't be allowed to go on.

I PUSHED THE library door open, wanting to find out what Nathan knew but scared at what I might find out. Tess had said at the time that there was something dodgy about Tom, and from Nathan's reaction when I mentioned Countervaillence, he probably thought the same too.

It was busy inside, lots of browsers. A queue at the desk. A reaction to the first earthquakes? Distract yourself by getting lost in a book? Nathan looked up when he heard the door swing shut behind me. Smiled, looked pleased to see me. I smiled back, felt my shoulders drop down, as a tension I hadn't been aware of released. He wasn't angry with me, or offended, like I'd thought.

I pointed up to say I'd be looking around in the fiction section when he had time to come find me. I found myself drawn to the science fiction. I'd always read sci-fi avidly when I was younger but my reading habits had been focused more on relationship dramas in recent years. I had enough of them going on at home with Dawn so thought a trip into other worlds could be the perfect antidote. I pulled down a novel called *Make Room! Make Room!* by Harry Harrison. I'd never heard of him, but the title intrigued me.

It had been written nearly one hundred years ago and was set in 1999 in a New York City where thirty-five million people lived. The blurb said it was a story about unchecked population growth's impact on the planet. Interesting. I wondered if he'd got any of it right, as even now, if you could believe the screens, the population of New York was still only twenty-four million. Only, I grinned to myself. Amazing how the brain adapts to crazy things. I sat down on the floor with my back against the shelves and started to read. By the time Nathan came to find me, I was gripped. If only my mum and all those other millions of deluded, non-contraceptive-taking Catholics had read it.

'Evie, sorry. It's been the busiest in ages today. I've shut up shop. Let's go and get some lunch.'

It had started to rain so we hurried to his house next door. His kitchen didn't seem to suit him. It was stark, hardly anything on the worktops, just a single pot with utensils in. A glass jar with herbs in sat on the windowsill. The only signs that anything ever happened in the room.

'Sit, I'll rustle us up something.' He opened the fridge and pulled out lettuce, tomatoes and peppers. All of which had come from our gardens. Then he chopped up some leftover potatoes, some rosemary, thyme and parsley and added them, stirred it all together and dished it up into two bowls.

After lunch we went into his study. This was more

like it. A floor to ceiling window looked out onto the garden. In front of the window a big desk was covered in notepads surrounding a huge computer screen. One whole wall was bookshelves, despite having his own massive library next door. The other walls were covered in prints of old movie posters, book covers, and famous artworks. There were original paintings too from local artists, and black and white landscape photographs. A fireplace had old ashes in it and a box of twigs on the hearth. A faded red, winged armchair close to the fire was covered in squashy cushions, a beaten up leather footstool in front of it.

I sat in the armchair and Nathan sat at his desk facing me. My stomach fluttered and clenched. I had a feeling I wasn't going to like what he had to say.

'You still want to do it then?' he asked.

I nodded. Told him about the blogs, the secret app that Tess had sorted.

'All great stuff. Online seems like a good place to start. You've not been out in the world in a long time, Evie. It's going to be different to what you remember.'

'I can handle it. I'm going to go with Tess and Matty into Bristol on their next march. I can't keep burying myself down here pretending none of it's happening. Especially when the fracking is on our doorstep now.'

He nodded.

'What did you mean about Countervaillence the other

day? What do you know about them?'

Nathan spun on his chair and gazed out into the garden, as if he had to carefully choose what he said next. Then he turned back to me.

'You obviously know Tom if you worked there. I have a contact in London, a young woman, probably not that much younger than you, five or so years maybe. She's known him her whole life.'

He stopped, a grave expression on his face. The reality of what he'd said sank into my brain. Tom did know people in London. Just like Tess had thought all along. But how had he appeared in my life down here? Although in the form of Dawn he'd always been here. But most of the time I lived with the belief that Connor was her dad and the past could be forgotten.

'But how? Can she get out? How do you know her?'

Nathan hesitated, weighing what to say next but before he could speak there was a hammering on his front door.

'Evie, are you there? Evie!' Lloyd's voice called out.

What was he doing here?

We ran to the door and when we pulled it open, Lloyd was climbing onto the back of Smokey, the horse we used to pull the cart when we went to the markets to sell our fruit and veg.

'Lloyd, what's going on?'

'It's Michael. There's been an accident.'

Parade

By the time we arrived home, Michael had been rescued and was in bed up at Rachael's, his left arm in a sling, stitches in his head above his right eye, and scrapes and grazes all over him.

Connor was sat next to the bed and he smiled up at me as I came in. 'It's alright, he's okay.'

'What the hell were you thinking, Michael?' I shouted. Fear, relief and happiness surging through me at seeing his tiny face and body all battered on the bed. But alive.

'I'm sorry. We just wanted to try it.' His bottom lip quivered and I rushed over to him wanting to gather him up in my arms but afraid of hurting him more. Settled for stroking his hair.

'Well, now you have. You won't be doing that again in a hurry will you?'

We left him there to rest and went down to the kitchen where Rachael was chopping onions, the pungent sting making my eyes water along with the tears of relief.

I sat down at the table next to Lloyd. Connor went

and helped himself to some tea from the pot that was always ready to drink on the range.

'What happened?' I said to nobody in particular.

'They tied a rope to one of the old apple trees right next to the cliff,' Lloyd said. 'Michael went first, abseiling down to the beach. The branch snapped and down he went.' He gestured towards the door to outside, 'First thing we knew about it Joe's standing in the doorway screaming. I had to go down and get him back up.'

'What if none of us had been here and the tide had come in?' I could hear the terror in my voice at a scenario I was creating in my head that hadn't happened and forced myself to get a grip. 'Sorry, that doesn't help.'

'It's over now, Evie. He's going to heal fine. He was even fine when we got him back here. Telling us how he was convinced that nobody had ever stood on that little bit of beach before and he'd be like the old explorers he's read about.' Rachael said wiping her hands on the checkered apron she was wearing over a spotty dress. My head hurt looking at her.

I laughed then. Allowed the relief to take over from the fear.

THE NEXT MORNING Tess turned up. 'Come on. We're going into Bristol. There's a march planned and you said you wanted to come.'

Connor smirked at me like I was a teenager going through a rebellious period when I stood up to go with her.

'Don't patronise me. I used to do things that mattered before we came here. I can do it again.'

'You were a kid playing at protest, running through shopping malls and tipping up tables in coffee shops. And why are you doing this anyway? We're safe here. We have everything we need.'

'It's not just about us though is it? What about all the other people who are being trampled over, who are going to end up with nothing, have no chance?'

'Why is it up to you to save them? We made our own way, saved ourselves. They can do the same.'

'No, they can't. We were lucky that Shona had come here. We had somewhere to escape to. But that's my real point. People shouldn't need somewhere to escape to.'

Tess stood and watched, her head swinging backwards and forwards between us as each of us spoke. We were going around in circles again, so I left. As we marched up the hill to where Matty was waiting in the car, Tess grabbed my arm. 'Hold up, slow down.'

I slowed my pace, turned my anger over and over in my head instead of stomping it into the ground.

When Tess had caught her breath, she said, 'Are things alright with you and Connor?'

I snorted. 'Yes, fine.'

WE ARRIVED AT the car cemetery in Bristol several hours later after a very bumpy drive. We had to walk from there and I trailed after Tess and Matty, distracted by what I was seeing. I hadn't been in a city in fifteen years and it was surreal to see all these people crammed in together. The noise, the litter, the smells, the heat. How did they handle it? Music and shouting poured out of the windows of almost every house we passed. Piles of rubbish were heaped up in the middle of the street. Rats scurried around everywhere, and nobody took any notice. People sat on doorsteps shouting to neighbours across the street. It was a cacophony and I felt like my head might explode.

'C'mon, Evie, keep up.' Tess turned around to wait for me. When I caught up with her she linked her arm though mine. 'You okay?' she asked.

I nodded, then shook my head, then nodded again. I didn't know. I couldn't think straight. There was no way anyone could think clearly in a place like this.

We walked for ages then we passed through an old railway tunnel and Matty stopped in front of a huge metal gate with razor wire on top and several thick chains and padlocks holding it closed. He shook the gates. 'Hey. It's Matty. Open up,' he shouted.

I stared in confusion. We were going in here? Through the gates I could see what looked like a shanty town. Tin huts crammed in next to each other. A big wooden building with boarded up windows. Kids sitting in the dirt below a big wind turbine, which was turning slowly even though the day was completely still.

A young woman came to the gate. She had one blue eye and one brown and dirty blonde dreads hanging down her back. She was wearing the same kind of tie-dye dress that Tess had taken to wearing and a matching scarf that tied her dreads back.

Tess stepped forward and hugged her. 'Lets, this is Evie. Evie, this is Scarlett, Lets.'

She unlocked the gates and we filed in. We followed her in to the big wooden building, one big room with a huge table in the middle, covered in placards, leaflets, laptops. A few chairs were shoved up against the table in front of the laptops and around the edges of the rooms, squashy old sofas and chairs were covered in people wearing the same tie-dye clothing. Dresses for the women and kaftan style tops over straight leg trousers for the men. I looked down at my jeans and waterproof jacket. Should I ask if there was a spare tie-dye outfit for me?

As if she read my mind, Lets took my hand and led me upstairs. Showed me into a small room filled with clothes. 'Help yourself. It has more impact if we all look the same, like an army.' She smiled and her teeth were tiny, like milk teeth.

Downstairs, a man with a bald head, Darren, showed us the map of the route we were going to take. 'Memorise it, in case you get split from the group,' he said.

Placards and leaflets gathered, we set off in a small procession and walked into the city centre. The heat didn't seem nearly as intense in my tie-dye dress. In Castle Park there was another crowd of tie-dye wearing protesters, about sixty of them. More arrived and they kept on coming until after about half an hour there were about two hundred of us. See, Connor? People do want change. There was a festival atmosphere to start with. People sitting around on the grass drinking and smoking, soaking up the sun, chatting and laughing, placards abandoned beside them.

Then Darren made his way to a bench and climbed up on it. Banged two placards together to get everyone's attention.

'Right. It's time to go. We're going to head down to Cabot Circus then through the shopping centre and down to the "Entertainment Hub".' At his air quote marks, sniggers rippled through the crowd. 'Then back in a loop to here. Hopefully we will have gathered people on the way. Then we'll have the speeches. Lets has one prepared and so does Tess but anyone that wants to speak can.'

Lets jumped up beside him and punched both fists in the air. 'Come on – we have to wake up the world!' she shouted.

Everyone cheered, stood up, waved their placards in the air and started to move towards the gate on the other side of the park, chanting 'Wake up world! Before it's too late.'

I fell into step beside Matty and joined in the chant. Adrenaline coursed through me to be with so many people after so long in the bay with just a few of us. To feel like I was doing something that was going to make a difference. Even if it took years.

But when we got to the Cabot Circus shopping mall I realised how unlikely that was. Even though lots of the shops were closed down there were shoppers everywhere with bags stuffed full of cheap clothes and more tat to fill their homes, not caring that where they were manufactured the air and the rivers were so polluted by factory waste that nothing and no one could live there anymore. The media and the corporations had brainwashed them into believing to consume was what we were here to do. That if we didn't the world would end, economies would fail, people would die. When the truth was that if we carried on like we were then there was no hope of a future that was safe, secure or anything like what they were used to. Why couldn't they see that?

As we paraded past a Coffair, a group of young people chucked the dregs from their coffee cups at us and the crusts from their sandwiches. 'Fucking freaks!' a man wearing a Mexican poncho over leather trousers shouted at us. He must have been boiling in such an outfit but I remembered from my days in Reading that it didn't matter to lots of people how uncomfortable they were as long as they looked the part. I'd thought it would be different in Bristol though. It had always been known as a forward-thinking place. A green city doing everything it could to be more sustainable. What had happened to change that?

Matty moved up to walk next to Tess but she shoved him aside and confronted the man, shouting, 'Fucking mindless idiot,' at him. We continued on with our chanting, which reverberated around the mall, bouncing off the glass ceiling.

People looked down from the upper floors, dropping cups on us and throwing water, sweets, all sorts. We were quite far back in the procession so couldn't see what was going on at the front but slowly we ground to a halt and the chanting died down.

'Security,' said Tess. 'They stop us every time and then escort us out, tell us never to come again.'

The people in front of us started to move forward again and we were led out to Penn Street and continued on our planned route down Newgate past Castle Park towards the waterfront. It was the same all the way there, with people jeering at us and throwing things. Pushing some of us off the pavement and into the road in front of approaching buses.

By the time we got to the waterfront it had started to rain and the dye from the dress was leaking down my legs. Everyone around me looked the same and I realised how

we must look to people. Like nutters. Nobody was ever
going to take any notice of people dressed like us,
chanting and waving placards in the air. They would have
to be reached in a different way.

Before we could carry on down to the walkway alongside the bars and restaurants which overlooked the water,
several riot vans of armed police turned up and they
jumped out shouting and pointing guns at us.

Matty grabbed my arm and Tess's and shouted, 'Run!'
He pulled us in the opposite direction to the riot vans and
we pushed through the crowd, ran up the hill that led
away from the city and the water. I couldn't run properly
in the stupid dress and soon I was lagging behind, my
chest burning from the pollution in the air that I wasn't
used to. Matty and Tess were getting further and further
away and I started to panic. I had no idea how to get back
to the shanty town, or where the car was. Without that I
had no way of getting home. But I had no breath to shout
loud enough to make them hear me over the din of bus
traffic and the shouts and sounds of trouble coming from
the procession we'd just left.

But then I felt a hand in my back pushing me gently
forward. 'Come on, just keep going, take deep breaths.'
Lets took my hand and jogged gently with me. When we
got to the top of the hill and turned the corner, Tess and
Matty were there waiting. Panting, hands on knees. Red-
faced. We looked at each other and then we were all

laughing. I hadn't felt so alive in years and I knew that I would be carrying on protesting, but not wearing badly tie-dyed dresses in pointless parades. I was going to come up with other ideas. How could we reach people, make them care?

Reaching

BACK AT THE wooden house, everyone who had managed to get away from the police was gathered in the big room and on the veranda outside, drinking, smoking, celebrating, it seemed. But I couldn't see what there was to celebrate. What had been achieved? Nothing as far as I could tell. I sat in a corner picking at a loose thread on my stupid tie-dye dress. Tess and Matty were setting up their instruments in the big area in front of the boarded-up window and it looked like the party would go on for the rest of the day and night. I sighed, thinking about my babies and Connor back in Woody Bay with no idea of the things that went on in places like Bristol. Well, Connor did obviously as he grew up in Reading. But Dawn and Michael had been kept safe in our little commune. The biggest place they'd ever been was Lynton and that was hardly a buzzing metropolis.

Lets came and sat by me, handed me a cup with warm, sickly sweet cider in it. I sipped, not wanting to appear rude.

'You think it's a waste of time, don't you?' she said.

How did she keep reading my mind? I smiled to take the edge off my words. 'Honestly? Yes, it seems pointless. I can't see what's been achieved.'

She pointed to a girl of about seventeen or eighteen, wearing the latest uniform of the fast fashion clones, who was chatting and laughing as she swigged from a can of lager, the boy with her obviously in her thrall. 'Those two have been recruited today. They were shopping in the mall, now they're with us. Every time we go, we get more. This is how we'll take it back. One person at a time coming to our cause.'

'But they're just kids, easily swayed. Who's to say when they get back with their mates later they won't just laugh at their exciting afternoon with the protesters and go back to their old ways? And what about the millions of people who are the parents of kids like this who don't give a shit, never have, never will? How do we reach them?'

'Through the young people. We show them there is another way and when they see, when they believe, then they start to spread the word too. Every single person whose mind we change will go out there and change more. It'll work, you'll see.'

I wasn't convinced, but I wanted to be. I wanted it to work.

I'd thought we would head back that night but it was obvious that there was no chance of getting home before tomorrow, so I sent an email to Connor, not that it was likely he'd see it. I went upstairs and cleaned the dye off my legs in the bathroom and changed back into my own clothes. I wasn't up for partying so headed out for a walk, following the same path we'd taken earlier to get back to the park. I needed some green. It was so grimy and grey in the city. Had Reading been this bad? Or did I just notice it more now that I lived in a beautiful, unspoiled place? Even in the park, litter marred the beauty. But if you ignored that, it was a lovely place to be. The old church covered in ivy was on one side and the river on the other. I sat down on a bench looking out over the park down to the water. Living next to it for so long, I seemed to only feel at home now when I was near water.

Was it true what Lets said, the young people had to be the answer? A group of teenagers sat down by the river, drinking from cans, laughing, shouting, surrounded by shopping bags. Or was Connor right, and Nathan, when they said people like me had been wanting to change the world forever and it didn't work as most people didn't want it to change? Sometimes I wished I could be like that. Switch it all off, stop caring. But I couldn't.

THE NEXT MORNING, I was sat at the table, waiting for Tess and Matty to get up so we could go home, when Lets came in the front door.

'Oh, hello. I'd assumed you were upstairs somewhere,

sleeping,' I said.

'I don't live here. I went home. I came back to see you. I've got an idea for us to work together, here in Bristol, using your self-sufficiency knowledge to reach the young people. Show them they can live in a better way, grow healthy food instead of eating the muck sold to them in the shops and while we're doing that, we can show them what's being done to us. That's how we can start to change it.' Her eyes were bright and she barely drew breath between sentences.

Her enthusiasm was infectious and by the time Tess and Matty got up in late afternoon, we had devised a whole plan. One that meant I'd have to come to Bristol a lot. Connor was going to be unhappy about it, but I had to do something.

It was almost dark by the time we reached the car and the journey home seemed to take forever. It was the early hours, silent and black, when I reached home and I expected the house to be in darkness, everyone in bed, but there was a light shining from the kitchen window. Connor. He must have been worried, and understandably so. But there was nothing I could have done about it. It wasn't my fault.

But they were all there, pinch-faced, huddled together around the table. Michael still pale, and bruised, his arm in a homemade plaster cast. Dawn ran to me and threw her arms around my waist, squeezing hard but saying nothing, her face buried in my shoulder. Michael sobbed, 'You came back. We thought you'd gone forever.' Connor smiled sadly and picked up the mug in front of him and went to stand at the sink with his back to me.

I hugged Dawn tight then eased her away from me. 'Hey, what's all this? Of course I came back. Why did you think I wouldn't?'

'Because you said you'd be back ages ago and you weren't, and you didn't tell us,' Dawn shouted, her tone telling me I was stupid not to realise. Then she ran off to her room, her feet pounding on the stairs then across the ceiling. Michael stood and slipped past, following her out of the door.

Connor was very still.

'I emailed you,' I said.

He sighed, gripped the side of the sink, but still didn't face me. 'I don't understand you, Evie. You knew I wouldn't read it. How often do I check emails? Why didn't you just come home when you said you would?'

'I'm sorry. I thought—'

'Not about us, that much is obvious.' He left then. Going off into the living room and shutting the door behind him.

I sat at the table and poured a cup of tea from the pot. It was tepid and horrible, like a punishment for upsetting everyone. But why should I have to explain myself to them? They knew where I was, what I was doing. So what if it took longer than I'd said it would? They'd thank me when our plans worked and they had a future filled with opportunities after all.

Arresting

CONNOR HADN'T SLEPT in our bed with me and when I came downstairs he was asleep on the sofa. I thought about waking him but took my tea outside instead. He'd come around. I worked outside all morning in the herb garden, despite the rain. Several times there were rumbles and shakes, but I just carried on. We'd got used to them now. What could we do? We had to just get on with it and hope we were far enough away from the fracking sites that they wouldn't get any worse. That our water wouldn't get poisoned, our houses wouldn't fall down.

I hadn't seen anyone by the time I went back in to get some food a couple of hours later. The kitchen was empty, but they'd obviously all been up as the dishes from their breakfast were piled in the sink. Connor's boots were by the door, so he was in the house. I thought when he heard me moving around he'd come to see me but there was still no sign of him, or the kids, by the time I'd tidied up and eaten. I hadn't heard them moving around either, so I went in search of them.

They were all still in bed, sleeping.

I woke Michael first, knowing he'd be the easiest one to deal with. 'Hey, sleepyhead. What are you still doing in bed?' I sat on the end of the bed, nudged gently against the heap of his body under the quilt.

His head lifted, and he squinted at me. 'Hello. We didn't sleep very much when you were away.' He croaked.

Guilt twanged in my chest but I pushed it away. They had to get used to it, had to understand that everything didn't revolve just around them and our life here. There were bigger things going on.

'Well, I'm back now and it's almost midday. You should get up.'

I left them to wake up properly and went back to the kitchen. By the time they joined me I'd got stuck into writing the plan that Lets and I had come up with. We were going to speak to teachers to see if they would let us come into the schools and give talks. Find a room or a hall somewhere in the city centre and start running workshops to teach the kids about self-sufficiency and at the same time show them how and where we'd all gone wrong, what we could do now to put it right. How important it was that we did. History from the late 20th century and early 21st, before I was born, was filled with empty promises from the government about their plans to manage climate change and resources, close the gap between rich and poor. They hadn't done any of them. We couldn't just keep waiting for them to do it when it was obvious they never would.

'What are you doing?' Dawn said as she sat in the chair next to me and looked at the screen.

'I'm writing a plan. This is part of what I was doing when I was away.' I wanted to go into it with her, get her caring about it too, but Connor came over and pushed the lid of the laptop shut.

'As important as all that is, there are things that need to be done around here too.' He sat in the chair by the stove and put his boots on.

'Come on, you two – let's get up to the gardens. We've got harvesting and planting to do. I'm sure your mum needs to get on with things in her garden too.'

They left me there with the distinct impression that they thought my plan wasn't important at all.

That night, Lloyd came to see us. 'Have you heard the news?' he said, sitting down on the sofa next to me.

'No, what?' I said.

Connor put down the book he'd been reading. 'Is everyone okay?'

Lloyd nodded. 'Everyone here is. I got an email from Leah. There's been riots in Reading. The police went and destroyed the King's Meadow shanty town and raided the old business park, threw everyone out. They all went mental and started burning shops in town. So the police started shooting. They killed hundreds and hundreds of people. She said Reading is completely trashed. No shops or restaurants are open, everyone's running out of food.'

'Oh my God.' My dad. 'What about my family, does she know if they're okay? What's she going to do?'

'She's gone. They left on the boat. They're somewhere north of Oxford. She didn't mention your family, Evie.'

I rushed off to get the laptop to email Dad. Please let them be alright. Even Mum.

But I didn't get a reply that day, or the next.

ABOUT A WEEK later, I still hadn't heard back from him. I'd been looking at the news online and it said all was under control again now. Who knows if that was true though. I kept telling myself that he would be fine as he wouldn't have been involved in the riots. But why wasn't he replying to my messages? I was driving myself mad worrying about it.

Connor and Dawn had been brilliant, telling me it was probably because communications were down there if everything had been set on fire, trying to put my mind at rest. But as soon as I said I was going to Bristol again, Connor stiffened and Dawn looked at me with big eyes.

'But why? Why do you have to go there? We need you here,' she said.

'I'll only be gone for a few days and you'll be fine without me.' I wasn't going to be talked out of it.

'But what if something bad happens while you're

there?' She banged her hands on the table. 'You are so selfish, always wanting your own way about everything. You don't care about us.'

'Don't be stupid, Dawn. It'll be fine and of course I care about you.'

She let out a howl of frustration and flounced off, slamming the door behind her. We heard her footsteps running down the path towards the beach. I went upstairs to pack a bag, leaving Connor to comfort her. They'd have to get used to it. After this trip to finalise the details, Lets and I were going to be busy and I was going to be away a lot more. What had happened in Reading had just made me even more determined.

I NEVER HEARD back from Dad and I used my grief to spur me on. Over the next couple of months, Lets and I put our plan into action and started working in the schools after hours, running youth drop-in sessions. We had statistics and images and videos to back up what we were saying and it was working. Many of the kids were seeing the truth. As well as educating them about what had happened in the past and what was happening now we had them making their own plans to change things. We'd started a community garden and were showing them how to grow their own food and many of them had gone home and started their own garden, even if it was just in pots. This was virtually unheard of in the cities. Allotments like my granddad had when I was very tiny had long been built over and it was rare for people to grow food, especially when they were encouraged to buy fast food so cheaply. It was all going well until a new lad turned up at a drop-in session.

'Lucas! You came,' Lets hurried over to him.

I looked up from the desk where I was preparing the day's presentation. Lucas looked to be about fifteen. He was short and dark, dressed all in black.

'Evie, this is Lucas. He wants to help.'

'Welcome, Lucas,' I smiled at him but when he smiled back it didn't reach his eyes. He's just shy, not used to being listened to, I told myself. I remembered how I'd felt growing up in Reading.

He sat at the back during our presentation, making notes in the pad he'd brought with him. When we finished and asked for questions he put his hand up straight away. 'How do you know that the statistics you've got are true? You talk about the news being propaganda and the screens telling people lies but where did you get this information if not from the screens? From the same places you tell us not to believe.'

'Great question, Lucas!' Lets said. 'Evie and I have got connections to networks of underground activists spread across the country. Scientists, writers, philosophers, who have all been working together to gather the truth. We have access to books and papers from the past, before the borders were closed, when we were able to share information with other countries, travel there and see things for ourselves.'

He nodded and made another note in his pad. 'And can we speak to these people, read these books? So we can make our own minds up?'

Lets smiled, her eyes on fire with the belief that he was going to be an important part of the future. 'Yes, when we feel you're ready we can get you more involved with them, but the majority of the books are not here. They're where Evie lives.' She turned to me. 'Maybe you could bring some of them with you next time?'

'I can certainly try. One or two anyway as they'll be too heavy to carry. Perhaps the best thing for now though is if you just read through the presentations Lets and I have been giving and see how you get on. I've got a blog as well that's filled with info. There's a lot to take in before you get to the stage where you can self-guide your learning.' How pompous and filled with self-worth I was. As if I knew best and if they all just listened to me and did things my way then all would be fine with the world.

But Lucas nodded and asked if we could email him copies of the presentations. 'We can't send them to you as they can see our communications unless you have a special app to hide them,' I said. 'But we can give you this booklet, which has all of the main points. Why don't you read that and when we see you again you can tell us what you think and what questions you have. A friend of mine can install the app on your phone so you can read my blog. I'll bring her with me next time.' I walked to the desk and pulled a copy of the booklet from my bag, warm in the belief that we had another convert.

That evening, Tess and Matty picked me up from Lets's house, where I stayed whenever I was in Bristol. She lived just around the corner from the shanty town where we'd first met but it was a different world. An old park-keeper's cottage surrounded by trees that blocked out much of the city noise, and created an enclosed haven. She'd filled the garden with flowers and it was a splash of reds, pinks, purples and yellows against all that relentless city grime.

When I got home in the early hours, I let myself into the cottage and found Dawn sat in the chair next to the kitchen stove, wrapped in a blanket. The room was lit by a couple of candles and the flames from the stove's open door. She looked so like Tom. She'd inherited his wavy golden hair and his height, towering above me already.

'Hello, Dawnie, what are you still doing up?' I dumped my bags on the kitchen table and went to the sink to fill the kettle. Part of me wished she was in bed as I was all talked out and in need of some time to myself after five days in Bristol in the company of others. Talking, preaching, planning and converting. It was so exhausting. In the car on the way home, Tess and Matty had been filled with more plans. They were writing and performing angry protest songs and had just come off stage before they picked me up so were all fired up with adrenaline from the performance. They barely paused for breath in the whole six and a half hours it took us to get home.

'I wanted to talk to you,' Dawn said. 'Without anyone else around.'

I put the kettle on the stove and sank into the chair nearest to her. 'Why, what's up?'

'I want you to stop this.' Her voice cracked and then she was sobbing into her hands.

I leaned forward and pulled her hands from her face, but she wrenched them away from me. 'Stop what?'

She took a deep breath. 'Going to Bristol. Doing all this stuff. You have to stay here.'

I sighed then launched into my usual speech about how important it was that people knew the truth.

'This, this is the truth,' she shouted. 'We are the truth, me and Dad and Michael. Rachael. Lloyd, everyone here. The plants, the sea. Why can't you see that?'

'I can see that you are, Dawn, but we are not the only people that matter. Everyone matters.'

'To you. Everyone matters to you apart from us. You're hardly ever here and even when you are, your head is somewhere else. Well, fuck you then.' She stood up letting the blanket fall from her shoulders onto the chair.

'Dawn, don't ever speak to me like that again!'

She shook her head and ran, sobbing, out into the dark of the garden.

'Dawn!' I shouted from the doorway but she'd disappeared into the night.

She avoided me for the next week, sleeping up at Shona and Marcus's, or Rachael's, and only seeing Connor and Michael in the garden. Then it was time for me to go to Bristol again. As I was packing my bags she appeared in our bedroom doorway.

'Nothing I say or feel makes any difference to you, does it? You'll just carry on doing what you want. I've got a bad feeling. Don't go. This is where you belong. Leave them to it. We're okay here.' Looking like Tom but sounding just like Connor.

'I can't, Dawn. I have to do this. It's for you and Michael too that I want the world to change.'

'No, it isn't. You just want to feel important, you think you're right about everything all the time. We all have to fit in with what you want.'

A FLAT TYRE on the way meant that we arrived in Bristol much later than planned, just as the sun was going down. The sky above the city glowed orange, red and purple, and as we walked from where we left the car, the reflection on the river made it look like a torrent of fire. Tess and Matty left me by the Watershed, heading straight to some pub in the north of the city for their gig, and I headed east to Lets's flat. I cut through Castle Park where I sat down on a bench to rest and drink some water.

As I turned the corner into her road, I saw a police van pulling away. Lucas was coming out of Lets's front door, a policeman patting his shoulder. I ducked into the nearest garden and crouched behind the wall.

'Well done, Lukie boy,' I heard the policeman say.

'Sorry that the other one wasn't here, Uncle Ryan.'

'Don't worry, we'll get her. We'll leave a couple of guys here and they'll nab her when she arrives.' He laughed but there was no joy in it. 'They'll bring her straight to the station. The message from London is she's the one they really want.'

I heard the car doors slam and the engine gun then fade into the distance. Where were they taking Lets? What would they do to her? What was I going to do now? Tess and Matty weren't coming to pick me up for another three days. I texted Tess, telling her what had happened. Why were people in London looking for me? Was this connected to Tom and what Nathan had been trying to tell me? I should have made the time to go back and see him, find out what he knew.

'What are you doing?' I started at the voice behind

me, jumped up.

A hard-faced woman was hanging out of the window above, staring down at me.

'Nothing. Sorry.' I walked quickly back to Castle Park not knowing where else to go. While I waited to hear back from Tess, the daylight disappeared completely. I felt scared and vulnerable sitting in a park by myself so headed into town. I had no money for food or drink as every time I came up to stay, I brought fruit and vegetables from our gardens to cook at Lets's. I sat on a bench opposite Cabot Circus and pulled a carrot from my bag, chewed on it as I stared at my phone, willing Tess to reply. Maybe I should go and see if anyone at the shanty town commune could help.

I couldn't remember how to get there from town so walked back to Lets's street instead, as I was pretty sure I knew the way from there. I stayed across the road in the shadows in case the police were still there waiting for me.

When I reached the commune, the gates were hanging off and the wooden meeting house was on fire, flames shooting up through the roof. The tin huts were smashed and strewn all over the ground. I couldn't see anyone around so crept through the gate, hoping that everyone who'd lived there was okay. What was going on? I stood looking around at all the chaos wondering what to do next. Where to go and how I could help Lets.

'Hey!' a man's voice shouted.

Where was he? Then I saw him coming out from round the back of the wooden house. He was silhouetted against the flames, so I couldn't tell who it was. Adrenaline surged and my stomach lurched. Was he the one that had done all this?

I ran. I leapt over the debris of smashed up homes and back out through the gate, turning right away from the route that would lead me back to Lets's house. I had no idea where I would end up but there were more houses that way. I'd be safer with more people around, wouldn't I?

I could hear footsteps pounding behind me but didn't stop to look back. When I emerged from the other end of the tunnel, I threw my backpack into a hedge. It was slowing me down. My phone started ringing, but I didn't stop to answer it. I had to get away. But I could hear the footsteps gaining on me.

'Evie. Stop!' the man called.

He knew my name. But it could be the police looking to bring me in. I carried on running.

'Evie. It's me, Darren. Stop!'

Darren. Darren. The man who gave a speech at the march. I slowed and glanced back, ready to carry on running if it wasn't really him. But it was. I stopped.

'Darren. You scared me.' I leant over with my hands on my knees, taking in big gulps of air.

'Ditto,' he said, stopping in front of me.

'What's going on?' I asked. 'Lets has been arrested.'

He shook his head. 'I came back and found it like that. There's nobody there. They must've arrested everyone, or they managed to get away.'

'I saw the police at Lets's and there was a boy there, Lucas, he's been coming to our sessions. His uncle's with the police. They were looking for me. Said someone in London wanted me. But why would they do this too? I've got no connection with the commune other than coming there for that march.'

'They'll be after everyone from there too anyway. What do they want you for? What have you been doing?'

'Nothing. Just the drop-ins with Lets. I don't even know anyone in London. I don't get it.'

My phone rang again then and I pulled it from my pocket. Tess.

She told me to come to the pub where they just played, they'd wait for me there.

I got my bag out of the bush and Darren and I set off. Both of us quiet. Trying to make sense of what was going on. The pub was up near the old university buildings and it took us about half an hour to walk there. Tess and Matty and the rest of the band were all drunk and stoned by the time we arrived and there was no food. Music was blasting from speakers and the place was rammed. I could barely hear myself think. I managed to fight my way to a spare stool in a corner and Darren came with me.

'Lets has been involved in all sorts so it makes sense that they arrested her. But why are they looking for you?' he said.

'What do you mean all sorts? What's she been doing?'

'They attack shops, security guards, police.'

'What? I don't believe it. Lets wouldn't do that. She believes in what we're doing. Changing things through the young people.'

'Go home to your little woodland, fairy Evie. You've got no idea what's really been going on. Your little presentations are just to make Lets feel better about the rest of the stuff she gets up to.' He made an explosion sound and gesture then fired his fingers at me like a gun before standing up and disappearing into the crowd.

Retreating

I SPENT THE next few nights trailing around various pubs listening to Tess and Matty's angry tirades, sleeping on benches in the bars, and eating bags of salty bar snacks and raw vegetables from my bag. I was exhausted, drained, and disillusioned. The crowds coming to the gigs were angry about how things were, yes, but they weren't going to do anything to change it other than get wasted and vent their anger on nights out listening to bands.

In the daytimes I walked past Lets's house to see if she was there, but I couldn't see any sign of life. They'd have to let her go soon, wouldn't they? After a couple of days of skulking past, I stopped two kids that were walking down the street and asked them to knock on the door for me.

'Why can't you do it yourself?' the girl asked.

'There were some people there looking for me that I don't want to see. But I just want to know if my friend's there.'

They looked at me as if I was mad, but they went and did it for me. Nobody answered the door. I didn't know what to do. How to find her. Was I never going to see her again? If the police took you away was that it? You vanished? What if they'd got me too? Connor would never know what happened to me. He'd told me not to get involved and maybe he was right. I clearly had no idea of what was really going on.

THE NEXT MORNING we set off home and it was early afternoon when I let myself into the cottage. Everybody was out, thank God. I slumped into the chair next to the range. The kitchen, tatty as it was, had never looked so lovely, so welcoming. My legs felt like they'd never be able to lift me up again and tears rolled down my face. How could I have been so blind? This, here, was what really mattered. Connor and Dawn were right all along. I'd been neglecting my family for what? Nothing had been achieved apart from getting myself in trouble with some unknown person in London who was now after me. Getting Lets in trouble too. Or did she do that herself? Did the police know where I lived? Were they going to turn up here next? My mind was spinning and I didn't know what to think anymore.

I ran a bath, thankful for the rain that kept our tanks full, and sank beneath the hot water, let it mingle with my tears. I was useless, stupid, delusional.

By the time Connor got home I'd got myself together

and was making dinner in the kitchen.

'Hey,' I said as he came through the kitchen door. 'Where have you been?'

He sat down at the table, pulling his boots off. 'Over to Lynton. How long are you back for this time?' His tone was weary. It had been a long time since we'd talked properly. Been together in the way that we used to.

'I'm not going again. I'm done. I'm staying here now.' I sat down in the chair next to his and took his hands in mine. 'I'm sorry.'

His eyes searched mine and whatever he saw there made him believe, brought him back to me. He leaned in and kissed me gently. 'I'm glad to hear it. I'm going to wash and change.'

Things weren't so easy with Dawn though.

'Why, what happened?' she said when I told her and Michael over dinner that I was going to stay at home from now on.

'Nothing happened. I just realised you were right,' I said.

'Liar. I can see it in your face. It's nothing to do with us.' She pushed her plate of food away and stood up.

'Dawn, sit down. Your mum is home, she's staying home. That's all that matters. Leave it. Now eat.'

I slept badly that night. Lying next to Connor in the dark, my mind was racing with questions about Lets and what she'd been up to. I was so stupid to think that my little workshops were going to change the world one young person at a time. Maybe I should have been doing whatever Lets had been doing. But then maybe I would have been made to disappear too. Maybe I still would. Was there any way Lucas could have found out where I lived? I focused on Connor's breathing and tried to make mine match his, so I could sleep. It finally worked as the light in the window started to move from pitch black to dark grey.

When I woke up light was filling the room. I lay and listened to the wind moving in the trees, the waves shuffling the stones on the beach. I thought I was alone but when I got up and went downstairs, Connor was washing up at the sink.

'How long have I been sleeping?' I asked.

He turned to face me, wiping his hands. The water gurgling down the sink was the only sound for a long moment.

'Not long enough, judging by how you look.' He smiled to soften the sharp edges of his words.

I sat down at the table, not knowing what to do with myself. For so long my time at home had been filled with making plans on what I was going to do when I left again.

'Dawn and Michael are up at Rachael's – we're harvesting some of the tunnels this week and replanting others.'

I nodded. I'd been taking food from the tunnels with

me to feed people that my family and community, who worked so hard to grow it, didn't even know. How selfish of me. Every time I was home Rachael had been trying to get me to focus back on the underlying messages that her herbalism and beliefs stemmed from. That everybody must find their own path to love and peace and oneness with nature. It can't be forced; but that had been my approach, trying to make everyone think what I thought, believe what I believed, live how I lived. What was wrong with me? History should have shown me that you can't change people if they didn't want to be changed.

It had, finally, sunk in.

Connor kissed the top of my head as he left to go and carry on with the work in the tunnels.

I went back to bed. If I could just have today to sleep and get myself back together properly then I would start again tomorrow. I slept the rest of the day and most of the night away. It was still pitch black when I woke, and I crept downstairs so as not to wake anyone. I felt more positive and determined to be a proper part of life in our Woody Bay again. I rummaged through the bookshelves in the sitting room, looking for the ones that Rachael had given me so long ago when she first started teaching me. Even though I'd been pretty good at looking after the herb garden and growing the food, I hadn't been thinking beyond keeping the plants alive since I'd started on my crusade. I had to focus my mind back on understanding how they could be used to keep us alive and healthy. Rachael wasn't getting any younger and I had to learn all I could to make sure we didn't lose her skills when the time came to lose her.

By the time Connor came down, I had been reading for hours. Remembering the wonder I'd felt when Rachael had first told me about the power of nature to heal us, heal itself.

He looked at all the books surrounding me on the sofa and smiled. 'This is good to see,' he said as he went off into the kitchen.

Connor returned ten minutes later, two steaming mugs of mint tea in his hand. He pushed the books aside and sat next to me. 'Don't take this the wrong way but I have to ask. Is this going to last?'

Instantly, I bristled. Why couldn't he just accept it? Why did he have to question everything I did? But, being honest with myself, which I was realising I hadn't been for a while now, I could see why. Even so, I sighed impatiently. 'Yes, it's going to last. I told you yesterday. I'm not going to go to Bristol anymore. I've realised you were right all along. I need to worry about us and our life here. Whatever is going on out there is out of my control and I was never going to be able to change things.'

I thought he'd be smug, agree with me, but he surprised me. 'That's not true, Evie. Give yourself some credit. There are lots of kids out there now who will be thinking differently because of you. They'll have new skills to be able to grow food, if they can find somewhere to do it and the seeds to start it from.'

I dropped my head onto his shoulder. He was always so good to me.

THAT DAY I worked alongside my family, Rachael, Lloyd, Shona and Marcus in the tunnels. Having my hands in the soil again felt so good. As the pile of shiny aubergines I was picking grew beside me, the wonder and awe I'd first felt on arriving here all those years ago re-grew with it. This was how I could make a difference. Feeding and nurturing my family, my friends, my soul, through the land and the wonders that nature provided for us if we worked with it.

By the end of the day we had boxes full of food – glossy courgettes, crisp lettuces, firm and pungent onions, muddy potatoes, crooked carrots, and more. My back ached, but it was a good pain, one that came from hard physical work, and my mind felt clearer than it had in ages. It had constantly been bouncing from one thing to the next with the anxiety I felt about converting everyone before it was too late. I sat on the wall outside Rachael's kitchen making the most of the final bit of sunshine before the hills blocked it out, She came to join me, handed me a glass of water.

'It's good to have you back, Evie. Really back.'

I leaned against her sturdy arm. 'It's good to be really back.'

'Tomorrow, we start again. In the herb tunnel after breakfast, let's get on with it.'

I nodded and we sat there until the light started to fade, listening to the robins chirping, the wood pigeons burbling, and the waves lapping the rocks below.

Liars

SEVERAL WEEKS PASSED. Long sunny days filled with growing and learning. I still wasn't completely sure about everything that Rachael believed in. The spells, the incantations. My mind couldn't go there fully but if I listened, took it all in, maybe it would come. But the homeopathy side I was definitely into. I went into Lynton to get more books to read up on the different plants from around the world that we were lucky enough to have and find out how they could be used too. For the first time ever, Nathan wasn't in the library and a man called Al was running things as Nathan was sick in bed with flu. I posted a note through his door wishing him well and saying I'd be back to see him soon.

We were settling back into being a family again. Dawn was less standoffish with me but I knew I hadn't completely won her back over. I was feeling content and hopeful when everything changed again.

Michael came bursting through the kitchen door. 'There's a boat coming. It's heading for the jetty, it's coming here!'

My stomach dropped through the floor. They'd found me. What was I going to do? I wiped my hands on the towel hanging on the back of the door then went out in the garden to look over the wall. He was right – there was a boat heading for us. But that didn't mean it was going to stop. Quite a few boats recently looked like they were coming but carried on past. So I watched and waited and when it became obvious that it was definitely coming to our jetty, I hurried back inside to get the shotgun we'd found in the basement when we moved in. I'd never fired it, didn't even know if it worked, but they wouldn't know that, wouldn't know that my hands were shaking so much I'd probably shoot myself by accident. Maybe I should run and hide instead.

'Go and get your dad,' I shouted at Michael.

Connor was up at Rachael's, helping on her latest building project in the garden.

I ran down to the wall where the steps led to the jetty and pointed the gun down at the man that was pulling his boat alongside our crumbly old pier.

'Don't stop here. Go away,' I shouted.

He looked up and said, 'Evie. It's me.'

I almost blacked out when I saw his face. It couldn't be. How could he be here? 'Tom?' My voice was tiny and was lost on the breeze so he didn't hear me.

'Evie, it's me, Tom,' he said.

The gun had dropped down by my side in my shock,

but I lifted it up again now and pointed it back at him. 'What do you want?'

He held his hands up in the air as he stepped from the boat onto the pier. 'I want to see you. See my child.'

BY THE TIME Michael came back with Connor, I was walking up the hill with Tom behind me. He was puffing and red-faced, unfit. Not like me. He wouldn't take no for an answer and short of shooting him, I couldn't stop him climbing up the wall and following me.

Connor stopped when he saw us. 'Who's this?' he said.

I looked up at him. 'Tom.'

I didn't need to say any more. Connor's face went white and pinched. 'Why is he here?'

I shrugged. I wasn't going to answer for him and Tom had no breath to tell Connor himself.

'Michael, go up to Rachael's and stay there until we come to get you.' Thank God, Dawn had gone into Lynton. She wouldn't be back for hours so maybe we could get rid of Tom before she came back.

'But, Mum—,' Michael started.

I cut him off. 'No arguments just go.'

Connor pushed him gently and nodded. Michael ran off, looking back over his shoulder several times before he disappeared up the wooded path to Rachael's house.

We all stood in the kitchen, looking at each other. Tom held his hand out to Connor. 'Hi. I'm Tom. Sorry to just descend on you like this.' As if he'd just popped round to see a neighbour, not travelled half way across a country that was in the process of imploding.

Connor didn't shake his hand or tell him his name.

'This is Connor.' I stepped up behind him and put my arm around him. Best to make it clear how things were from the start. But Connor stepped away from me.

'How did you know we were here?' he said to Tom, then looked at me. 'Did you tell him? Have you been in touch with him?'

'Of course not! Why would I do that?'

Tom shook his head. 'I've always known where you were, Evie.'

I stared at him, swallowing down a wave of nausea. How could that be? 'What? What do you mean?'

'Did you really think that I'd let you disappear on that boat without knowing where you were going? You were pregnant with my child.'

'Yes, but you didn't want it.' I sat down on the nearest chair. My legs couldn't hold me up anymore.

'Well, we need to talk about that. I was young, my priorities were wrong. I've come to see that now. I was torn. I did want you, and the baby too, but at the same time I didn't. I was caught up in things you knew nothing about. Things I thought were more important. But when

I realised you were really going to leave with the boat people, I had to make sure I knew where you were going.'

I remembered him standing on his balcony, speaking to me on the phone, and me throwing my mobile into the river. Thinking that he'd never be able to contact me again. How had he known where I was all along? And if he really felt all of these things why had it taken him fifteen years to come and tell me?

'So why are you here now after all this time?' Connor said. Coming to stand by me now that he knew I hadn't been in contact with Tom.

I wanted to move away this time. How could he have thought that of me?

'Look, there's much we have to talk about but I've had a long journey. Do you think I could have some food and drink, a bath, a rest? Then we can talk.'

'No!' I shouted. 'You can't stay here. You have to go.' I jumped up to hustle him out the door.

'I'm not going anywhere, Evie, not until I've seen my child.'

'But she doesn't know,' I gripped Connor's arm. 'She doesn't know about you.'

CONNOR TOOK HIM upstairs after we'd given him a bowl of soup, to show him into the room we used for Tess when she stayed. What would she make of this? Why were we being so civilised? We should just chuck him out. Force him back onto his boat with the gun. Make him go. How dare he do this after so long? Fifteen years and he'd never bothered before, so why now? How could we tell Dawn this? What would it do to her to discover that Connor, who she'd always adored and been so close to, wasn't her Dad after all? To find out that this arrogant man with his huge sense of entitlement, who she'd never seen or heard of before, was. It couldn't happen. But how could I stop it?

I shouted up the stairs that I was going out.

Connor appeared at the top. 'Where are you going?'

'To meet Dawn on her way back. Take her to Rachael's while we figure out what to do.'

'What will you tell her?'

'I'm not sure yet, I'll think of something on the way.'

I CLIMBED THE hill leading to the Lynton path really slowly. As if delaying when I saw Dawn would make it easier. At the bench by the waterfall I stopped and sat down. Watched the water tumbling, like my thoughts. Had someone followed us on Bhav's boat when we left Reading? And what about when we got on the boat with Shona to come here? There were no other boats behind us that day. There was no way someone could have followed us to the sea at Bristol and then known where we went when the boat picked us up. So it had to be someone that was with us. Someone was telling Tom all along. But who? Definitely not Connor. Tess? She was on her laptop all the time. Had been working with Tom before we left. But she wouldn't do that, would she? She was my closest friend apart from Leah. There's no way that Leah would have told Tom anything. What about Bhav? I didn't really know him, but that didn't mean it was him. Lloyd? No, no way. But it had to be one of them.

When I got to Shona and Marcus's house, she was in the porch piling up wood.

'Hey Shona,' I called.

'Evie, hello. You OK?' She walked down to the gate where I stood looking into her garden. Her afro had gone grey now and it made her look much older than she was.

'Not really. Tom has turned up. Wants to meet his daughter.' The last word came out in a croak.

'Jesus. What a nightmare,' Shona said, opening the gate and pulling me through into the garden. 'Come in and have a cuppa.'

We sat on her sofa with our tea, made from nettle leaves from her garden, keeping an eye on the path where Dawn would appear on her way home, and I told her what had happened. How it must have been someone who came from Reading with me that told him.

'No, none of them would have done it.'

'That's what I thought. But how else does he know

where we are?'

I ONLY WALKED for five minutes up the path before I saw her. My heart ached – for the first time in ages, she looked genuinely pleased to see me.

'Hey Mum. Look what I got.' She rummaged in her bag and pulled out a big bar of chocolate.

Despite everything I smiled. It was a rare treat indeed. 'Yum. Where'd you get that?'

'I traded it for some of the veg. With some man who had a whole bag of them. He said he'd been trading them for fresh food all the way. He's walked from somewhere called Cheltenham and he's going all the way to Land's End. He showed it to me on a map. It's a really long way.'

'Make sure you share it with Michael.'

'Of course. How come you're here?'

'To tell you to go to Rachael's. We've got a visitor. A man that wants to talk to your dad about something, so you and Michael can stay up there tonight.'

'What man? What does he want Dad for?'

I should have thought it through more. We never had visitors. Of course she was going to want to know all about it. But my brain was so filled with questions, I hadn't planned what to tell her.

'Oh, just someone that wants advice on building things like we've got in the gardens.'

It was a poor lie and she didn't look convinced.

'So why can't me and Michael be there?'

'Because I said so. Now go up to Rachael's. Michael's there already.'

She moaned and whined, like she did so often nowadays whenever we spoke to each other, but she went, and I headed home. Part of me hoped that by the time I'd got there, Connor would have lost it with Tom and made him leave, or shot him. Anything to just make this stop. Dawn was angry with me already about so many things, there's no way she would ever forgive me for this.

But when I walked in through the back door, Tom was sat at the kitchen table as if it was his home and Connor was nowhere to be seen.

'Where's Connor?' I said, not meeting Tom's eye. Despite everything that had happened since I last saw him and everything I'd achieved, I felt like the gauche teenager I was when I first met him. He looked so slick in his expensive city clothes. Very different to the earnest, social reformer look he'd had back then. I was conscious of the dirt under my nails, my old, often mended clothes.

I busied myself at the cooker, putting more wood into the fire box to keep it going. Anything so I wouldn't have to talk to him. I could feel his eyes following my every move, though he didn't answer my question. So I asked again, turning to look at him this time.

He shrugged. 'He went out. He told me I have a

daughter. Dawn. Where is she?'

'She's not coming home tonight. We need to talk before you see her.'

'Come away with me, Evie. You and Dawn. I can keep you safe.'

What? Where had this come from? Who did he think he was? 'I don't need you to keep me safe, Tom. I can look after myself. And I have no intention of going anywhere with you.'

'Rough times are coming and lots of people are going to die. I can make sure that you're not one of them.'

'Oh please, do you think I don't know that already? Don't you think that people have already died? There's not enough food, or water, or homes. I know this already. But we have plenty here. And anyway, where are you going to take us? How come you can survive when others can't?' But deep down I already knew the answer. He wasn't who I'd thought he was.

He smiled. 'Because I can take you somewhere where people are going to start again.'

Start again? He was talking nonsense. 'Why now, Tom? Why are you suddenly so interested in having a daughter now?'

'Because I made a lot of mistakes. Because I've realised how wrong I was, and I want to make up for it. And she's mine.'

There was something so creepy about the way that he

said that, my skin broke out in goosebumps. Where was Connor?

'She is not yours. She's very much her own person. And Connor is her dad. She loves him.'

Tom stood up. 'That's as maybe but he's not her dad, is he? I'm not going to leave here without seeing her. Giving her the chance to come with me.'

I flew at him then, screeching and flailing, hitting him on the chest, the head. He pushed me away and went upstairs, as if he had the right to make himself at home in my house.

I went down to the beach. Connor was sat by the rock pool, chucking stones in and watching the ripples until they subsided and then doing the same again. The tide was way out. The dense cloud hung low, hiding the Welsh coastline. Everything was still and muted. It should have been stormy, the waves and the trees crashing around like my thoughts. I sat down next to Connor and he put his arm around my shoulders and pulled me close.

'Why is he here?' he said.

'He wants to take her away with him. Said he can keep her safe now that everything is going so wrong.'

Connor shook his head. 'But she's safe here. And he doesn't know her. It doesn't make sense. Why does he think he can keep her safer than we can?'

'He said he's going somewhere people are starting again. I think he's connected to the corporations, the government. He has been all along. Tess said something ages ago when we first left Reading, but I didn't want to know. Then Nathan was trying to tell me something, but I've not seen him again since to find out what.'

We stared up at our little cottage hanging on the cliff overlooking the bay. The first building we'd seen on the day we'd arrived here so long ago. Smoke curled out of the chimney and lamps glowed in the windows. It looked like home always did but it was as if we'd been turned out. Tom had taken over and we couldn't go back in.

It was starting to get dark when we heard shouting coming from the garden. Dawn. We both leapt up and scrambled across the rocks to the path. When we reached the garden she was standing there, chest heaving as she threw rocks at him.

'Get out. I don't believe you,' she screamed.

When she saw us she ran to Connor and he cuddled her close. 'Dad, who's this? He's been saying crazy things.' She looked up at him and the expression on his face stopped her dead. She slumped in Connor's arms then straightened up and shoved him away. Ran back up the lane towards Rachael's. Connor started to go after her, but I grabbed his arm.

'Leave her for now.'

Tom was standing in the doorway, frowning, and Connor stepped forwards and punched him hard in the stomach. As Tom buckled, gasping for breath, Connor shoved him to the side and went indoors. I had never seen Connor be violent in all the years we'd been together. He was the most peaceful person I knew. Both of us physically attacking someone in the space of a few hours. How had everything changed so quickly?

'Why would you do that? Why couldn't you wait until we'd had a chance to talk?' I spat at him as I turned to go after Dawn.

I hurried up to Rachael's. I could see them through the window as I approached, Dawn crying and ranting. Rachael trying to calm her. I walked up to the window and tapped. When she saw me, Dawn screamed at me to go away then ran from the room. Rachael shrugged, mouthed, 'Come back tomorrow.'

So I turned and walked away.

Fathers

THE NEXT DAY Tess came. Tom hadn't got up yet, Connor had left early to go and speak to Dawn, and I was curled up in the chair next to the stove trying to get warm. It wasn't cold, the sun was shining and, if anything, it was close and sticky, but I was icy from the inside out.

I looked up as the door opened, expecting Connor. But Tess stood there. Her face was drawn, snow white, except for two hectic red spots on her cheeks. Both of us started crying as soon as we saw each other.

'Evie, he's gone,' she wailed. I could see now that there was blood mixed in with the tie-die on her dress, streaks of it dried on her forearms.

'What, who?'

'We were partying after the gig then suddenly there was gunfire and Matty was hit. Shot in the head. Dead. He's dead.' She stumbled towards me.

I sat her down in the chair I'd been sitting in, 'Jesus. Tess. My God. I'm so sorry. Are you hurt?'

She shook her head and slumped back in the chair. I

fed her blackberry wine diluted with hot water. She didn't say anything else. Just huddled over her mug sipping the wine.

When she'd finished, she stood up. 'I'm going to bed. I'm exhausted.'

'You can't go in your room. Tom's in there.'

She didn't twig who I meant.

'Tom who?'

'Tom.' My tone got through to her this time.

She sat back down in the chair. 'What the fuck is he doing here?'

'He turned up in a boat yesterday. Said he wants to take me and Dawn away with him, keep us safe as everything's about to go mad, madder.' My voice cracked. 'He told Dawn he's her dad before we could speak to her.'

'Bastard.'

'You should see him, Tess. He's rich, powerful. Not who he said he was.'

'I know. I know who he is. What he's been doing.'

We both jumped as the door from the hall opened and he walked in.

'Well done, Tess, for figuring it out. Not that it makes any difference now. And I am sorry. I do know I was wrong.'

She looked at him with complete contempt. 'I'll go and stay at Rachael's.' And she just walked out.

Tom started to speak, but I ran out the door after

Tess. I didn't want to deal with him, especially not on my own.

At Rachael's, Tess went upstairs to find a bed and I sat in the kitchen with Rachael.

'Dawn's very upset,' she said, 'but she went off with Connor this morning and she was quite calm. She was listening to him at least.'

I knew where they'd have gone. They had a spot up in the top of the woods, on the edge of the waterfall where they always went together. Connor had built them a bench. I'd got the distinct impression that I wasn't welcome there. Should I go there now, or leave them to it? Before I could decide, Michael came bursting in the door, ran over to me and for the first time in years climbed on to my lap.

He hugged me tight, spoke with his face pressed into my neck, 'Is Dad not my dad either?'

'Of course he is! Yes, Michael. Never think that.'

I looked at Rachael over his head and she smiled sadly.

'And he is Dawn's dad too, in every way that counts. I knew Tom when I was very young, only a couple of years older than Dawn is now, and when I got pregnant he sent me away. I met your dad soon after that and by the time Dawn was born we loved each other, and we were living here, and we were a family.'

I wanted to kill Tom for turning up here and upsetting everything. Rachael and I took Michael home. There was no way that I was going to let Tom drive us out. Rachael said I could put him in one of the barn cottages, but that he wasn't to come in the house as Tess was there. He was still in the kitchen, when we arrived.

'Tom, this is Rachael. She's got a cottage you can stay in. You can't stay here any longer.'

He looked up and smiled at Rachael, then at Michael, who was staring at him as if he were a creature from another planet.

'Okay. I can see it's hard for you all that I've turned up like this. I'm sorry. I should have handled it better. But I do still want to talk to Dawn. Give her the chance to make this decision for herself.'

Rachael stepped forward. 'Tom, hello. Come on. We can talk about this later.'

He stood and followed her out. I could breathe a bit more easily for the first time since he'd looked up from the jetty and I'd realised it was him.

Michael went down to the beach but around lunchtime the sky turned black, the wind whipped up and the rain started pelting down. He came running in about ten minutes later, soaked and splattered in mud.

The trees were creaking and flailing in crazy winds. The house rattled and the rain was coming down in sheets not drops. Something crashed onto the roof. The rain was relentless for hours. Michael and I stared out the window and saw the garden crack in half and slide off down the cliff, taking a birch tree and several bushes with it. Please let Connor and Dawn have got indoors.

I lit a fire and Michael and I huddled together on the sofa in the living room under a blanket. When the sun went down, the wind was still howling and battering the windows, there had been no let up in the rain and I was getting really scared. What if a tree fell on the house? What if the house slid down the cliff with us in it? Were Connor and Dawn safe?

I heated up some leftover soup and we ate it next to the stove. The temperature had dropped dramatically and away from the stove and the fire in the living room you could see your breath. It was the coldest it had ever been. Afterwards, I sent Michael back to the sofa and went and got more blankets and pillows from our bedrooms. We made a nest and after I loaded the fire up with wood, we snuggled up together on the sofa and lay there, listening to the storm. Michael drifted off to sleep but it was hours before I slept, and the storm raged the whole time.

When I woke it was just getting light. I could see blue skies through the window and everything was still. Michael was fast asleep, so I eased myself out from under his arm then tucked the blankets back round him. Out in the garden it looked like the apocalypse had finally come. Trees were split, branches hanging down. The huge pots by the door where we grew lavender and rosemary were gone. I couldn't see them anywhere and they were big, heavy – it took two people to lift them.

Even more of the garden had collapsed and slid down the cliff, there was barely any grass left to stand on. The path outside the garden was covered in clumps of soil, broken tree limbs. A whole fern had been ripped from the ground and had landed across the gate, which was smashed and hanging off its hinges. The silence was unnerving. There was no bird song. No sound of waves on the beach below. Michael and I might be the last people left on earth.

I dressed in a warm, waterproof coat and wellies. Left a note for Michael, telling him I was going to see if everyone was okay and he should not go outside until I came back, then I set off to Rachael's. I tried to pull the fern tree from the gate but it was too heavy, so I shoved it until it was low enough for me to clamber over. The path was littered with barely grown vegetables that had been ripped out of the ground and a large sheet of poly tunnel was in shreds, hanging from a splintered oak tree.

Up at the house, roof tiles were smashed all over the ground and the garden looked as if someone had ripped everything up and chucked it around. There was no sign of anyone. I let myself into the empty kitchen. 'Rachael?' I called.

No reply. I looked in all the downstairs rooms but there was no sign of her. I climbed the stairs, calling her name, remembering all those years ago when we'd first arrived and climbed these stairs. Nothing on the staircase or in the landing above had changed in all that time, but we were different people now.

'Rachael?' I shouted as I headed for her bedroom door.

When I pushed it open, she was sleeping peacefully in her bed. Relief flooded through me, making me light-headed for a moment.

I left her to sleep and set off up the long driveway that would take me up the hill to Shona's. The path to Connor and Dawn's waterfall went up through the woods from out the back of her house, a little way along the main track to Lynton. Maybe they'd had to stop there when the storm got too violent for them to carry on.

Shona and Marcus were in their garden, looking be-wildered at the mess. They were alone. Dawn and Connor hadn't made it to their house. So where were they? Had they been outside in the storm all night?

'Shona,' I screamed as I ran towards them. 'We have to find them, they didn't come home. They were in the woods when the storm came.'

I tripped and sprawled across the path in front of their gate, scraping my palms and banging my chin hard so that my teeth clanked together, biting my tongue. Marcus came running and pulled me up.

'Are you okay?' He brushed my clothes down, making

me feel like a child again. 'Who's in the wood?'

'Connor and Dawn. They went up there yesterday morning. We have to go and find them.'

He looked at Shona, and she looked at him, their expressions saying it all.

Buried

SHONA AND MARCUS tried to make me stay behind but I wouldn't. We didn't have to go far up the waterfall track before we saw Connor. He was face down under a fallen tree, trapped by the heavy branches that had broken his back as they hit him. The angle of him was all wrong and when we lifted his face, his nose and mouth were clogged with mud and leaves. I slumped down on the soggy ground next to him, lay across his crooked back, my face buried in his hair. He already didn't feel like Connor. My breath hitched and caught in my throat then I was wailing, screaming, howling. How could this be? This wasn't supposed to be. I don't know how long I was there before Marcus pulled me up and into his arms, then I was sobbing into his chest, wrenching the sobs from the pit of my stomach, as if I cried hard enough I could bring him back. Shona rubbed my back, her own sobs barely registering in my shattered mind.

When I finally calmed down, Marcus moved back from me and took my face in his hands. 'We have to find Dawn. We'll come back and get Connor once we've found her.'

We called her name but there was no reply. We clambered up to the bench, climbing over fallen trees and rock falls, the stream raging and roaring down the hill making it difficult to hear if Dawn was answering our calls. Shona found her in the end. She'd huddled into a hollow old oak trunk that had somehow survived the storm. She was unconscious. Blood on her temple and a huge lump. Marcus lifted her into his arms as if she was as light as a baby and stumbled back down to the house, where he laid her on the sofa.

'Is she breathing?' I whispered.

Marcus felt for her pulse, nodded. She opened her eyes as he pushed her sodden hair away from her face and I rushed over and knelt down next to her. But she couldn't, or wouldn't, speak. Her eyes were vacant as if she couldn't see us. Then they closed and she was gone again.

Shona led me into the kitchen. 'She'll be OK. You need to go and see Michael and we need to get Connor down from the woods. I'll look after Dawn.'

I stumbled back down the path towards Rachael's. As I rounded the last corner of the drive and the house appeared in front of me, Lloyd came out of the front door. I ran towards him crying and he caught me as I hurled myself at him.

'Lloyd you're back.' I sobbed into his chest. 'Connor's

dead.'

He took me into the kitchen. Rachael sat me down at the table and wrapped a blanket round me. I hadn't realised how cold and wet I was. My teeth were chattering and my trousers were icy and clinging to my legs.

'What's happened?' Lloyd said, rubbing my arms through the blanket. 'Rachael, get her some dry things.'

When Rachael came back in he took the clothes from her and told me to get changed then he hustled her back out the door. I could hear their voices murmuring. Then Rachael came up behind me and hugged me and we cried together. When we were calmer she said, 'Lloyd's gone up to see Shona and Marcus. You wait here and I'll go get Michael. Tess is still sleeping.'

When she came back with Michael, after we'd told him and he had cried himself out, we all sat around the table in silence.

Nothing would ever be the same again.

I don't know how long we'd been sat there when we heard Tess moving around upstairs. Soon after, she came into the kitchen and she looked awful. Pale with black smudges under her eyes. She looked around at us all. 'What's going on?'

Before we could answer, the back door opened and Tom was there. I screeched, making a raw and guttural sound that I had never heard come from me before, even when I was giving birth, and charged over and shoved him back out the door, so hard that he went sprawling on the ground. When I saw him lying there in his shiny city clothes and completely inappropriate slip-on shoes, something in me flipped and I started kicking him. I had never attacked anyone physically in my life before, but this was the second time he had pushed me to it in twenty-four hours. It was all his fault. If he hadn't have come here, told Dawn, they wouldn't have been outside. Connor would still be alive.

Tess and Rachael pulled me away and in the kitchen, I briefly saw Michael's shocked face before Rachael took me through the door to the living room, where she held my arms down at my side until I calmed down.

WE BURIED CONNOR the next day in our back garden. I'd cleared it up as best I could and chosen a spot under the weeping willow tree in the sunny corner. He loved that tree and we often lay under it with the willow fronds gently tickling our faces as they waved in the breeze.

After we had filled the grave with soil and put the sods of turf back on top, I lay down on top of it, staring up at the sky through the swaying branches. The tears had dried up. It was as if I was watching everything from far away. A running commentary in my head. There I am, lying down on Connor's grave. There's Lloyd putting the tools away. There I am, lying down on Connor's grave. His grave. It couldn't be.

Michael and I went to stay at Rachael's. Funny how I always thought of it as hers even though Lloyd had lived there too ever since we'd arrived. Them getting together a few years after we arrived had seemed weird at first, as she was fourteen years older than him, but there was something about her that was ageless.

Tom stayed away from us, just seeing Rachael when she took him food. Shona said Dawn had moved into their spare room. She told them to keep me away but Michael was welcome. He went to see her but wouldn't tell me anything about what she'd said, why she didn't want to see me. I didn't care anyway at first. I was too numb with the shock of losing Connor. I didn't have anything much to say to anyone for a while.

I'm not sure how many days later it was that Rachael came in and said that Shona had cleared the path enough to get down to the jetty. Our boat and the one that Tom had come in were both gone, smashed to pieces and sunk by the jetty. So now he had no way of leaving. Not that Tom was showing any signs of going apparently. He'd asked Rachael for some more suitable clothes and had been helping clear away the storm damage. She spoke of him as if she liked him and that made me hate him even more.

A few days later, Shona came and told me that Dawn had gone with Tom to live in the old place up the lane on the way to Hazel's that had been empty for years. This jerked me out of the daze I'd been floating around in and I got dressed and went up there. What was she doing? It must be the shock making her do crazy things. They were in the garden when I got there, tidying it up. Dawn was raking leaves and smaller branches into a pile. A heap of larger branches in a corner was being turned into firewood by Tom, who looked more like he did when I first met him now that he wasn't in his city clothes. When Dawn saw me, she dropped the rake and ran into the house. I went to follow her but suddenly Tom was in front of me, barring the way.

'Leave her. She doesn't want to talk to you.'

'But why? What have I done?' I resented having to ask him that. How had this happened that the daughter he didn't want, and I'd spent fifteen years looking after, was now living with him and I was the bad guy? 'And why are you still here?'

'Because I want to be with my daughter. I'm hoping that we can get to know each other then she'll want to come away with me.'

'And what if she doesn't? Are you just going to leave her again? You didn't even want her to be born. Does she know that about you? That you told me to kill her?'

He looked at me with a fake hurt face. He wasn't fooling me for one minute.

'And I thought you had to get back quickly, how long

are you going to wait for her to decide?'

A shriek from the doorway stopped me and I looked round to see Dawn.

'Just go away. It's none of your business what I do. You haven't given a shit about what I've been doing when you've been off trying, and failing, to save the world, so why pretend you do now?'

'But Dawn—'

'Leave me alone!' Then she turned and went back in the house, slamming the door behind her.

Tom reached out as if he was going to comfort me, but I walked away.

THAT NIGHT I took Michael back to our house for the first time since Connor died. We went to bed early, both of us together in the bed Connor and I had shared. I was woken by a deep rumbling sound. Michael half woke but snuggled deeper under the covers and went straight back to sleep. I couldn't figure out what it was at first. Then it got louder and louder and everything started to shake and roll. Another earthquake. I turned over to face Michael and closed my eyes again, thinking that it'd just be like all the others. But then there was a huge snapping sound in the distance somewhere and the shaking and rolling got a lot worse. The bed shifted along the floor.

I grabbed Michael. 'Come on, we have to go in the

basement.'

We ran down the stairs, which seemed to be moving up and down under our feet like a fairground ride I remembered going on when I was very small.

In the basement I pushed Michael under the table, which was covered in all the things I'd been collecting in preparation for the time when the shops were no more. I grabbed some quilts, blankets and pillows and stuffed them all around him then grabbed some more for me and joined him.

The whole time the snapping, rumbling and shaking were constant. What was going on? Usually the fracking quakes lasted no longer than five, ten minutes, max. Was it something else? I wrapped the quilt around my ears to try and block it out then lay half on top of Michael. He tried to push me off but I made myself into a dead weight, so he couldn't shift me. Slowly we realised that the noise was lessening and the shaking wasn't as violent, then it stopped. We carried on lying there in the basement, afraid to go and look. Afraid that this time we really might be the only ones left. It was then that I remembered that you should never go into a basement during an earthquake in case you got trapped. Basements were for hurricanes. What had I done?

Broken

WE WAITED UNTIL we could see a sliver of light coming through the gap at the bottom of the door into the kitchen.

'Stay here,' I said.

Michael grabbed my hand. 'Don't leave me.'

'I'm not. Just wait while I look through the door to see what's happened.' I tried to sound confident. As if I was absolutely certain that the door would open. Pretending that I wasn't terrified that my stupid mistake had trapped us under a ton of rubble.

I crawled out from under the table, dropped the quilt I was wrapped in to the floor and grabbed the torch. Slowly made my way to the stairs. My legs shook and cramped after so long huddled up.

I shone the light on the steps, there was a crack running through them that hadn't been there before but it didn't look deep. They looked safe to walk on. The first step up was fine but as I placed my foot on the second one, and the staircase took my body weight, the crack widened in front of my eyes. I froze, watching it expand.

But it didn't break completely and I tip-toed up to the door.

I twisted the handle and pushed but it only went a little way before it came up against something. I pushed harder and it gave a little but still didn't open. On the third shove, it opened enough for me to stick my head through. The table had moved across the room and was wedged in front of the door. There was broken crockery all over the floor, mixed with the glass from the window.

'Come and help me with the door.'

WHEN WE GOT outside, the sun was coming up behind the cliffs. We ran to Rachael's house. I expected the worst but when we got there it looked okay apart from some broken windows.

'Rachael, Lloyd, Tess!' we shouted.

Inside the kitchen there was broken crockery everywhere but there didn't seem to have been any structural damage.

We shouted again and then we heard Lloyd calling us from upstairs. I opened the door into the hall and saw that the staircase had collapsed. Lloyd stood at the top of it.

'Is Rachael okay? Tess?'

He nodded. 'We're fine. Go and get the ladder from the barn so we can come down.'

Rachael wasn't fine. She had a broken wrist and a huge gash on her arm that was bleeding a lot. They'd wrapped a towel around it, but it needed stitching and her wrist needed setting. Tess was still in bed. She wouldn't get up.

'Michael, run back to the house and get my box.' I'd been creating a box of magic since I'd been spending time with Rachael again. It was filled with dried herbs but also with bandages, needles, dressing pads, which I'd traded for our fruit and vegetables at the shop in Lynton.

While I sewed Rachael's arm up and made a temporary splint for her wrist, Lloyd went off to check on the others. I hoped Dawn was okay. That house they were staying in was higher up on the cliff. If we'd been shaken about as much as we had down here, what would it have been like up there? Would it be worse?

Lloyd came back with Shona and Marcus. It was best for us all to be together for now. Their house was mainly fine, a bit shaken up. But the path leading up to where Dawn and Tom were living had been covered by a landslide. It would take a while to get over there.

I ran to the top corner of the garden where it met the bottom of theirs and shouted Dawn's name over and over again. Would the dense trees and bushes stop her from hearing me? But after about five minutes she shouted back.

'Mum! I'm here. We're alright. Are you okay?'

Relief surged through me and I gripped the wall, tears welling in my eyes. 'Yes, we're all fine. Wait there and we'll come and get you. We'll have to dig through the landslide.'

MICHAEL AND I went down to our house and brought back clothes and all the fresh food we had in the kitchen, along with lots of paper to make mâché for a cast for Rachael. It was amazing that this was the only injury among us. Our old houses were sturdy and had kept us safe, or maybe, as Rachael believed, something in the universe was looking out for us. What was it going to be like in the rest of the country? Despite the noise and how much we'd been shaken about, we couldn't have been anywhere near the centre of the earthquake. But it had been huge and was by far the biggest one we'd experienced since they first started happening. Why had it gone on for so long? After we had some hot soup, we took spades and went up to clear the landslide so we could get to Dawn.

It took a couple of hours to clear a path and when we got through the other side we could see further up there were more landslides covering the road that led to Hazel and Stan's, but they were beyond the gate to the house Dawn was in. I started to run, desperate to know that she really was okay. The gate was hanging crooked and it wouldn't open so I shouted for her.

The others joined me at the gate and Marcus started fiddling with it so we could get through. Before he could get it open, Dawn appeared in the doorway of the house with Tom behind her.

'Oh, Dawn, thank God you're okay.'

'Mum!' She ran towards me and all the anger seemed to have been shaken off with the quake and she hugged me over the top of the gate.

When Marcus got it open she fell into my arms, sobbing. 'Where's Michael? Is he alright?'

'Everyone's fine. Rachael's arm is hurt but that's it. We're all alright.'

Tom came halfway towards the gate. I hated him and wished he had been killed, not Connor, but even so I knew we couldn't leave him behind. So we all went back to Rachael's together and started to clear up as best we could.

We went to check on the polytunnels first. As long as most of our food had survived, we'd be okay. We had seeds so we could plant more but we'd need time for them to grow and we'd already lost lots in the storm. Maybe we would have to use the stores now. Maybe this was the time we'd been saving them for. The greenhouses were shattered and everything inside them covered in glass, but that could be picked off. Some of the planters in the polytunnels had shifted and everything was haphazard, but it could have been so much worse.

We worked all day, straightening and sweeping, gathering the food that had been unearthed and putting it in the barn. That night the nine of us sat around the kitchen table, grimy and exhausted, but there was elation underpinning the tiredness. We'd survived. Rachael tried to get some news on my screen, but it was just the downtime message. Sorry, the page you're trying to access is not available at the moment. Please try again later.

After we'd eaten and put water on to heat for baths, she tried again and this time it was just completely blank.

When we went to bed that night, me, Michael and Dawn all in the same room, the moon shone brightly through the curtains. When they'd fallen asleep I got up and went to the window. A movement caught my eye and I squinted towards it. Tom was in the garden, sitting on a stone wall, his head in his hands. He looked as if he was crying. My first thought was to go and see if he was okay but almost immediately I changed my mind. He deserved to feel bad.

But was this the time to hold onto grudges? We had no idea what damage had been done outside Woody Bay. Our little group might need to pull together more than ever before. Holding onto hating him wasn't going to bring Connor back. So I wrapped myself up in a warm coat and woolly socks then joined him in the garden.

He looked up and wiped away the tears on his face,

but they shone silver in the moonlight momentarily. It reminded me of a creepy old picture that my nana had on her wall when I was little. We'd been so certain that we were building a better life than the one the old people had but now look.

'Tom, are you okay?' I sat down on the wall next to him.

He gave a half snort, half laugh. 'Oh yes, I'm really great. How about you?'

'There's no need to be like that.'

He grabbed for my hand. 'Sorry. I'm always like that. Sarcasm as first defence. I was just thinking about my people. My parents, sisters, nieces and nephews, friends. I'll probably never see them again.'

'They might be alright.'

We both fell silent then. I think we both knew deep down that nothing was alright anymore.

The moon went behind a cloud and we couldn't see a thing. I realised we were still holding hands and even though I wanted to pull mine away, I made myself squeeze his reassuringly. Tom leaned in and tried to kiss me. His lips hit my cheek to the side of my nose though as he couldn't see me.

I shoved him away. 'Don't do that.'

'Why not? We don't have anyone else now, Evie. We've got a daughter together. You loved me before.'

'No, I didn't. I was young, naive and infatuated. And

you definitely didn't love me.'

'Maybe not, but I liked you a lot. I think I could love you now.'

I chose to ignore this. 'Who was your spy?'

'It doesn't matter now, does it?'

'I suppose not. I'd like to know though.'

'It wasn't anyone. I put a tracker on the boat before you left.'

'What?'

The moon came out from behind the clouds again then and I could see him.

'It really doesn't matter.'

He was right and although I still felt anger and re-sentment towards him I pushed these feelings away. We had to start afresh if things really were as bad as we suspected. We couldn't have bad feeling in such a small community.

'Is this what you were talking about? Things getting rough?'

'Yes. This is it.'

'What's happened?'

'It was the final push. They wanted all the gas they could get and now they've gone.'

'They?'

'Yes, they, them.'

'Where have they gone? What do they want the gas for?'

He shook his head. 'It doesn't matter.'

I wasn't sure if he even knew what he was talking about. He had a strange faraway tone in his voice. Whatever had happened he was right. It didn't matter to us here, just like Connor had always said. 'You should go to bed,' I said, standing up. 'I'm going back in.'

'Night, Evie,' he said and gave a funny little smile that I couldn't figure out.

I walked back to the house but he carried on sitting there and when I got up into the bedroom I looked out the window and he was still there. It looked like he was crying again. I climbed into the bed and snuggled up against Michael. Was it a good thing for Dawn that Tom was here? I wasn't convinced. Maybe it wasn't a good thing for any of us that he was here. Just before I dropped off to sleep a question popped up in my mind. How had he kept track of us after we left Bhav's boat behind?

THE SUN HAD been shining for a whole week, drying out the soggy ground, giving the new seeds we'd planted much needed sustenance. We were all still living together in Rachael's house. After the quake were battered by more storms and almost non-stop torrential rain for the first couple of weeks. Lots of food was ruined but we'd saved as much of it as we could and made covers for the greenhouses with polytunnel sheets, as all the glass in the stores had smashed. We hadn't been able to get out past the landslides to check on Hazel and Stan because of the rain. More of the hillside had slipped down where we'd cleared it to get to Dawn and Tom.

I was working in my garden, sorting out the herbs as best I could. Our house seemed desolate, as if it had been empty for a lot longer than the time since the quake. I wondered if I'd ever come back.

After a couple of hours of digging, pruning and re-planting I sat down next to Connor's grave to eat my lunch.

'Things are so different now, Connor. You were supposed to be here with us when this time came. You were the one who was going to keep us safe, you who knew how to do everything. How are we supposed to fix it all up without you?'

I put my lunch to one side and lay down as if he was curled up next to me, like we'd lain in bed together so many times. The sun made me sleepy and the next thing I knew, Tess was gently shaking me by the shoulder to wake me up.

'Hey, Evie. Wake up.'

I rolled over and looked up, but the sun was behind her and I couldn't see her face. She'd been so quiet since she came back, spending most of her time alone, so I was surprised she'd come to find me.

'Alright, Tess?' I said as I pushed myself up to sitting

and leaned back against the trunk of Connor's willow tree.

She sat down beside me and put her head on my shoulder and grabbed for my hand. 'I'm pregnant.'

I swivelled round to look at her. 'That's great, Tess, isn't it?'

She nodded but tears rolled down her cheeks. 'I think so. I'm glad I've got something of Matty still but everything's all fucked up. What sort of life is this baby going to have?'

'I don't know. We don't know what's going on everywhere else.'

She snorted. 'It's fairly obvious, isn't it? The screens haven't come back on. And things were pretty fucked up before this happened anyway.'

'But we're still here, and we've got food, shelter, each other.' If only Connor could hear me now.

'I know. It doesn't matter how I feel anyway does it? I'm pregnant and that's that. But don't tell anyone else yet.'

With that she left again, and I realised I still hadn't asked what she knew about Tom. I'd wait until we found out more about what was going on outside our little bay. Because if this really was it, I didn't want to know. I'd need to just accept him and we'd all have to live together and get along.

But there had to be more than just us left. Otherwise

there'd be nobody for Dawn and Michael to fall in love with. No more children after the one Tess was carrying.

THE NEXT MORNING the sun was shining again. The ground should be dry enough now for us to go and see if Hazel and Stan and their kids were okay. At breakfast I asked Lloyd to come with me and help.

'Don't you think if they were okay they'd have tried to get down here to see us?' Tom said.

I shrugged. 'Maybe they can't. The storms have stopped us from trying.'

He didn't look convinced but after breakfast he came with me and Lloyd to the shed and we gathered up some shovels and ropes to take with us. Lloyd also strapped a shotgun to his back and told me and Tom to do the same. I filled a backpack with bottles of water and food and the three of us set off up the garden. We took the short cut and climbed over the wall, so we'd come out by the first landslide we'd cleared to get to Dawn.

Even though more soil had fallen down, it was still passable as the heavy rain had flattened it out and then the sun had baked it. We clambered over and walked up the lane. Just past the house Tom and Dawn had been in there was a huge oak fallen across the road. Lloyd started hacking at the branches with a small axe to clear a path so we could climb over the trunk. Once we were over the other side, we looked up to where the big house hung above us and it was still there. It looked like a big part of it had fallen off though. There was no sign of anyone. We hurried up the lane, which was covered in branches and leaves. The path leading out along the cliffs to the next valley was clear as far as we could see but we went straight past it and rounded the corner to climb the hill to the house. As we got nearer we could hear the dog barking but we couldn't see it.

We stopped at the bottom of the drive. 'Hello, hello,' I shouted. The dog's barking got more frantic and we could see the shape of it behind the glass of the kitchen door, running backwards and forwards. A man shape appeared behind it and the dog fell quiet. We waited but he didn't answer or open the door.

'Hello,' I called again. 'Stan, is that you? It's Evie. Are you okay in there?'

The dog gave another quick bark but it shut up as the door opened.

'Are you okay?' Lloyd said.

Stan's face crumpled but he pulled himself back. His knuckles were white on the hand gripping the door. A small grubby face appeared from behind him and an arm gripped around his thigh. Without looking he dropped his hand down onto the child's head. The dog ran to the top of the stairs leading down from the deck outside the door and barked frantically at us, his tail wagging.

'We're okay,' he said then stepped backwards, pulling the door open wider. 'Come in.'

Inside, the house was a mess. They'd obviously been hit harder by the quake than we had, and it didn't seem as if any attempt had been made to clear it up.

We followed Stan through the kitchen down a dim corridor and into the living room with its big windows looking out over the woods and sea. Amazingly the glass was still intact, but a big crack zigzagged right across it.

On the sofa a heavily pregnant Hazel looked up at us and smiled shakily. I hadn't realised she was pregnant again. I'd been so caught up in everything else I had stopped noticing what was going on in my home, my community. 'Oh thank God. We thought there was nobody else left apart from us. Evie, I haven't seen you in so long.' She pulled the child down to sit next to her. 'This is Eric, you've not met him yet, have you?'

He gave us a gappy-toothed smile. I put him at about a year old.

'Where are Olivia and Joe?' Lloyd said.

'They're out looking for food. A landslide fell on our vegetable garden and ruined it all.' Stan had sat down in an armchair by the window. 'I knew something like this was going to happen when they started that fracking.'

'Oh Stan, don't start that again now. What's the point?' Hazel sighed. She looked enquiringly at Tom, 'Hello. I don't believe we've met before.'

He stepped forward and shook her hand as if they'd just been introduced across a meeting table. 'No, we haven't. I arrived just before the big storm. I'm Tom. Dawn's dad.'

Hazel's eyes widened. Before she could say anything, Olivia and Joe arrived home. Despondent, grubby and hungry clutching a few straggly berries.

I opened my bag and shared out the food and water I'd brought.

'Come back with us, we have lots of space, food,' Tom said.

Lloyd glanced across at him, then at me. Who did Tom think he was, inviting other people to our place, where he'd turned up uninvited and caused no end of trouble? Not that we wouldn't have been inviting them anyway, but he had a real nerve.

Stan and Hazel's eyes met, and he shook his head, a tiny movement only intended for her eyes. But she ignored him, heaved herself up from the sofa. 'Thank you, we'll just put some stuff together.'

It was slow going on the way back, Hazel shuffled along, her enormous belly seeming to pull her forward as we headed back down the hill.

'There's a landslide down here blocking the path and a big tree trunk. You're going to have to climb up and over them both,' I said. 'Will you be able to do it?'

She nodded and gave a determined smile. But when

we got there and she saw how high and unstable it was the determination on her face faded. 'Oh.'

Olivia and Joe scrambled up and disappeared over the other side. Stan followed them, carrying Eric, and with the dog at his heels. He looked back when he got to the top.

'Lloyd, you go up and drop the rope down. Tom, you help him hold it and pull. I'll stay here and push Hazel up from behind.'

'I can't, Evie. There's no way I can get up there,' Hazel said.

I looked up and then at her belly. She was right.

'Go back to the house and wait while we clear an easier path,' Lloyd said.

So we turned back. Stan came back down and went with us. When we got there, Hazel lay down on the sofa, Stan went upstairs with the baby and I started clearing up a bit.

'When are you due?'

She smiled. 'Now.'

It was several hours before Lloyd came to get us. They'd made a channel through the landslide but the tree trunk had defeated them. We had to climb up the hill and round the root base that towered up in the air. We supported Hazel on each side, pushing and pulling her to keep her going. By the time we got back to the house we were all sweaty and covered in mud and grime.

Dawn and Shona were chopping veg for a stew.

Rachael was sat with her plastered arm resting on the table.

'We've brought everyone back with us,' Lloyd said.

Rachael smiled. 'Hello everyone. Come in, plenty of room for all.' She held her good arm out and Hazel stepped forwards and clasped her hand. 'Thank you for letting us come here, Rachael. Are you okay?'

'Yes. Just a little break. It'll soon be mended. No problem. Let me take you to one of the cottages. Looks like you won't be long.' Rachael rubbed her hand on Hazel's belly. It was a very intimate gesture that I had hated when people did it to me when I was pregnant but Hazel smiled, grabbed Rachael's hand and held it in place, saying, 'Feel?'

Rachael nodded and then the whole family followed her out across the courtyard to the cottage next to the one Tom was in.

I climbed the ladder and went and ran a bath. Connor's homemade plumbing, essentially hosepipes coming from the rain tanks on the roof directly into the taps, had survived the quake. The hot water hose came from the tank heated by solar panels. What were we going to do without him and all the ingenious solutions he came up with?

HAZEL WENT INTO labour early the next morning. Stan, Rachael and Shona stayed with her and as soon as it was light enough Lloyd took the children down to the beach to distract them. I spent the day in the poly tunnels, tidying and planting, putting the tiny, barely-formed vegetables that were strewn all around into a box and wishing that Connor was still with me.

Tess appeared blinking sleep from her eyes. 'Who's screaming?' she said.

'Hazel. We brought them all back yesterday. She's having a baby.'

Tess sat down on the plastic chair next to the water butt. 'Aren't we all.'

'Come on, Tess. Things will get better.'

She smiled weakly but tears fell down her cheeks. 'I've got a bad feeling.'

'Of course you have. It's been a terrible time. Terrible things have happened. But we're still here, we've still got each other.'

I thought that would help but she just got up and wandered back into the house, went back to bed again, where she'd been almost constantly since she'd returned.

Hazel had twin girls. I felt filled with hope again that we could build a new future for our little group on our woody cliffside by the sea. The kind of world I'd always been dreaming of where we made decisions together for the good of all. Nobody more important than anyone else, more entitled.

Gathering

THE NEXT DAY I decided to walk into Lynton to see if Nathan and his library had made it through. I packed enough food for about a week, not knowing what the path would be like and whether I'd have to camp out, and my box so I could help if I found people who were injured. I filled a small flask with water. I'd be able to get more from the streams on the way.

As I finished putting it all in my backpack, Tess appeared in the kitchen doorway. Her face was pale and crumpled, eyes red from crying.

'Where are you going?'

'Into Lynton to see what it's like there, see if Nathan's alright.'

'I'll come too.'

She went off to get dressed so I packed another bag with food for her too. When she reappeared she had a gun in her hand, which she tucked into the net pouch at the side of the pack.

'Why are you bringing that?'

'We have to be ready for anything.'

IT TOOK US two days to get to Lynton as the track was a mess, covered in fallen trees and landslides we had to climb around. We didn't see a single person the whole time. When we came off the track and walked down the hill that led to the top of the high street, we could see the town had been hit badly. The first few houses we came to were half fallen down and much of the street further along looked the same. All the houses on the cliffs at the back of the town were gone and the land was scarred and rough, tree stumps falling down the side and no sign of life anywhere. We stopped and looked down the cliff to Lynmouth and at sea level, the village was gone, completely covered in water. The bridge was submerged too and it was only as the road went up hill, way back from the shoreline, that the tops of chimneys started to poke out again.

Tess pulled the gun out from her bag and held it loosely down at her side and we instinctively drew closer together. I could smell smoke so either there was someone nearby who had lit a fire or fires had been smouldering since the quake.

Tess put her arm out across my body and drew me to a stop. 'Wait, shush,' she whispered.

Tess was tense, alert, but I couldn't hear anything. In the end, she motioned to move on.

'Let's check the library,' I said quietly right next to her ear.

We walked quickly, both of us looking to see if there was anybody around but there was no-one. We couldn't see any smoke but the smell was getting stronger.

When we rounded the corner on the road that led to the library, the Grand Hotel was to our right. The smoke was coming from a chimney there. It was a huge old building and still standing. A few windows were broken, one of the chimneys had fallen off and there was a huge crack running from the roof to the ground.

We stopped dead. Afraid of who might be inside even though we'd come to find people. Before we could decide what to do, the main doors to the hotel opened and a man stepped through. He looked to be in his early thirties and when he saw Tess with her gun he flinched. He let the door swing shut behind him, stepped forward, holding his hands up in the air. 'We don't want any trouble.'

I recognised him. The man who'd been working in the library last time I went when Nathan was sick. Al.

'Al, I'm Evie. You saw me in the library, remember?'

He tore his eyes away from Tess briefly to look at me. 'Yes, I remember. I've seen you around before that too. Selling your fruit and veg.'

'Is Nathan here with you?' I asked.

Al nodded. 'Yes. We got him out of his house and brought him here after the quake. He's really sick.'

Tess lowered her gun, but she didn't put it away.

We followed Al through a pair of frosted glass doors into a small bar area filled with squashy sofas and armchairs. More cracks covered the walls and piles of broken glass had been swept to the corners of the room. A young man and woman, probably about twenty, sat feeding small sticks into the fire. They had different versions of the same face. Twins.

'This is Evie and—' Al looked at Tess questioningly.

'Tess.' She had finally put the gun away.

Al gestured towards the couple on the sofa, 'Karin and Dylan.'

I smiled but I was impatient. 'Where's Nathan?'

'Through here in bed. Follow me.'

HE LOOKED LIKE he was dead already, his face on the pillow a sallow grey tinged with yellow. I wished Rachael was with me. The room smelled of unwashed body and piss.

'What's wrong with him?' I knelt down next to him and put my hand on his forehead. Hot, clammy.

'I don't know. He said he had the flu weeks ago, but he never got better. His stomach is all swollen. I've been looking after him as best I can with some pills and powders I managed to find in the rubble of the pharmacy. But he's not getting any better.'

'Nathan?' I said softly. 'Nathan, can you hear me? It's

Evie.'

There was no response.

'Does he wake up?' I asked.

'Yes. Not for long, and he's often confused but he wakes up every day. I've been feeding him broth. It's all we've got really.'

What on earth did I have in my box that could be of any help? I was way out of my depth. Why hadn't I brought the book with me as well? The one with all my notes in? I shook myself. Get a grip, Evie. What does he look like? He looked like his liver was failing with his skin all yellow like that. Okay, what had Rachael taught me? What's good for the liver? I didn't know. I haven't learned enough yet.

'Are you okay?' Al said from behind me.

'Yes, yes, sorry, just trying to think how to help. I have herbs but I can't think which ones to give him.' I dropped my head, the flowers on the cover blurring through my tears. I wasn't going to be able to save him. But then the flowers triggered something in my mind. I saw Rachael in front of me. 'Look for links to help you remember. People with liver problems go yellow and yellow things can help them.' Dandelion root. Turmeric. I had them both in my box.

I ran back downstairs to get it. 'Al, show me where the kitchen is,' I called as he came running behind me.

ARMED WITH A boiled concoction of grated turmeric and dried dandelion root I returned to Nathan's room to find him awake.

'Evie?' His voice was tiny.

I placed the bowl on the bedside table and helped him to sit up. 'This will help you feel better.'

He smiled sadly. 'I doubt it. I think I'm too far gone this time.'

'This time. What do you mean?'

'The liver. It's shot. Not enough healthy living. I've had bad turns before but I don't think I'm getting over this one.'

'Of course you are.' I spooned the liquid into his mouth and he managed almost half the bowl before slumping back down in the bed. 'Enough?'

He nodded.

'Go back to sleep now. I'll come back in a few hours and see how you are.'

TESS WAS SLEEPING on a sofa in the foyer so I went to a bedroom and got a cover and placed it over her. Back in the bar, Al and the others were still sat there.

'Is he alright?' Al asked.

I shrugged. 'I don't know. We'll keep feeding him remedies and see how he is in a couple of days.'

Dylan stared at me. 'Look, I don't mean to be rude

but if you're planning on sticking around we don't really have enough food for two more people.'

'Dylan! I'm sorry,' Karin said. 'We can manage. We can go out looking for more.'

'It's okay. We've brought food from our gardens.' I stood. 'Can somebody else cook it? I'm knackered.'

I lay down on a sofa next to the one Tess was on and the next thing I knew, she was shaking me awake.

'Food's up.'

We ate in the bar area, sitting around the log burner, gazing at it even though it wasn't lit. The food was hot and filling but that's about all that could be said for it. Whoever had cooked was not a natural in the kitchen.

After we'd finished, Dylan and Karin took the bowls off to the kitchen.

'Is there anyone else here, in Lynton?' I asked Al.

He shook his head. 'Not that I know of. If there is, we haven't seen them. You've seen what it's like.'

'You must come back with us, to Woody Bay. We have plenty of room, food, enough for everyone. It's better if we stick together. We'll go in a few days when Nathan can get up.'

Al nodded and gave me a sad smile.

Nathan didn't wake up again until the following morning. He was disorientated and confused. Could barely speak more than a few words without tiring. He kept calling me Ada.

'No, it's Evie, Nathan. Evie.' I sat at his bedside holding his hand. His stomach was hugely swollen under the covers and he was even more yellow. Was this my fault? Had I given him the wrong remedies?

'Ada? It's you? You're the one. She's the one.'

I figured she was an old love so in the end I just went along with it, let him think I was Ada.

'Do you think you can drink some tea, Nathan? It will make you feel better.'

But he pursed his lips, turned away from the spoon. I left, feeling like I was making things worse. Agitating him.

I sat down on the top step outside. I didn't want the others to see me crying. He was right. He wasn't going to get over it this time.

Later that evening, he slipped away. He gripped my hand at the end and looked at me properly it seemed, like he was seeing me. 'Evie, you have to find Ada. She's the one.'

Ruptured

WE LEFT THE next day after burying Nathan in the old graveyard next to the hotel. When we arrived home, strangers were there—a man and woman wrapped in blankets sat on a bench in front of the house. The woman was holding a baby, about three months old. Lloyd appeared with a tray with two steaming bowls on it.

'Evie. At last. We were wondering if we were going to have to come and look for you.'

'Who's this?' I asked as I stopped in front of them.

The strangers looked up at me but neither of them spoke. They looked dazed, shaky, blinking in the bright sun like underground creatures experiencing it for the first time.

'Later. Come inside, everyone's been worried. But there's something I need to tell you first.'

Tess took Al, Karin and Dylan inside and when they were gone, Lloyd said quietly, 'Dawn has been spending all her time with Tom. She's been staying in his cottage since you left. They seem to be getting on very well.'

My heart sank. I'd have to go and have it out with

Tom. Dawn was vulnerable and needy, and he was making the most of that to get his own way, as always. My thoughts must have shown on my face as Lloyd said, 'Evie, think before you react. You know how things are with you two. Don't say the wrong thing and make it seem like Tom's the one she can turn to.'

I linked his arm. 'Oh Lloyd. Always so Zen – what should I do then?'

He laughed. 'I have no idea but going and shouting at either of them, which is what you were thinking of doing, is not it.'

Perhaps I should have stayed and looked after her and Michael rather than going into Lynton. Their Dad had just died and I went off and left them. What was I thinking? But they had Rachael, Lloyd, Hazel, Stan, each other. It's not like I'd left them all alone. Maybe I wasn't really cut out to be a mother. I didn't seem to have that bit you're supposed to have where you always put them first, no matter what.

I went to Tom's cottage and knocked on the door, taking deep breaths to keep myself calm. Not sure what kind of reception I'd get even though the quake had brought Dawn and me closer again. She opened the door a crack.

'Hi,' she said without opening the door any further to invite me in.

'Are you alright? Are you coming home with me and

Michael?' The deep breaths hadn't stopped me from blurting out the one thing I should have waited to say.

Dawn shook her head. 'I'm going to stay here.' Her tone was friendly, no trace of her old defiance.

'Why?' I couldn't understand why she was so instantly accepting of Tom. None of the anger I'd expected about his abandonment of her. His part in Connor's death.

'Because I want to. Because I'm going to make my own decisions from now on. You lied to me, over and over again. I can't trust you. You put yourself and your ideals, other people, strangers, before me all of the time. Before all of us. So, carry on. You do your thing and I'll do mine.' Then she shut the door, very softly.

But it was as if she'd slammed it. I blinked back tears. What had I done? Maybe she'd come round. I'd have to prove to her that she could trust me again.

THAT NIGHT, ALL twenty of us crammed round the table in the dining room, which never usually got used but we couldn't fit in the kitchen. Despite everything, there was a slight feeling of celebration in the air. We'd lost loved ones but we were all still here, alive, together, with food and shelter, love.

I took a seat between Lloyd and one of the strangers, smiling at him as I sat down. 'Hello, I'm Evie.'

He looked slightly less glazed and confused than he

had earlier and gave a small smile back. 'Bob. Thanks for this.' He flicked his eyes round the table and the room. He gestured to the woman sitting on his other side still holding the baby as if she was never going to let it go. 'My wife, Nora, and son, Ben.'

'You're welcome. Where have you come from?'

'Over near Barnstaple. We needed to find food. We'd been walking for days without finding any. Then we ended up here.'

'What's it like out there?'

His face went pinched again and he swallowed loudly. 'Bad.'

A COUPLE OF weeks later more strangers appeared. Olivia and Joe had been out on the bridle path gathering blackberries, and came running into the garden where Tess and I were working in the poly tunnels. Tom was helping Lloyd fix the staircase in the house.

'People, people, they're coming here!' Olivia shouted as she sprinted down the garden, Joe clambering over the wall behind her.

I felt a surge of fear. We couldn't know that they would be friendly. God knows what was going on out there. The memory of the sirens, Connor getting stabbed, flooded my mind.

Tess ran off behind the house, calling to Lloyd and

Tom. The three of them came back out, each with a gun in their hand.

'No!' I shouted. 'We don't know who they are.'

They ignored me and went to wait at the start of the drive, where the strangers would appear if they were coming here. I sat on the wall behind them and waited.

Eventually we saw them. Three women, two men and two children. When a woman who was walking slightly ahead of the others saw us, saw the guns, she stopped dead and put her arms out to stop the others.

We all stared at each other.

'What do you want?' Tess called.

'Nothing. We're on our way to Heddon and saw the children. We thought they might be alone so came to see if they needed help,' the woman at the front shouted.

'Well they're not alone and they're fine. So you can carry on your way.'

I jumped up and ran forward then. 'Tess! Stop it. Please, come, don't be afraid. Have a rest, a drink. It's a long walk to Heddon.'

I took them into the kitchen and gave them all a glass of water and some of our precious salad. They gulped it down.

'So you're going to Heddon's Mouth?' I asked.

The woman who'd spoken outside put down her cup and nodded. 'My mum and dad live in the valley by the old hotel. I'm hoping they'll be okay but even if they aren't we're going to stay there.'

I filled her cup with more water and pushed the salad bowl towards her. 'Help yourself to more. Where have you come from?'

'Minehead way, but it's gone. Luckily, we were up high on the moors. Everyone else will have drowned. We didn't know what was happening. The sea was rushing in. It's all cut off.'

'What do you mean?'

'The earthquake. It's broken us off. We're not connected to England anymore.'

'That can't be. We must be,' I said. There was no way that could be true.

'We met a couple who'd come from near Bristol going to Cornwall to see if they could find their families. They said they had to walk east and south for days to get round the water. Said there was just a sliver of land left that led them by Salisbury then up to Taunton. Water on both sides as far as they could see.'

'My God.' It was all I could find to say.

They left shortly after and I went to find Rachael and Lloyd, tell them what the woman had told me.

'We're going to get all sorts turning up here now,' Lloyd said. 'We can't take them all in. There's not enough space, nor enough food.'

I thought Rachael would disagree but she nodded thoughtfully. 'You're right. With Bill, Nora and Ben there's already nearly twenty of us. And people are going to have more kids too. The stores were planned with a lot fewer people in mind. We could all end up starving if we keep letting them come.'

'What? I said. 'No. We can't turn people away. We have to help whoever we can.'

'Evie, be realistic. We can't do that. We just can't,' Rachael said.

THE NEXT MORNING Tom, Al, Lloyd and Dylan took saws and axes and went up past Hazel and Stan's house and chopped down trees, dragged them over the turning at the top of the hill. They covered them with leafy branches, twisted them together and around the trunks to make it look like a natural hedge. Piled it up high and then made another pile exactly the same behind it, again and again until the whole road was covered right down the hill to Hazel and Stan's driveway. Cutting us off. It made me remember hiding Bhav's boat all those years ago on the way here. What had happened to Bhav and Leah? Where had they been when the quakes hit?

The piles of foliage didn't stop there either; they went out along the bridle path that led to Heddon and covered the paths leading to our homes. I couldn't bring myself to help. What was the matter with us? We should be trying to find survivors, not hide from them. Cut ourselves off from whoever had made it through.

As if we hadn't enough to deal with, Shona and Marcus were killed a few days later. They were walking on the cliff path with Karin to collect blackberries, when a landslide swept them down into the sea. Karin had lagged behind and that's what saved her.

There was no point in even trying anymore. My daughter, although polite when we spoke, didn't want to know me. Connor was dead. Matty and Nathan too, and now Shona and Marcus. Mother Nature was fighting back with a vengeance. Against us too, who had been making sure our impact was minimal. For the first time since the quake, I went back and slept in the cottage at the bottom of the hill that had been mine and Connor's home. I crawled into the bed we'd shared for fifteen years and cried myself to sleep.

The next day I couldn't bring myself to get up, nor the day after that. For weeks, I lay in bed, crying and sleeping. People kept coming to see me, made me eat and drink, tried to coax me out of bed, but I wouldn't get up. What was there to get up for? We were stuck down here on our cliff face, dreaming that we could re-build a better world and look what happened at the first chance we got. Cut ourselves off and refused to help people that might need it. There was something wrong with us humans and it was better if we just died out. We'd ruined the planet that was the only home we had. Spent the whole of history killing and hurting each other, while thinking we were special. Well, we weren't. We were just animals with consciousness and thumbs that enabled us to build things. We believed we were better, more intelligent. But look what we'd done with that awareness, that intelligence.

It was Karin that got me up in the end. She came early one morning as the sun was just starting to light up the bedroom window. The knock on the bedroom door startled me as I'd been dozing and not heard her on the stairs. She opened the door without waiting for me to answer.

'Hello Evie,' she said as she walked towards the bed. 'Come on now. That's enough.' She pulled the covers back and grabbed my arm. 'Your children need you. We all need you.'

I tried to resist, make myself heavy, but she wouldn't give up. Kept pulling at my arm until I had to sit up or she'd have pulled it from my shoulder socket.

'Get off me,' I muttered. Even in the state I'd got myself in I could hear that I sounded like a sulky child and I was ashamed. So I got up and washed and dressed. Went with Karina to breakfast in Rachael's house.

I supposed I had to get on with life, or what was the point in having survived?

Part IV

Later Still
2062

Schooling

WE DID MORE than survive over the next twelve years. Our little community thrived. We replanted, rebuilt, grew. Children became adults, babies were born, including my first grandchild, Jonah, and Tess's daughter, Berry. Dawn had moved in with Dylan, in the house she'd first run away to with Tom, when she was seventeen. Then not long after that, Jonah came along. It made me think about the future. To make it a bright one we had to preserve the knowledge from the past. We couldn't just let it all go. We had to keep the things that were worth preserving.

The TV. Internet. Mobile phones. Governments. Credit ratings. Retail Parks. Banks. Pubs. Cars. Celebrities. Gyms. Anti-wrinkle creams. Coffee shops. Corporations. Everything we'd thought we needed and thought we knew about civilisation—all of that was gone. But we could still have the knowledge that helped us to create all that. Use it for good this time. Nathan's library was still there. We had to get the books back so that we could remember what came before. Learn from it. But how would we do it? The paths between our Woody Bay and Lynton were terrible and the books would be heavy.

It was Joe who offered to go and get them. He was a quiet young man now and he'd read every book we had in our houses more than once and was excited at the thought of getting hundreds more, no matter how long it might take. So he got a backpack and he went backwards and forwards bringing as many as he could carry each time. Sometimes other people went with him and helped but it was mainly him. It took a very long time to get them all but then one day Joe dropped a box down on the table in the schoolroom, which used to be the sitting room in Rachael's house.

'That's the last of them. The rest are in the basement. But here's the ones you said you wanted up here.'

'So they're all here now?' I said.

'Yep, every single book that was in that library is now here, just like you wanted. Although lots of them are not in a great shape. Probably not even still readable.'

I grinned at him. We might be all alone, but we had the history of the world at our fingertips now we had the books. We had the knowledge from before. I was going to make sure that the kids here grew up understanding how we wasted it, but now we had a chance to use it right. Nathan would be so happy that his books were going to be used again and the knowledge that he'd worked so hard to gather and keep safe was here with us.

I emptied the box out onto the table. 'Enough will be.'

Joe picked one up. 'The Witch Trials of the 17th Century.' He looked up at me. 'Are you sure we need to be learning about all this stuff?'

'Yes, it's a good way to show them how we got things wrong. Witch hunts never actually ended, they just morphed into other things over time. They need to know how women were persecuted, and men to a lesser extent, how everything was driven by fear, mistrust, and hatred of anybody perceived to be different. Then I'll give them another example to show how some, many, humans were filled with love, compassion and beauty. Created beautiful music, art, cared for other people. So we can make sure that is how we all stay now. And anyway, what do you mean "we"? Are you coming back to school?'

'No. But I plan to read all the books I've just spent years collecting.'

By the time the kids arrived for their lesson a few hours later, I'd drawn a crude picture of a witch as they used to be depicted on Halloween tat and stuck it up on the wall. They filed in and sat down. It was hard to believe sometimes that our community had grown so much, so fast. Ten kids in our school and we'd been having lessons for almost two years now. In that time, Hazel and I had taught them to read, write and do arithmetic. We'd covered the big things in human history—religion, the wheel, industry and capitalism, the digital revolution, but only at a basic level as we'd had hardly any books here.

'Right, everyone. Today we're going to be learning about witches.'

'What's a witches, Nan?' Jonah said.

Dawn and I were still not close, but I thought I could make up for my failures as a mother by being a great grandmother. Jonah and I spent a lot of time together, being silly, playing games, swimming in the sea. I'd tried to win Dawn over via Dylan after they'd become a couple, and he tried, but she wasn't having it. She was polite but we never *talked*. I'd like to have been able to remember Connor with her, but she seemed to have replaced him with Tom. Although you could see that Tom was disappointed in her. She didn't live up to what he'd expected a daughter of his to be. Wasn't intellectual enough for him. Spent too much time talking about day-to-day things and went quiet when he tried to have philosophical discussions with her.

'A witch, if there's just one. Or witches, if there are more than one. In the past, some people would have said that I was a witch because I use herbs to help people. Rachael too, and now that Berry is starting to learn, she would have been called one too.'

Berry blushed and looked down at the table. She hated being singled out. Always so quiet in the corner but taking everything in.

'So they were good people then?' Jonah said.

'Yes, Jonah, they were. Although lots of silly people believed they weren't and some horrible men made up stories about them to make themselves seem more important and to try and control people. It was all tied into religion, the Christian religion. You all remember the lessons on the different religions that people believed in, don't you?'

When the lesson ended a couple of hours later they knew all about the Pendle witches. I said: 'Tomorrow we'll look at the Salem Witch trials, which happened in America. Tonight I want you to make a list of all the things people got wrong about the women they said were witches.'

Jonah came and hugged me as he left. 'People used to do very strange things, didn't they, Nan?'

THE BOXES OF books in the basement took up almost all the available floor space, even though it was getting bigger by the day as our stores steadily dwindled. There were almost thirty of us now. I'd have to talk to Rachael about rationing soon. When she was feeling better.

The bookcase Lloyd had built for me from old pallets covered one entire wall, but it wasn't enough to house all the books. We'd raided the house up on the cliff on the way to Lynton and found hundreds of pallets in the garage. I'd wanted to use them all to build bookshelves, but Lloyd insisted we save most of them to use in the gardens, and he was probably right. But how would I ever choose which books to put on the shelves and which to keep in the boxes? I'd already filled my cottage with novels and they covered every windowsill, shelf, fireplace, and there were quite a few piles on the floor too.

I sat in front of the nearest box and rifled through it. Self-help books. They were huge for a long time. Didn't look like they worked though, all things considered. They could stay in the boxes.

'Ah, there you are, Evie. I've been looking everywhere for you.'

I stiffened. Tom. I'd tried my best to get along with him but part of me still resented him.

'Tom. What can I do for you?'

'Just got back from one of my walks and I went right over to Heddon this time. Saw the people who came here that day, remember?'

I nodded. 'Are they alright? What's it like over there?'

'Pretty much what it's like here, although we've got more of everything than them thanks to Rachael. The kids have all gotten sick and they don't know how to help them. I said I'd ask if you would go over there and see what you can do.'

I frowned. Tom was always so presumptuous. Always

offering things he had no right to. I hadn't left here in years. Why would he think I'd want to now? I swallowed my irritation. Of course, I must go and help.

'I'll go tomorrow. Do you know what's wrong with them?'

He shook his head. 'When you get back there's something else I need to talk to you about.'

'Can't you talk to me about it now?' I closed the box of self-help books and stood up. I'd leave all this sorting until after I'd been to Heddon. My stomach lurched at the thought of it. I was safe here. I didn't know what it was like out there.

'No, it can wait.' He turned and left.

So arrogant. Everything had to be when Tom wanted it.

After I'd packed a rucksack with herbs and tinctures, clean clothes in case I needed to stay a while, and a few books to give them, I headed back up to Rachael's. I let myself into her room after knocking quietly and waited until my eyes adjusted to the dark before moving over to the bed.

'Rachael? Are you awake?' I whispered.

She turned to face me. Her eyes were tiny and sunken, her lids swollen and drooping but still shining with love. 'Hello, yes I'm awake.'

'Not feeling any better then?'

She just smiled.

'What's the matter with you, Rachael? It's obviously not just some bug. You've been in bed for over a week and not right for months.'

'No, it's not a bug. I've got a tumour in my stomach. It's not going to go away. It's been killing me slowly and painfully.'

I dropped onto the bed next to her, stifling an involuntary cry with my hand. The tears were instant, and the acceptance. I'd known.

'Oh Rachael.' I lay down next to her and wrapped my arms around her shrunken body. Rested my forehead on hers. 'Why didn't you tell me before? We could have tried to treat it.'

'I did try. It worked for a while. I've had it for a long time now.'

'Is there anything I can do?'

'No. Don't tell the others. I might rally for a bit yet and we don't want to upset everyone unnecessarily.'

'I'm going to be away for a few days from tomorrow.'

Rachael gave a breathless little laugh. 'Well, that's something I've not heard you say for a long time. I didn't expect to hear you say it ever again. Where on earth are you going?'

I laughed too. 'Over to the Heddon Valley. Tom has just been there on one of his walks and said the children over there are sick and he offered my help.'

'Always very helpful, isn't he Tom?'

'Always.' I smiled to soften the sharp tone that came out in.

She closed her eyes. 'You be careful, and I'll see you when you get back.'

'I will. We need to talk. I think we need to consider some serious rationing from now on. People helping themselves to whatever they want, whenever they want, is not really feasible anymore.'

This wakes her up again. 'No. Surely not. There was enough there for decades.'

'Don't worry about it now. I'll have a proper look at what we've got when I get back. Make a list of everything and we'll figure it out. Rest now.'

I pulled the door quietly shut. It was only just over a decade since the quake, but the stores were way more than half gone. There were more babies being born all the time and we had to be realistic. We were going to struggle to keep feeding us all.

Saving

MICHAEL DECIDED TO come with me. We rested in the shade of an old oak to eat our lunch. We'd been walking for a couple of hours and the path was very rough. Overgrown brambles and trees. Sometimes we could see where Tom had made a path through, sometimes not. It felt very strange to be leaving our bay after so long. To be heading to the unknown. We set off again as soon as we'd finished eating. If the path was this bad all the way, it was going to take us hours to get there and we had to make it before it got dark.

But once we had climbed the hill and rounded the corner, the views along the coast were as stunning as ever and looking like they always had. The path was much clearer too. We made good time and reached the top of the hill leading down to the valley in just over an hour. We could see smoke coming from the chimney of the old hotel.

In another forty minutes or so we were walking up the path to the door when it opened.

'What do you want?' A man's voice called out. It was

dark in the doorway and the shadows shrouded his face, so we couldn't see what he looked like.

'I'm Evie. This is Michael. We've come from Woody Bay. Tom told us you needed help.'

The door opened wider and a woman stepped out from behind the man. Amber, the woman we'd met before.

'I remember you,' she said. 'Come in. Thank you for coming.'

INSIDE EVERYTHING LOOKED the same as it had last time I'd been there, many years ago when we'd first arrived in Woody Bay. The tables were set up in the bar area as if the pub was still running. The view through the big windows, some of which were covered with plastic sheets where the glass had gone, showed the road outside was being taken over by nature though, plants poking up through holes in the tarmac and trees fallen down the banks. The old cottage in front of the hotel where Tess and Matty once lived was derelict, walls crumbled, trees growing through where the roof used to be.

'Would you like something to drink?' Amber gestured for us to sit at a table by the bar. The man had disappeared through a door that led to the hotel rooms.

Michael and I perched on wooden stools. For a moment, I thought she was going to make us a proper drink as if we were in the pub and nothing had changed, but she poured some water into two glasses. It had a reddish tinge to it.

She put a glass down in front of us then returned to behind the bar. Stood watching us gulp down the water. It had been a long walk. The heat and humidity making it seem even longer.

'Who's here with you, Amber?' I said.

'The people you met that day. My kids. My parents were here too but they died. And a couple of other families that lived in the houses further up the valley.'

'Have you been out anywhere? Do you know if there's anything, anyone, out there? What's going on? Have you had any news from anywhere else?' I hadn't even realised I was so keen to hear news of the rest of the country. If there was any to hear. I was happy and content in our little community, wasn't I?

She looked at me as if I was insane. Shook her head and went to speak but bit her lip to stop herself. But it burst out of her. 'News? News of what? There was barely anyone left when we came here. There will be nobody now.'

Michael said, 'You can't know that. Has anyone from here gone to see?'

Before she could answer, the door from the hotel area swung open and a child of about five stood there. A girl with blonde ringleted hair, a dirty face, and a dress that looked like it had been made from a pillow case.

'Mama?'

'Go back to bed, Willow.'

But the girl stepped forward. Her face was flushed red with spots and her eyes glazed with fever. Dried snot crusted around her nostrils.

'Hello, Willow,' I said. 'You look like you're feeling a bit poorly.'

She stared vacantly at me without answering.

Amber nodded. 'All the kids are. They've been feverish, vomiting, having difficulty breathing. Now these red spots have appeared.'

I racked my brains to recall what illness produced these symptoms. 'It sounds like measles but how could they have caught it? Has somebody been here? What have you been giving them for it?'

'Nothing. We have nothing to give.'

'Has anyone been here?'

'Only you, and Tom. Nobody else.'

Willow climbed onto Amber's lap and I couldn't stop myself from pushing Michael further away from them. He couldn't risk taking whatever it was back to Olivia and their unborn child.

'If it is measles, it's very infectious. We have to keep them separate. I can help. Michael, go find some ramson.'

Amber stared after him as he hurried out of the door.

'Are you sure nobody's been here? Have you been

anywhere else and seen other people?' They had to have caught it from somewhere, if that's what it was.

But she shook her head. 'No. I just told you. We haven't seen anyone in years. Apart from Tom. He comes here every now and then. But that's it.'

If nobody else had been here it couldn't be measles, could it? I wasn't a hundred percent sure though. But whatever was wrong with them the symptoms were similar to measles so the best I could do was to treat it as if it was.

WHEN MICHAEL CAME back with the ramson, Amber and I put all of the infected children together in one room. There were six of them in total. Willow the youngest at five and the eldest, Noah, nine.

I soaked cloths in cold water and we wiped them all down to cool the fever.

'Michael, you need to go. If you caught this and took it back…'

He shook his head. 'If it's infectious then it's too late. Let me help.'

I knew he was right and I cursed myself for letting him come with me. I handed him the bowl and cloth. 'Carry on wiping them down and I'll go and make a tincture.'

I found my way down to the kitchen. A woman was at

the sink, washing cups and plates.

'Hello. I need a large bowl and something heavy that I can crush these leaves up with. Some boiled water.'

She turned to me. 'What? Who are you?'

'I'm Evie. I'm from the bay along the path.' I gestured in that direction. 'I've come to see if I can help make the children better.'

'Oh. Okay.' It was as if she was in a daze. She stood staring at me.

I waited and when she didn't move, I said, 'Can you help me? Get me the things I need?'

She nodded and went to a cupboard, passed me a large ceramic bowl and a wooden rolling pin. Then she went to the large pot suspended over the flames in the fireplace that was big enough to stand in. She used a cup tied to a long wooden handle to take water from the pot.

I crushed up the ramson leaves with the rolling pin handle until they were an oily paste, savouring the aroma of garlic that filled the room. From my bag I pulled a pot of our precious honey, made by our own bees that I'd finally managed to get settled back into a hive after the quake, and put six spoonfuls on top of the paste. I poured the hot water on top, stirring until it was a thin broth. I took this to the bedroom and spoon-fed the broth to each child, making them chew the leaves and swallow even though they complained.

We kept the children cool with wet cloths and fed

them broth every day. I was so scared that we would show signs of the illness too, but it didn't spread to any of the adults. After a few days, the fever broke in all but one of the children and they all started to improve. Amos, who was eight but looked about half that age, wasn't strong enough to fight back like the others had. We moved him to a room by himself and his mother, Daisy, carried on the treatment.

A few days later, I decided that it was safe for Michael and I to head home. That we weren't going to take the illness back with us. We'd wash ourselves and our clothes in the river and camp out on the path for a couple of nights to be sure that any trace of the virus was gone from us. Before I headed off to bed, I told everyone we'd be leaving the next morning.

Daisy woke me a few hours later. Moonlight coming through the bare window lit up the room even though it was the middle of the night.

'He's burning up. Help me.'

She led me along the corridors and when we reached the dark room I put my hand to Amos's forehead. I didn't think he had much chance, but I told Daisy to fill a bath with cold water and then add enough hot water so that it felt tepid to her fingers.

When it was ready she carried him to the bathroom and placed him gently in the water. She cupped water in her hands and poured it over his head, again and again. His eyes fluttered but he was lost in his fever. In the kitchen I pulled the bag of dried yarrow leaves from my bag and made tea.

I took it to Amos's room and Daisy brought him back in and placed him in the bed. We dried him and covered him with a clean sheet and she held him upright while I helped him to drink the tea. Some of it dribbled out of his mouth but I managed to get most of it inside him.

'It's yarrow tea,' I told Daisy. 'Made from the plant that shares your name. It's the best cure for high fever.' She squeezed my hand and then lay down next to Amos on the bed. I returned to my room not expecting to see him alive the next morning.

When I woke the sun was coming up from behind the hill. I headed straight for Amos's room and when I pushed the door open I could see them both still there on the bed where I'd left them, deep in sleep. His colour told me that Amos had made it. The fever had broken. He was probably going to be okay. I pulled the door shut gently and went down to the kitchen.

I took bags of dried leaves and powders and the remaining honey from my bag and rummaged in a drawer until I found a pencil and paper and then I wrote instructions on what each herb was good for and how to use it and left it all on the table. I added a line telling them that they could come to see us and get more if needed.

Then I woke Michael and we ate some berries before we set off on our journey back to our bay.

Dead

WHEN WE GOT there, Lloyd was sat at the kitchen table staring into space. The first thing he said when I walked in the room was, 'Rachael's dead.'

'What? She can't be,' I wailed. I ran upstairs to her room, but she was gone.

'Where is she?' I said to Lloyd back in the kitchen.

'Buried her yesterday. Down in the woods.'

'How? I mean how did she die?' I wrapped my arms around myself as the tears came.

It was as if my sobs broke the ice Lloyd was frozen in. He stood and took me in his arms and we cried together for the woman we'd both loved, who had given us a home, given us her love.

When we were all cried out, Lloyd said, 'She wrote you a note. Said to tell you she was sorry she couldn't hang on until you got back.' He pulled it from his back pocket, gave a melancholy little laugh. 'She joked right up until the end, and said that's if you came back. Maybe you'd found you liked it over in Heddon more than you liked it here.'

I took the note and put it in my jacket pocket. I'd read it later, when I was alone. 'Take me and show me where she is,' I said.

WHEN I LET myself into my cottage later, it was chilly and there was a damp feel to the air. I lit the kitchen stove and a fire in the living room then sat on the sofa in front of it with a cup of tea and opened Rachael's letter. It was her writing but a shakier, more uncertain version than it used to be.

My dearest Evie,

I'm sorry I didn't get to see you again. I wasn't sure how long you would be gone, or how long I could keep going. The pain has got very bad now. I'm going to take something to help me on my way.

I have been thinking about what you said about the stores, and the rationing. If it has to be done then so be it, but this is not a way I imagined we would have to live here. I hope it doesn't cause a rift. It is not my place to tell people how they should live but you could also encourage people to think about birth control – there are many herbs that can help. Queen Anne's Lace and Pennyroyal are both effective. Now that so many years have passed maybe it is safe to open up the paths properly again. You could use the old fields at the top of the hill to grow more crops to feed our growing population.

Now to the important part of my note—farewell, my lovely friend. I have felt blessed by the universe bringing you here, and I have enjoyed our life together. Try not to grieve for too long. If you have understood everything I've been telling you over the years, you will know that the essence of me will live on, it's just this container that has worn out. I hope to see you again somewhere, in some form. In the meantime, know that my love will always be surrounding you.

Keep well, love well, and enjoy what the universe gives us.

All my love,
Rachael x

I put the letter down, wiping a tear away on my sleeve. I'd suspected that she'd taken something. I raised my mug in a salute. 'Farewell, my lovely Rachael.'

Lloyd arranged a remembrance gathering for her in the clearing in the orchard so that everyone could say goodbye and share memories of her. Jonah came to see me the night before, clutching a notepad, pencil and, of all things, a bible.

'What are you doing with that, Jonah?'

'I've been reading it.' He sat down on the floor in front of the fire. 'It says that Rachael will be in heaven now, if she'd been good. Was she good? Is that where's she's gone?'

I sat down on the floor next to him. 'You remember what I said about religions when we learnt about them in lessons? There were loads of different ones and they all believed different things. Well, heaven is a belief of the religion that created the Bible. It's not what Rachael believed. And all the religions were made up by people.'

'But how can it all be different? Don't we all go to the same place?'

'Nobody knows, Jonah. Until they die.'

'But it says in here that God created the world and us.' He patted the cover of his bible, which he appeared to be getting quite attached to. Keeping it close the whole time, I'd noticed.

'It's just a story, Jonah. If you read a Buddhist book, or a Sikh one, or one from any other religion, apart from Islam, which has a lot of the same stories and people as Christianity, then they would tell a different story about who and what God is and how the world came to be. Scientists used to say it came from a big explosion. It's all just people telling themselves stories to try and figure out why we are here. But nobody really knows.'

He sat quietly for a while gazing at the floor, pro-cessing, then he gathered up his things. 'Okay. I'm going home. I was going to write something to say about Rachael tomorrow but now I'm confused.'

I pulled him into a hug. 'Life can be very confusing. Try not to worry too much and if you want to say anything tomorrow then just say how you felt about Rachael, it doesn't have to have anything to do with heaven and hell.'

He wandered off, his head down. Only six and having his first existential crisis. I chuckled as I watched him go, glad to be able to find something to laugh about.

I made a little bouquet to take with me to the remembrance, some lavender and rosemary, both herbs that Rachael had loved and the first ones she taught me about. It was the first time in ages that everybody had been all together, and it hit me again how big our community was getting. I sat down cross-legged on the grass between Tess and Hazel.

'Hear you've been over to Heddon,' Tess said. 'What's going on over there?'

'Not much. The kids were sick so I went to help. There's a few families living in the old hotel. They're doing alright.'

Lloyd stood and clapped his hands together to get everyone's attention. 'Thanks everyone, for coming to remember Rachael. Whoever wants to speak can, but Jonah has asked if he can go first.'

Jonah sprang up from where he'd been sitting next to Dawn, still clutching his bible, and stood beside Lloyd, who squeezed his shoulder before coming to sit by me, leaving Jonah standing alone in front of us, looking so small and vulnerable. Was he going to be able to speak?

His face reddened but when he spoke his voice was clear and confident. 'I loved Rachael, she was always very nice to me and she had lovely hair.' Smiles appeared everywhere. 'Even though she was a witch, and the Bible says they are evil, I think she'll be in heaven now as she didn't mean anything bad by it.'

We all laughed. He was so gorgeous and innocent. If only we'd known where it was all leading.

Vanishing

A FEW DAYS later, Lloyd, Tess and I were sat at the kitchen table in Rachael's house drawing up a plan for the rationing. It was hard. How could we possibly figure out how much food was the right amount to allow people? And how were we going to make sure people stuck to it? There was no way of keeping people out of the basement. If they wanted to just go and help themselves they could. But surely everyone would know that we had to do this for the good of all and stick to it?

'Rachael had some notebooks somewhere from years ago,' Lloyd said. 'From when she first thought of making the stores. She showed me them once. I can't remember exactly what was in them but if we found them maybe they could help?'

I nodded. 'Definitely. I'll see if I can find anything in the library books too. What are we going to do until we have a proper plan worked out though? We need to be really careful with the stores from now on.'

Before either of them could answer, Tom came through the back door, just walked in without knocking, and sat down at the table with us. I swallowed my irritation but Tess let hers shine through.

'Come in, Tom, join us,' she said, the sarcasm obvious in her tone. She'd never liked him. After the quake when she'd finally started to tell me how he was connected to the corporations, what he'd really been doing at Countervaillence, I stopped her. 'It really doesn't matter now, does it?' I'd said. 'None of it exists anymore. This is it, so we just have to get on with it.'

She'd tried to protest. I'd cut her off though. 'No, Tess. Just let it go.'

So she'd never told me but she'd also never made peace with Tom and avoided him as much as she could.

He ignored her and looked straight at me. 'Evie, you remember before you went to Heddon I said I needed to talk to you about something? Well I have to do it now. It has to be today.'

Lloyd made a huh sound and shook his head. He wasn't one of Tom's biggest fans either.

'I'm sure you feel whatever you have to say is very important and very urgent, Tom, but I'm actually in the middle of something here. We're having a meeting to decide how to make sure we're all going to have enough to eat. Which, I'm sure you'll agree is very important and something that we really need to focus on.' Part of me was filled with righteous glee at putting him in his place like that.

'But—'

'No, Tom. I'm sick of the way you always think what-ever you want is the most important thing. It isn't and to be honest, whatever it is you want to talk to me about, I'm not interested.'

I turned back to face Tess, picking up the pencil I'd been making notes with. 'Right, so we were saying.'

Tom's chair scraped violently on the tile floor as he stood up. 'Fine, have it your way. But when you find out don't say that I didn't try.'

Cryptic as ever and no doubt designed to make me give in and talk to him, but I didn't look at him again as he left the room.

A FEW DAYS later I was in the herb shed grinding some willow bark in the pestle and mortar when Tess appeared in the doorway. 'Tom's gone,' she said.

'Gone where?' I said absently. I wasn't that interest-ed—he was always wandering off then coming back again.

'Nobody's seen him since he burst in on our meeting the other day so we went in his cottage to see if he's alright and it's cleared out. He's taken a rucksack from the basement. All his clothes are gone and he took lots of food from the stores.'

I wasn't convinced. 'He'll come back.'

But he didn't.

Part V

Now
2073

Light

Moon Phase: Full

UNTIL NOW. I must have nodded off, I don't know for how long, because I'm woken by chanting and I'm still gripping his letter in my hand. I peep around the edge of the kiln and panic surges through me. They're on the path to the beach. There's no other way out apart from the sea and we'd have no hope of surviving a swim. I sit back down. 'Berry, they're here.'

She stirs, sits up and grips my hand. What can we do? How did they know we were here? I should've read the letter when I had the chance. Now I'll never find out what Tom had to say. They'll kill me this time.

There's nothing to do but face them. I pull Berry up and we leave the kiln, stand on the path, watching them come.

Jonah walks proudly in the front, his most devoted followers close behind. Dawn, of course. I try to catch her eye, but she won't look at me.

'Evie, Evie, Evie,' Jonah says. 'You must know that there is no escape from the eye of the Lord. He has led us straight to you. He will not allow your evil to roam free.'

'Please, leave me alone. I've done nothing to you, nor to harm anyone.'

He steps forward. His white robe glows silver in the moonlight. The shadows on his face make him wolf-like.

'Jonah. Please. You have to see that there's no need for this. We've gone. You don't need to do this,' Berry calls.

'Traitor,' he says. 'You are as bad as your evil teacher.'

I step back and press myself against the wall of the kiln but with a flick of his fingers he signals to his followers to get me. They step forwards and pull me away from the wall. More of them grab Berry and they take us up the path and lead us out above the kiln to the cliff edge.

'This is the time for your judgement,' Jonah shouts to be heard over the crashing and rushing of the sea and the river. 'We shall cast you into the sea and if you float you are a witch. If you drown you are clean and you will be cleansed as your soul rises to join Him.'

I can't believe it's happening.

They are going to throw me into the sea and I'll

drown. Are they going to do it to Berry too? But then I hear a different kind of shout bellowing over the chanting.

'Lights, lights, look.'

The men holding my arms let go and walk towards the cliff edge. Mesmerised by what they can see on the other side of the channel in the land that used to be known as Wales. Electric lights, coming on in waves. The chanting stops and everyone moves forward to watch. I gasp. Tom's letter. Read this when the lights come on.

As we watch more and more lights appear. Shining in the distance like the brightest stars you've ever seen. Even I am entranced. They twinkle and blink then a huge beam of light shoots up into the sky. A search light. What's going on over there? Then another beam of light joins it and they dance together.

Berry appears at my side. 'Let's go. This is our chance.'

We creep backwards along the path, keeping an eye on Jonah and his followers, but they've forgotten us as they watch the light show. When it's too dark for us to see them anymore we turn and run. I don't know how my body finds the strength but we run and run and run without stopping, the darkness not slowing us down, no rocks tripping us up. If I were a believer I would say that a benevolent God is helping us on our way.

We turn away from the path to the hotel, knowing it will be the first place they'll look for us, and head up the steep path that goes towards the Great Hangman cliff, where Connor and I had enjoyed walks so long ago. Still running, still finding the strength to keep going. Halfway up the path we run out of steam and slow to a fast walk, but we keep on going. When we get to the top, the path levels out and we stop to look at the coastline of Wales. All lit up. While we've been here going backwards, whoever is over there has been working to move forwards again.

We walk on until we come to an old wooden house that's still standing. Most of its roof is intact and inside it's full of furniture. Mouldy and damp but we set up camp for the night. We sit and watch the lights of Wales until the sun rises and one by one they go out. What's going on elsewhere in the country? People are out there, starting again.

Berry lies down to sleep and I pull Tom's letter from my pocket. Only open if the lights appear. How had he known? Part of me is terrified of what the letter will reveal but I have to read it.

Dear Evie,

I know you think I have done so much wrong, and I definitely have, but in the end I also tried to do what I thought was right. Countervaillence was a sham, a fake organisation that I headed up for the corporations, so we could know what people were doing.

Feed them the wrong information. I was a spy. But I promise you I came good. When you got pregnant I panicked. I wanted to keep you safe but I didn't know how. So when you left I put the tracker on the boat and the people who turned up, Mia and Erin, and the others who gave you the camping gear – they were working for me. There was another tracker in the tent they gave you. I always knew where you were.

I don't have time to tell you everything now but if you are reading this then the lights have come on. So come to us and I will finally tell you the full truth. This is where I wanted to take you and Dawn when I turned up all those years ago. Mia had a daughter, Ada. She is so like you in so many ways and she made me see that what I was doing was wrong. She is starting again in the way you always wanted to, with like-minded people, and the know-how and resources to create a good life, not like the one we were eking out in Woody Bay. I'm going there now. When the lights come on head to the beach at Combe Martin and wait out by the rock pools. We will come and get you in a boat and take you to the new place we have created. I promise you I won't let you down again.

Tom

I stare down at the letter then across the sea to where the lights had been. Ada. Nathan tried to tell me about her. He said he knew a woman who knew Tom. What was it he kept saying when he was dying? Ada, she's the one. I trusted Nathan and if he said Ada was the one and she trusted Tom, did this mean I could trust him too? Should I go and meet him, let him take me and Berry to Wales? To this Ada, who is like me? I don't know what is right anymore, or what will happen next.

While I gaze out across the water and ponder, Berry tosses restlessly in her sleep, murmuring and muttering at something, or someone, and as the sun rises higher on this new day the sea sparkles and shines. Then I see it. A tiny black speck at first, its shape slowly forming as it gets nearer. A boat. The first one I have seen on this sea in many years. Tom. Coming to get me just like he said he would.

I have nowhere else to go. I will have to trust him and hope that this time around, we use the knowledge and the power to take the right path. I don't know if Berry and I are safe yet, but I will wake her soon and we will head down to the sea. Wait for them to come and take us to the other side of the channel, to the light. To a future that looks nothing like the past.

Acknowledgements

When I started writing this novel it was early 2015 and Brexit had never been heard of. My vision of a future UK that had been cut off from the rest of the world and turned into a police state was purely imagination. Now as the book comes out, some of what I made up is coming true. I hope the rest of it doesn't.

There are always so many people to thank in creation of a novel so apologies if I miss anyone.

My huge thanks go to:

- Andrew Wille you made me slow down and really think about what I was writing and why. I'm forever grateful for your invaluable guidance and cheering on in the planning stages.

- Craig Taylor, Jane Elmor and Rose McGinty your critiques showed me the things I was doing right, but more importantly the (many) things I was doing wrong.

- Debi Alper this novel shines like the full moon on the cover only because of your brilliant editing.

- Anna Orridge the points you made in your beta read were excellent, and all bar one of them now appear here and the story is much better for it.

- Jennie Rawlings at Serifim Book Design – thank you for this gorgeous cover that really captures the heart of the novel.

As well as the people who worked with me on the writing and editing of the story, there are a number of online communities without whom this novel couldn't have been written as they were integral to my research. So thank you for all you do to share info with the world: all the preppers out there getting ready for the apocalypse; the green witches; the anti-fracking protestors; environmental activists; self-sustaining communities; and everyday people all around the world sharing news of how climate change is affecting their lives.

Thanks also to the myriad of print and online journals who have commissioned me to write articles for the past fifteen years or so about environmental sustainability, and the impact of consumerism and the changing climate on all areas of life. Without that knowledge to guide me, I don't think I could have had this vision for this novel.

Finally, the biggest thanks always goes to John, for being the best husband there ever was.

Retreat West Books

WHAT WAS LEFT, VARIOUS
20 winning and shortlisted stories from the 2016 Retreat West Short Story and Flash Fiction Prizes. A past that comes back to haunt a woman when she feels she has no future. A man with no mind of his own living a life of clichés. A teenage girl band that maybe never was. A dying millionaire's bizarre tasks for the family hoping to get his money. A granddaughter losing the grandfather she loves. A list of things about Abraham Lincoln that reveal both sadness and ambition for a modern day schoolgirl.

AS IF I WERE A RIVER, AMANDA SAINT
Kate's life is falling apart. Her husband has vanished without a trace – just like her mother did. Laura's about to do something that will change her family's lives forever – but she can't stop herself. Una's been keeping secrets – but for how much longer?

NOTHING IS AS IT WAS, VARIOUS
A charity anthology of climate-fiction stories raising funds for the Earth Day Network. A schoolboy inspired by a conservation hero to do his bit; a mother trying to save

her family and her farm from drought; a world that doesn't get dark anymore; and a city that lives in a tower slowly being taken over by the sea.

SEPARATED FROM THE SEA, AMANDA HUGGINS

Separated From the Sea is the debut short story collection from award-winning author, Amanda Huggins. Crossing oceans from Japan to New York and from England to Havana, these stories are filled with a sense of yearning, of loss, of not quite belonging, of not being sure that things are what you thought they were. They are stories imbued with pathos and irony, humour and hope.

IMPERMANENT FACTS, VARIOUS

These 20 stories are the winners in the 2017 Retreat West Short Story and Flash Fiction prizes. A woman ventures out into a marsh at night seeking answers about herself that she cannot find; a man enjoys the solitude when his wife goes away for a few days; two young women make a get rich quick plan; and a father longs for the daughter that has gone to teach English in Japan.

THIS IS (NOT ABOUT) DAVID BOWIE, FJ MORRIS

Every day we dress up in other people's expectations. We button on opinions of who we should be, we instagram impossible ideals, tweet to follow, and comment to judge. But what if we could just let it all go? What if we took off our capes and halos, threw away our uniforms, let go of the future. What if we became who we were always supposed to be? Human.

This is (not about) David Bowie. It's about you. This Is (Not About) David Bowie is the debut flash fiction collection from F.J. Morris. Surreal, strange and beautiful it shines a light on the modern day from the view of the outsider. From lost souls, to missing sisters, and dying lovers to superheroes, it shows what it really is to be human in a world that's always expecting you to be something else.

http://retreatwestbooks.com

Lightning Source UK Ltd.
Milton Keynes UK
UKHW021630270219
337848UK00005B/44/P

9 781916 448322